General Roffis said,

"When we have dealings with these Earthmen, we get carried off in a basket?"

"Yes, sir."

"How do they do it?"

"When they get through talking, everything looks different."

"How do they accomplish *that*?"

"I think they emphasize whatever favors their argument."

"Then they have a weakness. If they restricted themselves to truth, they would be strong. With this procedure, they will take up false positions."

"Nevertheless, we have a serious problem. They have gulled our men into giving up valuable space ships in return for—let's see—fancy ground-cars, cabin cruisers, vacation trailers, sauna baths, *The Collected Adventures of Sherlock Holmes*, airplanes, undeveloped real estate, a 'private ocean backyard swimming pool' . . ." Roffis looked up. "This isn't very promising."

Maklin growled. "And all this is against regulations. Every one of these transactions is a capital offense. . . ."

o o O

PANDORA'S PLANET

o O o

Christopher Anvil

DAW BOOKS, INC.

DONALD A. WOLLHEIM, PUBLISHER

1301 Avenue of the Americas
New York, N. Y.   10019

This novel was developed from a short story by
Christopher Anvil entitled, "Pandora's Planet,"
first published in *Analog* in 1956, copyright ©
1956 by Condé Nast Publications, Inc. The story
was republished in 1962 in *Prologue to Analog*,
edited by John W. Campbell (Doubleday &
Co., Inc.).

Cover art by Kelly Freas.

FIRST PRINTING, AUGUST 1973

1 2 3 4 5 6 7 8 9

PRINTED IN U.S.A.

"A Treat, Moffis"

Klide Horsip, Planetary Integrator, prided himself on being much more than a gaoler. Each advance of the Integral Union meant more occupied planets, and each one of these planets, like a single tiny component in a giant magnet, must be brought into line with the rest. This was Klide Horsip's job, and he settled to it now with relish.

"Phase I is *complete?*" he insisted, emphasizing the word.

Brak Moffis, the Military Overseer, smiled ruefully. "Not quite as complete as it often is on these humanoid planets."

"Then give me a brief summary of the details," said Horsip. He cast a quick glance out the landing boat's window at the curve of the blue and green world below. "Looks promising enough."

"Well," said Moffis, "as far as that goes, it is. It's a Centra-type planet, mean diameter about 0.8, with gravity, oxygen, and temperature ideally suited to human and humanoid life. The percentage of water surface is higher than on Centra—about 75 percent—but it's well distributed, and helps moderate the climate. There are plenty of minerals, including massive quantities of deep nickel-iron that hasn't yet been touched."

Horsip nodded. "And the inhabitants?"

"The usual types of plant and animal life—and, the humanoids."

"Ah, we come to the main point. What stage were the humanoids in when you landed?"

Brak Moffis looked at Horsip and gave a wry smile. "Technologically," said Moffis, "they were very near Centra 0.9, and in some areas higher."

"You aren't serious?"

The Military Overseer shook his head and looked away.

"You wouldn't ask me that if you'd been in on the invasion. Perhaps you've heard of Centralis II?"

"The 'hell-planet.' Who hasn't heard of it?" Horsip let his voice show impatience. "What of it?"

"Well," said Moffis, "that gives us ground for comparison. This was worse—30 percent of the initial landing parties were vaporized the first day. Another 50 percent had their sites eliminated by the second day, and were pinned to the earth that day or the day after. The whole second wave had to funnel through the remaining 20 percent of sites in isolated regions, and of course that meant the natives retained effective control of the situation everywhere it counted. If you'll imagine yourself wrestling one of the giant snakes of Goa, you'll have a good idea of our position." He raised a hand as Horsip, frowning, started to speak. "Let me summarize: 30 percent of our selected sites were eliminated, 50 percent were in desperate straits, and the remaining 20 precent were jam-packed, overloaded, and only meant for secondary purposes in the first place. . . . All this, mind you, despite the fact that the natives let off a couple of incomplete attacks on *each other* during the initial stages."

"Hysteria?" Horsip scowled.

"Regional rivalries," said Moffis.

"Well," said Horsip, "give the censorship another silver nova for efficiency. All I ever heard of this was that it was proceeding 'according to schedule.' "

"It was," said Moffis, "but it wasn't our schedule."

"I see," said Horsip, his face disapproving. "Well, what did you do?"

"Organized our established sites as fast as possible, and improvised new ones in chosen locations connecting the outer sites to form a defensive perimeter."

"*Defensive!*"

"That was what it boiled down to."

"What about the other sites—the 50 percent under attack?"

"We supplied them as well as we could. When we were built up enough, we started a heavy thrust to split the enemy—I mean, native—forces, and at the same time ordered a simultaneous break-out of the surrounded units toward common centers. The idea was to build up strong enough groups so they could fight their way to the perimeter."

"You were actually *giving up* the original sites?" Horsip looked at the Military Overseer with an expression of offended disbelief.

Moffis looked back coldly. "I'm telling you all this in detail so you'll understand it wasn't the usual matter of slaughtering a molk in a stall, and so you'll be ready in case *you* run into anything. I'm telling you we had a rough tossing-around in the beginning. Maybe you'll have a better idea when I tell you one of our northern groups of initial landing parties ran into this routine:

"The natives vaporized the center of each site with a nuclear bomb, contained the troops remaining in each site with minimum forces, then switched a heavy reserve from one landing party to the next, slaughtering them one after the other, in succession. This wasn't brilliance on their part. This was their usual level of performance."

Horsip swallowed and looked serious.

Moffis noted Horsip's reaction and nodded. "I'm no more used to being on the defensive than you are, and I can assure you I didn't enjoy a minute of it. But that's what we were up against. We managed to recover just one large group—about 18 percent—of the original landing parties, then we pulled back into our perimeter under heavy attack. We had to bring the Fleet down into the atmosphere to get at their communications. At that the ships took losses of better than one in five despite the meteor guards. It was touch-and-go for weeks, then we got the edge, and finally we had them hamstrung. Then we had some terrific fighting when we broke out of the defensive perimeter. But we won. At the end, we crushed them piecemeal."

"How long did this take?" asked Horsip.

"A hundred and twenty-seven of the planet's days," said Moffis. "Their day is roughly the same length as a a day on Centra."

"I see," said Horsip, "and ten to twelve days is considered average."

"Averages don't count with something worse than Centralis II."

Horsip looked out at the planet, growing big as the landing boat swung closer. As he watched, he saw a region of pits and craters, a part of the globe that looked as if an angry giant had beat on it with a sledge hammer. He turned away, as if to change the subject.

"What," he asked, "do these humanoid natives look like?"

"A lot like us. They have a pair of anterior and a pair of posterior appendages, one head, but no functional tail. They walk upright, and have opposable thumbs on the anterior appendages."

"Many significant marking differences?"

Moffis swallowed. "A few."

"Good," said Horsip, relaxing a bit. "That will save us the trouble of marking them." When Moffis remained quiet, Horsip turned impatiently. "Well, don't just sit there. Enumerate them. What are the differences?"

"A bigger skull," said Moffis, "with a larger brow and a less prominent nose. The females are practically hairless over the greater portion of their bodies, and so are the males, though in less degree."

"Very good," said Horsip, nodding approval. "What else?"

"A vestigial tail that's almost completely absorbed. And the head is set more nearly erect on the body."

"Splendid! Yes, very good indeed." Horsip looked vastly pleased. "You realize the implications?"

"I don't see anything good about it," said Moffis.

"Oh, come, man," said Horsip. "You've had a difficult experience, but don't let it distort your values. This is a propitious start for Planetary Integration. This folk are self-marked, by nature. We'll have no mixed-race trouble here, nor any of the usual marking difficulties, either."

Horsip paused in thought, snapped his fingers, and added, "For instance, look at the words that apply to these natives—big-headed, hairless, flat-nosed—"

"But they aren't flat-nosed."

"What does that matter? Didn't you say their noses were smaller?"

"Well, yes. But not flat."

Horsip waved his hand. "Never mind that. We'll call them flat-nosed. Now let's see. Big-headed, hairless, flat-nosed. . . .Wasn't there another. . ."

"Tailless," supplied Moffis, without enthusiasm.

"Yes, tailless. Well . . ." Horsip leaned back, and a smile of creative enjoyment crossed his face. "We'll call them 'puff-skulled, hairless, flat-nosed, top-tails.' Let's see any of our rowdy young bloods try to mate with them after that!"

"They will," said Moffis tonelessly.

"But not officially," said Horsip. "And that's what counts." He looked down with pleasurable anticipation at the planet grown large beneath them. He rubbed his hands. "Well," he said, "this is going to be pleasant work. A treat, Moffis."

Moffis shut his eyes as if to ease a pain.

"I hope so," he said.

❀ **II** ❀

Puff-Skulled Lop-Tails
in Action

A strong guard of heavily armed soldiers awaited them in the landing area, itself ringed by several formidable lines of spike-bar barriers, thickly sown with leaping-mine trip wires, and covered by deeply dug-in splat-gun emplacements.

Horsip looked the defenses over curiously as he walked with Moffis to a heavily armored ground-car. He noted that the soldiers carried out their orders readily enough, but without a certain verve usual on newly conquered planets. "Trouble?" he asked.

Moffis glanced around uneasily. "Roving bands," he said. "You think you've got them wiped out, and they pop up again somewhere else."

They got into the ground-car, an order was shouted outside, and the convoy began to move off. It wound out onto the road like a giant chuffing snake, moving jerkily as gaps opened and closed between vehicles. The going was bumpy until they got out onto the main road, then the car moved smoothly along. At this stage, Horsip raised up to peer out a shuttered slit in the side of his vehicle. For a hundred yards back from the side of the road, the vegetation was a burnt black. He scowled.

Moffis read his thoughts. "Yes, clearing the roadside *is* an unusual precaution. But it's either that or get plastered with a can of flammable liquid when you go by in the car."

"Such an unnecessary width might indicate fear to the natives."

Moffis suppressed a snort.

Horsip looked at him coldly. "Isn't that so?"

"Maybe," said Moffis. "And maybe it indicates fear to a molk when you put heavier bars on his stall. But the main idea is, not to get gored."

9

"We've already conquered these lop-tails."

"Some of them don't know it yet. That's the whole trouble."

"We won't convince them by acting frightened."

"We won't convince them by being dead, either."

Horsip looked at Moffis coldly. His heavy brows came together and he opened his mouth.

There was a dull boom from somewhere up ahead. Their car slowed suddenly, swerved, and then rolled forward so fast they were thrown hard back against the cushions. Something *spanged* against the side of the car. The snapping *whack* of a splat-gun sounded up ahead, was joined by others, and rose to a crescendo as they raced forward and passed to one side of the uproar. Acrid fumes momentarily filled the car, making Horsip cough and his eyes run. Somewhere in the background there was an unfamiliar hammering thud that jarred Horsip's nerves. There was another explosion and another, now well to the rear. Then the car slowed with a loud squeal from the machinery. Horsip was thrown forward, then slammed back hard as the car raced ahead again. As they settled into a fast steady run, he turned to Moffis with a thoughtful frown. "How much farther do we have to go?"

"We should be about a quarter of the way."

Horsip sat, pale and thoughtful, beside Moffis, who sat, pale and gloomy, all the way to Horsip's new headquarters.

The site of the new headquarters was not well chosen to convey the effect of untouchable superiority. The site consisted of a large, blackened mountain with a concrete tunnel entrance at the base. The mountain bristled with air-defense cannon, was pocked and lined with shellholes, trenches, bunkers, and spike-bar barriers. Around the tunnel entrance at the base, the barriers, cannon, and splat-gun emplacements were so thick as to excite ridicule. Horsip was about to comment on it when he noted a huge thing like a monster turtle some 150 yards from the entrance. He felt the hair on his neck, back, and shoulders bristle.

"What's that?"

Moffs peered out the slit. "One of the humanoids' traveling forts."

Horsip stared at the long thick cannon that pointed straight at the tunnel entrance. He swallowed. "Ah . . . is it disarmed?" The ground-car's armor plating suddenly seemed very thin. "It is, isn't it?"

Moffis said, "Not exactly. Our engineers are studying it."

"You don't mean the humanoids are still in *control* of it?"

"Oh no," said Moffis. "The concussion from our bombardment apparently killed them. Our experts are *inside* it, trying to figure out the mechanism."

"Oh." Horsip, as his angle of view changed, saw an armored ground-car gradually come into sight, parked near the alien fort. He damned himself for his scare. Of *course*, the thing was disarmed. But he could not help noticing how ineffectual the ground-car looked beside it. He cleared his throat.

"How many of those, ah, 'moving forts' did the humanoids have?"

"Hundreds of them," said Moffis.

They rode in silence through the massive concrete entrance, and Horsip felt an unexpected sense of relief as the thick layer of earth, rock, and cement intervened between himself and the alien world. They rode downward for a long distance, then got out of the ground-car. Moffis showed Horsip around his new headquarters, which consisted of a large suite of rooms comfortably fitted out; several outer offices with files, clerks, and thick bound volumes of maps and data; and a private inner office paneled in dark wood, with Horsip's desk and chair on a raised dais, and a huge flag of Centra hanging behind it.

Horsip looked everything over in complete silence. Then he looked again around the private office at the desk, dais, and flag. He cleared his throat.

"Let's go into my suite. Do you have the time?"

"I suppose so," said Moffis gloomily. "There isn't a great deal I can do, anyway."

Horsip looked at him sharply, then led the way back to his suite. They sat down in a small study, then Horsip got up, scowling intently, and began to pace the floor. Moffis looked at him curiously.

"Moffis," said Horsip suddenly, "you haven't told me the whole story."

Moffis looked startled.

"Go on," said Horsip. "Let's have it."

"I've summarized—"

"You've left out pieces. Perhaps you've told me the facts and left out interpretations. We need it all." He faced Moffis and pinned him with his gaze.

"Well . . ." said Moffis, looking uncomfortable.

"You're my military deputy," said Horsip, his eyes never leaving Moffis. "You and I must work together, each supplying the other's lacks. The first rule of planetary integration is to apply the maximum available force, *in line with itself*. If you apply force in one direction, and I apply force in another direction, the result will be less than if we both apply force in the same direction. That can be proved.

"Now," he said, "you have had a difficult time. You hit with all your strength, and the blow was blunted. The natives showed considerable low cunning in using the brute force at their disposal. Because we are accustomed to swift victories, the slowness of your success discouraged you. I was somewhat surprised at the situation myself, at first.

"However," said Horsip, his voice swelling, "a molk is a molk no matter how many bars he kicks off his stall. He may put up a struggle. It may take twenty times as long as usual to strap his neck to the block and slam the ax through. But when he's dead, he's just as dead as if it was over in a minute. *Right?*"

"Truth," said Moffis, looking somewhat encouraged.

"All right," said Horsip, pacing. "Now, we've got this molk into the stall, but apparently we're having some little trouble getting his head in the straps. Now, we can't strap a molk in the dark, Moffis. The horns will get us if we try it. We've got to have light. You've got to light up the beast for me with the lantern of knowledge, Moffis, or I can't do my part. Now, how about it?"

"Well," said Moffis, looking interested and sitting forward on the edge of his chair, "I'm willing, now you put it that way, but where should I start?"

"Start anywhere," said Horsip.

Moffis cleared his throat, and looked thoughtful.

"Well, for one thing," said Moffis, "there's this piecemeal filing-down they're doing to us." He hesitated.

"Go on," prompted Horsip. "Talk freely. If it's important, tell me."

"Well," said Moffis, "it doesn't *seem* important. But take that trip from the landing boat to here. That wasn't a long trip. Yet they knocked out at least one ground-car. If it was the same as other trips like it, they put fifteen men out of action, and three ground-cars, at least for now. . . . Now, say we have three hundred men and fifty ground-cars we can spare as escort between here and the landing-boat place. Each time, they're likely to get hit once, at least. It seems like just a small battle. Not even a battle. Just a brush with some die-hard natives.

"But in two trips, we've lost one man out of ten and one car out of eight."

Moffis paused, frowning. "And the worst of it is, we can't put it down. It's like a little cut that won't stop bleeding. If it just happened here it would be bad enough. But it happens everywhere and anywhere that we don't have everything screwed down tight."

"But," said Horsip, "see here. Why don't you gather together five thousand men and scour that countryside clean? Then you'll have an end to that. Then, take those five thousand men and clean out the next place." He grew a little excited. "That's what they did to our landing parties, isn't it? Why not spring their own trap on them?"

Moffis looked thoughtful. "We tried something like that earlier, when all this started. But the wear on the ground-cars was terrific. Moreover, they moved only a few scores of men, and we had to move thousands. It was wearing us out. Worse yet, they only had small bands in action, so we couldn't always find them. We'd end up with thousands of men milling around in a little field, and no humanoids. Then, from somewhere else, they'd fire into us." Moffis shivered. "We tried to bring the whole army to bear on them, but it was like trying to shoot insects with a cannon. It didn't work."

"Well," said Horsip, "that was too bad; but still, you had the right idea. But you overdid it."

"I wouldn't be surprised," said Moffis. "None of us were in very good form by then."

Horsip nodded. "But look here, take five thousand men, break them up into units of, say, five hundred each. Train the units to act alone or with others. Take six of the units, and send them to troubled places. Hold the other four in your hand, ready to put them here or there, as needed."

Moffis looked thoughtful. "It sounds good. But what if on their way to the trouble place, *these* men get fired on?"

Horsip suppressed a gesture of irritation. "Naturally, the five hundred would be split up into units. Say it was ten units of fifty men each. One fifty-man unit would clean out the nest of snakes, and the rest would go on. When they were finished, the unit that had stopped would go after the rest."

Moffis nodded. "Yes, it sounds good."

"What's wrong with it?" demanded Horsip.

"The natives' stitching-gun," said Moffis dryly.

"The which?" said Horsip.

"Stitching-gun," said Moffis. "It has a single snout that the darts move into from a traveling belt, like ground-cars on an assembly line. The snout spits them out one at a time and they work ruin on our men. If this five-hundred-man team you speak of was hit on the road, and just fifty men from it tried to beat the natives, we'd probably lose all fifty. The only way to win would be to stop the whole five hundred, and let the men fire at them from inside the ground-cars."

"But listen," said Horsip, "just how many natives would they be fighting?"

"Twenty, maybe."

Horsip did a mental calculation. "Then you mean one of their men is worth two to three of ours?"

"In this kind of fighting, yes."

Horsip made a howling sound in his throat, let out the beginning of a string of oaths and cut them off.

"I'm sorry," said Moffis. "I know how you feel."

"All right," said Horsip angrily, raising his hand and making gestures as if brushing away layers of gathering fog, "let's get back to this stitching-gun. It only shoots one dart at a time. How does that make it better than our splat-gun, that can shoot up to twenty-five darts at a time?"

"I don't understand it exactly," said Moffis, "but it has something to do with the way they fight. Well, and then, too, the stitching-gun shoots the darts out *fast*. It shoots a *stream* of darts. If the first one misses, the humanoid moves the gun a little and maybe the *next* one strikes home. If not, he moves it a little more. This time, five or six darts hit our man and down he goes. Now the humanoid looks around for someone else and starts in on him. Meanwhile, another humanoid is feeding belts of darts into the gun—"

"But our splat-guns!" said Horsip exasperatedly. "What are *they* doing all this time?"

"They're heavy," said Moffis, "and it takes a little while to get them into action. Besides, the enemy—I mean, the humanoids—have had all night to set *their* gun up and hide it, and now they pick out their target at will. We have to stop the vehicles to go into action. And that isn't the worst, either."

"Now what?"

"Now the splat-gun operators can't see the enemy. I mean, the humanoids. They'll be dug in, and concealed. When the gunners do realize where they are, as likely as not the splat-guns can't get at them, because there's nothing but the snout of the stitching-gun to fire at. It's likely to be someone firing from inside the ground-cars that finally picks off the humanoids."

Horsip looked at Moffis thoughtfully. "Are there many more difficulties like this?"

"The planet is full of them," said Moffis. "It seems like heaven compared to what it was when the full-scale fighting was going on, but when you get right down to it, it's hard to see whether we've made any headway since then or not. The maddening part of it is, we can't seem to get a grip on the thing." He hesitated, then went on. "It's too much like trying to wear down a rock with dirt. The dirt wears away instead."

Horsip nodded, made an effort, and looked confident. "Never mind that, Moffis. You've got the molk in the stall for us. He's still kicking, but that just means there's so much the more meat on him."

"I hope so," said Moffis.

"You'll see," said Horsip, "once Planetary Integration gets started on the job."

❊ III ❊

A Significant Datum

The staff of Planetary Integration came down on the planet the next day. Soon they were coming in from the landing field in groups. They were talkative people, waving their hands excitedly, their voices higher-pitched than most. Their faces were smug, and in their eyes was a glint of shrewdness and cunning as they regarded the new world around them. Moffis did not look especially confident at their arrival, but Horsip brimmed over with energy and assurance. He began to put the problems to them.

First, what to do about the ambushing on the road?

The answers flew thick as dust in summertime.

Small forts and splat-gun nests could be built along the chief roads. Light patrols could scour the fields alongside to seek out the lop-tails before they got their guns in place. Strips of leaping mines could be laid alongside the roads at a distance, so the lop-tails would have to cross them to do any damage. Light air-planes could drop explosives on them. The problem was easy.

What about the stitching-gun?

Simple. Capture as many as possible from the lop-tails, and teach our men how to use them. Find the factories that made them, and induce the manufacturer to make more. And the same for the place that made their darts. Minor details of the gun's outward appearance could be changed, and a big seal attached, reading "Official *Centra* Stitching-Gun."

Now, the big question: How to end this creeping war?

The Planetary Integration staff had a simple answer for that one. Every time a human was killed, ten of the lop-tails should lose their lives. If that didn't stop the foolishness, then *eleven* lop-tails should die. If it still went on, then twelve lop-tails. Each time the ratio was raised there should be an impressive announcement. Placards should be scattered over the country, saying, "If you murder a Centran, you kill *ten* of your own kind."

The lop-tails should be offered full humanoid equality, local self-government and all the other inducements, on the condition that they were peaceful, and disciplined the rowdy elements that were causing trouble.

Horsip gave the necessary commands to set the machinery in motion.

For a full week, everything worked splendidly.

Horsip was enjoying a hot scented bath when Moffis came charging in. Moffis had a raised black and blue welt on his head, his uniform was torn open at the chest, and he looked furious.

Horsip put his hands over his ears.

"Stop that foul-mouthed cursing," said Horsip. "I can't understand a word you're saying."

Moffis shivered all over convulsively.

"I say, your integration program isn't working, that's what I say!"

"Why not?" Horsip looked stunned.

"How do I know why not? Nothing works on this stinking planet!"

Horsip clambered out of the tub into the drip pan. "What's wrong? What's happened?"

"I'll tell you what's wrong! We built the small forts and splat-gun nests just as you told us to. The crews in them have been living a horrible life. They're harassed from morning to night. And just what is the advantage, I'd like to know, of having five hundred men strung out in two dozen little packets that each have to be supplied separately, instead of all together where you can do something with them?

"And then, this stitching-gun business. We can't *find* the manufacturer. Everyone says someone else made it. Or they say they used to make them, but not that model. Or they haven't made them for years. Or we blew up their factory when we attacked. And—hairy master of sin!—by the time we get through going from one place to the other—they talk a different language in each place, you know—we don't know whether we're standing on our hands or our feet. Now let me just give you an example.

"We took this stitching-gun we captured around to find out who made it. Wouldn't you think they could just look at it and tell us? No, sir! Not them! We showed it to the Mairicuns first. One of them said, No, this didn't look like one of their jobs. He thought the Rushuns made it. The Rushuns said, Hah! This wasn't one of theirs. Theirs had wheels on them. Try the Beljuns. The Beljuns said they didn't make it. Maybe the Frentsh did. The Frentsh looked it over and said, Oh no, that was a Nazy job. And where were the Nazies? . . . They were wiped out years ago."

Moffis stared at Horsip in frustration. "Now what do we do? And listen, I'm just giving you a summary of this. You don't know what we went through. Each one of those places had bureaus, and branches, and departments, and nobody trusts anyone else.

"The Rushuns say about the Mairicuns, 'What can you expect of those people? Pay no attention to them.'

"The Mairicuns say about the Rushuns, 'Oh, well, that's just what the Rushuns say. You can't believe that.'

"Now what do we do?"

Horsip decided he had dripped long enough, wrapped a bath blanket around him and began drying himself. Evading the issue, he asked, "How's the casualty rate?"

"We haven't had a man *killed* since we made the edict."

"Well," said Horsip, brightening, "that worked out, didn't it?"

Moffis looked like he smelled something unpleasant. "I don't know."

"Well, man, why not? What's wrong with that? That's what you wanted, isn't it?"

"Well . . . I guess so."

"Well, then. We're getting a grip on the thing."

"Are we?" Moffis pulled a sheet of paper out of his pocket. "Since we gave the edict, we have had 3,768 slit or punctured tires, 112 blown-up places in the road, five unoccupied cars rolled over the side of a hill, eighteen cars stuck in tarry gunk on a steep incline, and a whole procession of twenty-six cars that went off the road for no known reason at the bottom of a hilly curve. We have also had breakdowns due to sand in the fuel tank, holes in the fuel tank, and vital parts missing from the machinery. Is that an improvement or isn't it? The tires, injured roads, and damaged machinery have to be repaired. That takes work. In this same period we have had"—he turned over the paper—"112 men out for sprained backs, ruptures, and so on, and eight men in bad shape due to heart trouble. Also, the men are getting rebellious. You know as well as I do, Centran soldiers *hate* drudgery. Not only that, but you should see those roads! How do they make them like that in the first place? We can't repair them as well as they're made. I tell you I'm getting fed up with this!"

Horsip scrubbed himself dry, then dressed and went off to

see his Planetary Integration staff, now working happily on plans for final integration of the planet into the Integral Union some twenty years in the future. Moffis went along with him. Horsip explained the situation.

A precocious-looking individual, with large eye-correctors and thin hair on his hands, addressed Moffis in a peevish voice:

"Why," he demanded, "do you fail to assure proper protective precautions for these vehicles?"

"Because," snarled Moffis, "we have all these stinking rattraps to supply, that's why."

"I presume your troops are in possession of all their senses? How can damage be inflicted upon the vehicles when your men maintain proper precautions?"

"What? I just told you!"

"I fail to understand how it can be possible for the natives to approach the vehicles without being apprehended."

Horsip put in quickly, "He means, why aren't they seen?"

Moffis, whose face was glowing red, said fiercely, "Because it's night, that's why! They can't be seen!"

"A simple solution. Carry the operation out in daytime."

Moffis gritted his teeth. "We *can't*. Every time a car slows down in the daytime, some sharpshooter half a drag away puts a dart through the tires."

Moffis' precocious-looking questioner stared at him as if in a daze. "Oh," he said suddenly, looking relieved, "exaggeration-for-conversational-effect."

"What?" demanded Moffis.

"I supposed you to be serious about the half-drag accuracy of the projectile."

"About," Horsip hastily interpreted, "how far the native's gun could shoot with accuracy. He thought you meant it."

"I did mean it," said Moffis.

There was a sound of uneasy movement in the room.

"Theoretically impossible," said someone.

Moffis glared at him. "Would you care to come up and lie down behind a tire?"

Horsip, noting an undesirable effect on the morale of his staff, suggested they put a team to work on the new problem, while the rest continue what they were doing. He ushered the growling Moffis out of the room.

By the time Horsip had Moffis soothed down, and finally got back to his staff, an uproar had developed over the "meaning" of the "significant datum" that the lop-tails could shoot a gun half a drag and hit something with it. This fact seemed to upset a great number of calculations, in the same way that it would upset calculations to find two different lower jaws for the same prehistoric monster.

The arguments were many and fierce, but under Horsip's skillful prompting, they seemed to boil down to a choice between two: (a) the lop-tails possessed supernatural powers; or (b) the lop-tails used methods of precision manufacture on their ordinary guns and munitions such as humans used only—and then with great difficulty—on their space ships.

The possibilities resulting from the acceptance of (a) were too discouraging to think about. Those resulting from (b) led by various routes each time to the same conclusion, that the lop-tails were smarter than the humans.

This unpleasant conclusion led to one that was really ugly, namely, of two races having humanlike characteristics: Which race is human, the smart race or the dull race?

At this point in the argument, an unpleasant little man in the back of the room rose up and announced that on the basis of an extension of standard comparative physique types from the humanoid to the human, the lop-tails were more advanced than the Centrans.

But that was the low point in the argument. Soon the hypothesis of "pseudointelligence" was introduced to explain the lop-tails' accomplishments. Next, a previously undistinguished staff member introduced the homely simile of passing over the brow of a hill. If, he said, one went far enough in one direction, he at last came to the very top of the hill. Any further motion in that direction carried one down the slope. True, he said, these lop-tails might go further in certain physical characteristics than the Centrans themselves. But to what point? The Centrans were at the peak, and any ostentatious exaggeration of Centran traits was merely ridiculous.

The excitement abated somewhat, and Horsip got his staff back to work on the pressing problem of supplying the road outposts without losing vehicles in the process. Then he hunted up Moffis.

The Military Overseer was in a room with five humans and a number of lop-tails. Plainly, Moffis was trying to question the lop-tails about something. But the lop-tails were arguing among themselves. Moffis left the room when he saw Horsip, first instructing his subordinates to carry on.

Moffis, wincing as if with a severe headache, said, "What a relief! I'm glad you came along."

"What's wrong?" asked Horsip.

"Interpreters," said Moffis. "These lop-tails all have different languages, and interpreters never agree on what's being said."

"Hah!" said Horsip. "You should have heard what I've just been through."

"This was worse," said Moffis.

"I doubt it," said Horsip, and described it.

Moffis looked gloomy. "I don't care what you call it. This pseudointelligence is going to be the end of us yet. Of all the planets I've helped capture or occupy up till now, I've generally had the feeling of outplaying the natives. You know what I mean. After the first clash of arms, you play a *deeper* game than they do. You manipulate the situation so that if they go against you they're swimming against the current. When you have that advantage, you can use it to get other advantages, till, finally, you have complete control of the situation."

"They're integrated," said Horsip.

"Yes," said Moffis. "But it isn't working that way here. Ever since the initial clash, we've been *losing* advantages. We're spread thin. The natives act in such a way that we spread ourselves thinner. I have the feeling *we're* the ones that are swimming upstream."

"Still," said Horsip, "we're the conquerors."

"I just hope they stay conquered," said Moffis fervently.

"I have an idea," said Horsip.

❊ IV ❊

"They Are Smarter
Than We Are!"

Horsip and Moffis spent the next few hours discussing Horsip's idea.

"It's the best thing yet," said Moffis, as they strolled down the hall afterward. A smile of anticipation lighted his face. "It should tie them in knots."

Horsip smiled modestly.

"We'll need plenty of reinforcements," said Moffis, "so I'll send out the request right away."

"Good idea," said Horsip.

They strolled past the office of the Planetary Integration staff. A sound of groaning came from within. Horsip spun around.

"Excuse me," said Horsip. Scowling, he went into the room.

As he entered, he saw the whole staff sitting around in attitudes of gloom and dejection. A number of natives were in the room, and one was talking earnestly to several members of the staff.

"No! No! No!" the native was saying. "You can't do it that way! If you do, the cars will lurch or even fly off the track every time you get up past a certain speed. You've got to have a transition curve first, see, and then the arc of a circle."

Horsip stopped, dazed.

Beside him, a staff member with his head in his hands looked up and saw Horsip. Horsip glanced at him and demanded, "What's going on here?"

"We got the natives in to study their language, and—and to worm their tribal taboos out of them." His face twisted in pain. "And we wanted to find out the limits of their pseudointelligence." Tears appeared in his eyes. "Oh, why did we do it?"

"Will you stop croaking?" snapped Horsip. "What happened? What's all this about?"

"They're *smarter* than we are!" cried the staff member. "We tested them. And they're smarter. Oh, God!" He put his head in his hands and started to sob. Several other staff members around the room were crying.

Horsip let out a low growl, stuck his head into the corridor, and bellowed, "Guards!"

A sergeant came running, followed by a number of soldiers.

"Clear these natives out of here!" roared Horsip. "And hold them under guard till I give the word!"

The sergeant snapped, "Yes, sir!" and began to bawl orders.

The natives marched past with knives and guns in their backs.

"Listen," said one of the natives conversationally, as he was hustled out of the room, "if you'd just put holes in the guards of those knives, you could slip them over the gun barrels, and it would make it twice as easy . . ." His voice faded away in the corridor.

Horsip, furious, turned to glare at his staff. With the natives' voices taken out of the room, the sobbing and whimpering was now plainly audible.

"Stop that!" roared Horsip.

"We can't help it," sobbed several voices in unison, "they're smarter than we are."

"Gr'r'r," said Horsip, his face contorted. He reached out, grabbed one man by the uniform top, and slapped him hard across the face. The man stiffened, his eyes flashing reflexive rage.

"Listen to me!" roared Horsip. "You limp-spined, knock-kneed boobs! You yellow, cowardly, worthless sons of unwed humanoid mothers, pay attention here, before I—"

Slap!

"Look up, you slack-jawed—"

Slap!

"Straighten up, before I—"

Slap!

"Look up, you—"

Slap! . . . Slap! . . . Slap! . . .

Massaging his fingers, Horsip returned to the head of the silent room.

"Morons," he said angrily, "you boobs, you simpletons, you subhuman—"

"That's just it!" cried one of the men. "The things you just said are—"

"Shut up!" Horsip glared at him, then let his glare roam over each of the others in turn.

"Here you sit," he went on, "the elect of Centra. Not the smartest, by a long shot, but good enough to be in Planetary Integration. And you moan because the lop-tails are smarter. Do you make your own minds stronger by putting your heads in your hands and groaning about it? Do you make a muscle stronger by complaining that it's weak? Do you climb a hill by lying down, putting your hands over your eyes, and rolling to the bottom—all because someone else seemed to be a little higher up? Do you?"

There was a feeble scattering of No's.

"No!" said Horsip. "That's right. Now you're starting to think. If you want to be stronger, you use your muscles, so if you want to strengthen your grip, do you let things go loose and sloppy through your fingers? No, you grip down tight on something suited for the purpose. And if you want your mind to grip stronger, do you let it stay limp and loose with self-pity? Do you? *No!* You grip with it! You take hold of something small enough to work with and grip it, fasten your attention on it, and then you've exercised your mind and you're stronger. Right?

"Now"—he turned to the nearest man—"fasten your mind on what you've learned from these natives. Hold it steady and think on it. Nothing else. The rest of you, do the same. What an opportunity for you! Then, when you've squeezed all the juice out of what you've learned, boil it down, and put the essence of it on a sheet of paper so I can look it over. Now I am going to be busy, so get to work."

Horsip stalked out of the room, closed the door firmly, strode down the hall to his suite, and locked the door behind him.

"My God," he groaned. "They *are* smarter than we are!"

He stripped off his wet clothes, soaked himself in a steaming hot bath, fell into his bed in a state of exhaustion, and slept sixteen hours without a break.

He awoke feeling refreshed, till he thought what had happened the day before. With a groan, he got up, and some time later appeared in the Planetary Integration offices, smiling confidently. A stack of papers twice as thick as his hand was waiting for him on his desk. He greeted his staff cheerfully, noted that if they were not exuberant at least they were not sunk in despair, then picked up the stack of papers and strode out.

Back in his private suite, he plopped the papers down, looked at them uneasily, chose a comfortable seat, loosened the collar of his uniform, got up, checked the door, sat down, and began going through the papers, peeping cautiously at the titles of each report before looking further. Clearly, the natives had unburdened themselves of a vast amount of information. But most of it was very specialized. About a quarter of the way down the list, Horsip came on a thick report labeled "Love Habits of the Lop-Tail Natives." Firmly he passed over the paper, moved on, and found one headed "Why the Lop-Tails Do Not Have Space Travel." He separated this from the rest, put one labeled "The Mikeril Peril" with it, set it aside, and went on.

When he was through, he had a much smaller pile of papers that he thought worth reading, the lot headed by a paper on "Topics the Lop-Tail Humanoids Avoided Discussing." Before starting to read them, he thought he should just glance through the pile to see that he hadn't missed any. About a quarter of the way through the heap, he came on a thick paper labeled "Love Habits of the Lop-Tail Natives." H'm, he thought, there might be important information in that. You never knew. . . . Firmly, he passed over it and searched through the remaining sheets. He set the pile aside, it slipped off the table, and as he bent to pick it up he came across "Love Habits of the Lop-Tail Natives."

He decided to just glance at the first page.

Fifty-one minutes later, Moffis rudely interrupted Horsip's wide-eyed scrutiny of page eighteen by hammering on the door.

"Now what?" demanded Horsip, opening the door.

Moffis strode in angrily, a large piece of message paper fluttering in his hand.

"The double-damned boob won't reinforce us, that's what! Look at this!" Moffis thrust out the paper.

Horsip read through the usual dates and identification numbers, passed through some double-talk that all boiled down to "I've thought it over," and then came to the sentence: "Requests for such massive reinforcements at this date would create a most unfavorable atmosphere, and insofar as the Sector Conference on Allocation of Supplies is about to begin, it seems highly inadvisable at this end to produce a general impression of disappointment and/or dissatisfaction concerning the performance of any units of this command."

Horsip's teeth bared involuntarily. He took a deep breath

and read on. There were vague hints of promotion if all went
well, and subtle insinuations that people would be jammed
headfirst into nuclear furnaces if things went wrong. It ended
up with double-talk designed to create a sensation of mutual
good feeling.

Moffis glared. "Now what do we do?"

Horsip controlled his surging emotions, and took time to
think it over. Then he said, "There's a time to smile all over
and be as slippery as a snake in a swamp, and then there's a
time to roar and pound on tables. Go find out when this Sector Conference meets, and where."

Moffis hurried out of the room.

Horsip went into his office, yanked down a book on protocol, and began drafting a message.

Moffis found him some time later and came in. "I've got
the location and time."

"All right," said Horsip, "then send this." He handed over
a sheet of paper. "If possible, it ought to be timed so it will
arrive just as the conference opens."

Moffis looked at it and turned pale. He read aloud:

"Situation here unprecedented. Require immediate rein-
forcement by two full expeditionary forces to gain effective
control of situation, which has exceeded in violence and
danger that of Centralis II."

Moffis swallowed hard. "Do I sign that or do you?"

Horsip glared at him. "I'm signing it. And it would be
much more effective if you signed it too."

"All right," said Moffis. He smiled grimly and went out of
the room.

Horsip shivered, went back to his suite, wrapped himself
up in a blanket, and began reading "Topics the Lop-Tail Humanoids Avoided Discussing."

Horsip was very thoughtful after reading that paper. Apparently the humanoids were slippery as eels regarding any
discussion of military principles or problems. They professed
also a great ignorance concerning questions of nuclear fission.
They were evasive concerning a glaring discrepancy between
the numbers of cannon, traveling forts, etc., turned over to
the Centrans, and the number that were estimated to have
been used in action. Horsip made brief notes on a pad of paper, and turned without pleasure to the next report.

This was a paper headed "The Mikeril Peril." As usual, he
felt the hair on the back of his neck rise at mention of the
word "Mikeril." Uneasy tingling sensations went up and
down his back, probably dating from the childhood days

when his mother warned him, "Klide, do you know what happens to bad boys who don't do what they're told? ... The Mikerils get them." The Mikerils ate Centrans. Or, at least, they *had* before the Centrans wiped them out in a series of wars. Horsip pulled the blanket around him and began reading the paper.

"I was discussing problems in statistics with one of the lop-tails," the paper began, "and while searching a test problem to put to him, I came across some old data concerning the numerous outbreaks of Mikerils on Centra and other planets we have occupied.

"On the basis of the partial data I gave him, the native was able to accurately date other outbreaks that preceded and followed the period concerning which I had given him information. I was preparing to concede the correctness of his calculations, when he screwed up his face, put his head on one side, and said, 'I should estimate the next probable heavy outbreak to take place sixty-seven days four hours and thirteen minutes from now, plus or minus 7.2 minutes.' "

Horsip looked up, the hair on his back rose, and he experienced a severe chill as he seemed to see a big hairy Mikeril sinking its poison shafts into its victim, its many legs spinning him around and around as it bound him helplessly and carried him off inert.

Then Horsip sank down in his seat, looked over the prediction again, and his eye caught on "plus or minus 7.2 minutes." Horsip decided the native was either vastly overenthusiastic, or else just liked to poke people in the ribs to see them jump. He turned to the next paper.

This one, on "Why the Lop-Tails Do Not Have Space Travel," made difficult reading. Horsip could not reconcile the straightforward title with the involved argument and minute dividing of hairs in the body of the paper. After a hard fight, Horsip got to the last paragraph of the report, which read:

Summary: In summary, this author states the conclusion that the beings provisionally known as "lop-tailed humanoids" failed to acquire space-traversing mechanisms owing to a regrettable preoccupation with secondary matters pertaining principally to interests other than those regarding the traverse of interplanetary and interstellar regions, primarily; and secondarily, owing to use of that characteristic provisionally known as "pseudointelligence," the aforesaid beings were enabled to produce locally satisfactory working solutions to certain difficult and specialized problems the solution of which, in a different state of affairs, might well have even-

tuated in the discovery of the principle known briefly in common professional parlance as the positive null-void (PN-V)
law. With these conclusions, the native known as Q throughout this paper was in complete accord.

Horsip, dazed from the rough treatment the paper had
given him, stared at it in vague alarm. Unable to pin down
the exact point that bothered him, he moved on, fuzzy-
brained, to the next report.

This one started off as if it consisted of vital information
about the very core of lop-tail psychology. But on close inspection, it turned out to contain a collection of native fairy
tales. Horsip read dully about "Pandora's Box, the highly significant, crystallized expression of the fear-of-the-unknown
syndrome, the reaction of retreat-into-the-womb; the tale
symbolizes the natives' attitude toward life and their world.
The protagonist, Pandora, receives a box (significance of angular shape of typical native container), which she is not
supposed to open (see taboo list, below), and a variety of
afflictions emerge *into* the world (Pandora's world). . . ."

Horsip looked up angrily to hear a knock sound on the
door. He let Moffis in.

"I sent it off," said Moffis.

"What?" snapped Horsip.

"The message to the Sector Conference, of course." He
looked sharply at Horsip. "What hit you?"

"Oh, these stinking reports," said Horsip angrily. "Come in
and lock the door."

Horsip went back to the reports and told Moffis about
them.

"Some are good, and some are bad," said Horsip, "and
some are written so you need a translator to explain them to
you. It's always been like that, but on this planet, it seems ex-
aggerated. . . . I suppose for the same reason that a ground-
car makes more trouble in rough country."

"Well," said Moffis, "maybe I can help you. Let me look
over that bunch you've finished. That business about the significant quantities of guns, etc., that are missing makes me
uneasy."

"Help yourself," said Horsip.

Moffis picked up the pile and leafed through it. He paused
at one report, looked at it, started to pull it out, put it back,
scowled, looked at it again, shrugged, pulled it out farther,
held his place in the pile with one hand, and pulled it out all
the way to look at it.

Together they read the reports, Horsip uttering groans and curses, and Moffis saying "H'm" from time to time.

At last Horsip threw down several reports with a loud *whack*, and turned to speak to Moffis.

Moffis was absorbed.

Horsip looked impressed, turned away considerately, stiffened suddenly, turned back, got down on his hands and knees, twisted his head around, and looked up from below at the title of what Moffis was reading. The letters stared down at him:

"Love Habits of the Lop-Tail Natives."

Horsip untwisted himself, stood up, brushed himself off, and disgustedly left the room. He strode down the corridor, resolved on action. He was fed up with this feeling of struggling uphill through a river of glue. He was in charge of this planet and he aimed to make his influence felt. The first thing obviously was to take these natives the staff had been questioning, get one of them alone with some guards, then put the questions to him. This business of getting it second- or third-hand was no good.

He turned a corner, walked to a door marked "Prison," said, "At ease," as the guard snapped to attention, and started in.

"Sir," said the guard desperately, "I wouldn't go in there just now. Things are a little confused right now, sir."

Horsip's brows came together and he strode through the doorway as if propelled by rockets. He halted with equal suddenness on the other side.

Several dazed-looking soldiers were working under the direction of a red-faced officer who was barking oaths and orders in rapid succession. The general direction of the effort seemed to be to get three soldiers who were tied up untied. The trouble was that the three were off the floor, strung by their middles to the upper tier of bars in a cell. When one soldier was successfully pulled to the floor, overenthusiastic soldiers working on the other side of the bars would make a leap upward, seize one of the other soldiers, and haul him down, whereupon the first soldier would fly up out of the hands of the men trying to untie him.

"Captain," said Horsip dryly, "concentrate your effort on one man at a time."

The officer was apparently shouting too loudly to hear.

Wham! Down came one soldier and up went another.

The officer paid not the slightest attention to Horsip's order.

Horsip noticed one of the three tied soldiers slowly bending and unbending from his middle.

The first soldier came down and the second jerked up.

The officer screamed in frustration: threats, oaths, and orders mingled together in a rage that drove the soldiers to jerking frenzy.

Down came the second soldier. Up went the first.

Now the first was down again. Now he was up. Now down again.

Up ... down ... up ...

Every small detail of the scene was suddenly crystal clear to Horsip, as if he were seeing it under thick glass. He felt detached from it all, much like a third person looking on. When he spoke he did not feel that he gave excessive force to the word. He was hardly conscious of speaking at all. He merely said:

"CAPTAIN!"

The officer halted in mid-curse. He turned around with the glassy-eyed expression of a fish yanked out of the water on a hook.

The soldiers froze in various postures, then jerked to attention.

The outer door opened and the guard presented arms.

Horsip said, "Captain, take the two nearest soldiers. Have them pull down that man on the *outside* of the cell. Now have them hold tight to that rope that's looped up over the bar. Now, take the next two nearest soldiers and have them untie that man. . . . All right. Now, have those next two soldiers stand on the opposite side of those bars, *inside* the cell, ready to catch that other soldier when the rope is lowered."

The captain, using his hands to move the soldiers around, was following out Horsip's orders in a sort of dumb stupor. The first soldier was untied. The second soldier was cut down. The second soldier was untied. The third soldier was untied, and sat chafing his wrists and hands and massaging his abdomen.

Horsip motioned the captain into a little cubicle containing a desk and a filing cabinet.

"What's happened here?" said Horsip.

The captain merely blinked.

Horsip tried again. The captain stood there with an unfocused look.

"Report your presence," said Horsip.

The captain's hand came up in a salute, which Horsip returned.

"Sir, Captain Moklis Mogron, 14-0-17682355, Third Head-quarters Guards, reports his presence."

The captain blinked, and his eyes came to a focus. He seemed to really see Horsip for the first time. He turned pale.

"What happened, Captain?" said Horsip.

"Sir, I . . ." The captain stopped.

"Just tell me what you saw and heard, as it happened," said Horsip.

"Well, I . . . sir, it all boils down to . . . I just don't remember."

"What's the first thing you do remember?"

"I opened that outside door, and I came in, and . . . wait. No. The guard came to me and told me the prisoners needed attention. I came in, and . . . and . . ." He scowled fiercely. "Let's see, I came in, and, let's see, one of the prisoners . . . yes! The prisoners were out of their cells! . . . But they said that's what they called me in for. The lock design on the cell was no good, and they wanted to show me a better one. One of them was holding a shiny key on a string in the bright light from this desk light—Now, what was that doing out there?—and he said to look at it, and watch it, and keep my eye on it, and he'd explain why I should . . . should . . ."

The captain looked dazed.

"Report your presence!" snapped Horsip.

The captain did so. Horsip tried several times, but could not get past the point where the natives showed the captain the shiny key in the bright light. Horsip became vaguely aware that he was wasting his time on scattered details, and, as usual on this planet, coming away empty-handed. He sent the captain out to learn from the three soldiers how they had come to be tied up in the air that way. The captain returned to say the natives had told the soldiers about a rope trick, had gotten them over the bars with a coil if rope, and that was all the soldiers remembered.

Horsip sent out orders to comb the place for the prisoners, and for anyone who had seen them pass to report it.

The prisoners weren't found, and everyone was sure *he* hadn't seen them.

Horsip went back to his rooms feeling more than ever as if he were struggling uphill through layers of mud.

❈ V ❈

Spike-Bars and Fang-Wire

The next day passed in a welter of sticky details. The staff had finally figured out how to get supplies to the outposts without having the tires shot out in the process. An armored ground-car towing a string of supply waggons was to approach the outposts, traveling along the roadway at high speed. As the cars passed the outposts, soldiers on the waggons were to throw off the necessary supplies, which the men from the outposts would come out and pick up. In this way, the staff exulted, there would be no need for the cars to slow down; as the natives seemed reluctant to fire at moving vehicles—lest they kill someone and invoke the edict—there should be no more trouble from that source.

To protect vehicles from sabotage at night, the staff proposed the construction of several enormous car-parks, to be surrounded by leaping-mine fields and thick spike-bar barriers.

Meanwhile, another convoy of eighteen cars had shot off the bottom of the hilly curve with no known explanation. The staff advised the building of a fortified observation post, with no fewer than two observers on watch at all times, so it could at least be found out what happened.

But the old troubles were not the only ones to deal with. Just as the Planetary Integration team triumphantly handed out answers to thorny problems that had confounded them in the past, word came of something new and worse. The soldiers were getting hard to manage.

Always in the past, on conquered planets, the troops had had *some* sort of female companionship. The natives had often been actually glad to make alliances with their conquerors. But here, such was not the case. The females of the local species ran shrieking at the approach of a love-starved

soldier. This had a bad effect on morale. Worse yet, the lop-
tail authorities had been offering to help matters by showing
the soldiers instructive moving pictures on the topic, these
pictures being the very same ones used to instruct the lop-tail
soldiers on how to act toward females. Since seeing these pictures, it was a question who was more afraid of whom, the
soldiers or the women. Now there was a sort of boiling re-
sentment and frustration, and there was no telling where it
might lead.

While the staff, under Horsip's direction, was thrashing this
problem out, Moffis, red-faced and indignant, came charging
into the room.

Horsip sprang from his seat and rushed Moffis out into another room.

"Hairy master of sin!" roared Moffis. "Are you trying to
ruin me?"

"Keep your voice down," said Horsip. "What's wrong
now?"

"Wrong? That stinking idea for feeding the outposts, that's
what's wrong."

"But ... why?"

"*Why?*" Moffis growled deep in his throat. He stepped
back, his teeth bared and one hand out to his side. "All right.
Here I am. I'm on one of these stinking supply waggons your
bright boys say ought to be hooked up to the ground-cars.
We're racing along the road at 'high speed,' like we're supposed to. We go over a repaired place in the road. All the
waggons go up in the air. I have to hang on for dear life or *I*
go up in the air. Now someone yells, 'Three barrels of flour,
a sack of mash, three large cans Concentrate B, and a case of
.33 splat-gun darts.' "

Moffis glared. "I'm supposed to get this stuff unstrapped
and pitched out between the time we bounce over the repaired place and the time the outpost shoots past to one
side?"

Horsip hesitated.

"Come on," roared Moffis. "*Am* I?"

"Well, now, look," said Horsip. "You're not going at it the
right way."

"Oh, I'm not, am I?"

Horsip flared: "If you had the sense an officer's supposed
to have, you'd know better than to have the stuff strapped in
helter-skelter. You'd have a supply schedule strapped to a
waggon post, and the supplies all loaded on in reverse order,
so it would be no trouble at all—"

"But," said Moffis, "I'm not playing the *part* of an officer here! I'm one of our *soldiers!* I'm irked and griped because here I am, a soldier of the Integral Union, and I don't even dare speak to any of the native girls running around. There's no fighting going on—nothing definite—just an endless folderol that isn't getting anywhere. I'm about fed up with the thing. Every time I turn around there's some new makeshift."

"Yes, yes," said Horsip. "I see that—"

"All right," said Moffis, "the point is, the soldier is no mathematician in the first place. If you explain every point of the routine to him . . . okay, *maybe.* But if he isn't used to it, things are going to get snarled up. Well, he hasn't had any training for this routine and it's a mess."

"In time—" said Horsip, groping his way.

"In time, nothing," said Moffis. "It won't work, and that's that. I haven't even had time to tell you everything wrong with it. What do you suppose these barrels and cans *do* when they hit the ground, anyway?"

"Well—"

"They *burst,* that's what they do! And I'm here to tell you a soldier that sees his barrel of flour come out the side of a waggon, hit the ground, fly to pieces, and then get swirled all over the road by half a dozen sets of wheels is in no frame of mind worth talking about."

"For—"

"He has to sweep it up with a broom!" roared Moffis. "And by the Great Hungry Mikeril, I tell you, I don't want to be around trying to give that soldier orders until we've unloaded his gun and got his knife away from him. There's got to be some other way of supplying these outposts or I pull in every one of them and to hell with sharpshooters along the road. At least the men will be able to eat."

"Yes," said Horsip, feeling exhausted, "I see you've got a point there."

"All right," said Moffis. He stopped to swallow and massage his throat. "There's another thing. This car-park idea."

"Surely there's nothing wrong with that."

"No, the *idea* is all right. The plan on paper looks good. But how many million gross of spike-bars do your people think an army is equipped with, anyway? You're an officer. You know that. We have just so many for ordinary requirements, plus a reserve for desperate situations. And that's it. Well, this planet has been nothing but one big desperate situation since we landed on it. We just don't have the material to make any such big things as these car-parks."

"Couldn't you," said Horsip, desperately, "collect a few here and there from your fortifica—"

"*No!*" roared Moffis, his voice cracking. "Not on your life! Once we start gnawing holes in our own defenses—"

"All right, then," said Horsip, straightening up, "what about the natives? They had armies. *They* must have used spike-bars. Or, if they didn't, we can teach them how they're made, buy them from them . . ."

Moffis looked down at the floor gloomily.

"What's the matter?" said Horsip.

Moffis shook his head. "They didn't use spike-bars."

"Well, then, we can teach—"

"They had their own stuff."

Horsip looked apprehensive. "What?"

"Fang-wire."

Horsip felt himself sinking into a fog of confusion. With an effort, he struggled clear. "What did you say?"

"I said, they had their own stuff. Fang-wire."

"What in the world is that?"

"Thick twisted wire with teeth on it."

Horsip goggled. "Is it as good as our spike-bars?"

"As far as coming up against it, one is about as bad as the other."

"Then, why don't we use it?"

Moffis shook his head. "If you ever saw our soldiers laying the stuff out—it comes wound up on little wire barrels. You have to take one end of the stuff, without getting the teeth in you, and pull it free. It comes off twisted, it jumps and vibrates, and the teeth are likely to get you if you try to straighten it out. I saw half a company of soldiers fighting three rolls of fang-wire the only time we ever tried to use it. The wire was winning. The natives were dug in on a hill opposite from us, and they were having hysterics. No, thanks. Never again."

"Listen," said Horsip doggedly, "if *they* use the stuff, there must be some way to do it."

"That's so," said Moffis, "but if we take the time to train the army all over again in new ways of fighting, we aren't going to get anything else done."

Horsip paced the floor. "I hate to say this, Moffis, but it appears to me to be a plain fact that this victory is tearing the army to pieces."

"I know it," said Moffis.

"Everywhere we come in contact with the natives, something goes wrong."

Moffis nodded.

"All right," said Horsip, his voice rising. "What we need here is drastic action, striking at the root of the trouble."

Moffis watched Horsip uneasily. "What, though?"

"Reconcentration," said Horsip. "The iron rusts fast when it's cut in bits where the air can get at it. Melt it back into a bar and only the surface will rust. Then the bar will keep its strength." Horsip looked hard into Moffis' eyes. "We've got to mass the troops. Not just the road outposts, but the occupation districts. Everything. Take over a dominating section of this planet and *command* it."

"But regulations . . . in Phase II we *have* to do it this way!"

"All right," said Horsip, "then we'll go back to Phase I."

"But ... but that's never been done! That's ..." Moffis paused, frowning. "It might work, at that. The devil with regulations."

They gripped each other's arms. Moffis started for the door and walked into a hurrying messenger. They exchanged salutes, Moffis took the paper, looked at it, and handed it to Horsip. Horsip looked at it and read aloud:

"Hold on. Arriving in thirty days. Twenty million troops in motion. Your plan good. . . . Argit, Supreme Integrator."

"I guess we'd better stay put," said Moffis.

Horsip frowned. "Maybe so."

❊ VI ❊

The Ground Shook

It was a trying thirty days.

The outposts took to buying food direct from the natives. The road-repair crews fell into an ugly habit of getting out of work by exposing arms or legs and daring the lop-tails to shoot at them. There were so many flesh wounds that the aid stations began running out of supplies. Troops in the remoter sections began drinking a kind of liquid propellant the lop-tails sold in bottles and cans. It was supposed to cure boredom, but the troops went wild on it, and the reserves were kept bouncing and grinding from one place to another, thinking the war had broken out again.

Planetary Integration did have a few victories to its credit. The trouble on the hilly curve, for instance, proved to be caused by a gang of native boys who came out every few days and stretched a cable across the road at an angle. The speeding ground-cars spun around the curve, slid along the cable, and went over the edge. The boys then came out, rolled up the cable, and went home for breakfast. By the time this was discovered, the situation was so uneasy no one thought of asking any more than that the boys be spanked and the cable confiscated.

At intervals, by now, large concentrations of humanoid soldiers were observed in open maneuvers; their troops were fully equipped with stitching-guns, cannons run from place to place by their own engines, and traveling forts in numbers sufficient to turn a man pale at the mere mention.

Horsip watched one of these maneuvers through a double telescope in an observation post on his fortified mountain.

"Is that what you had to fight, Moffis?" he asked, his voice awed.

"That's it," said Moffis. "Only more of them."

37

Horsip watched the procession of forts, guns, and troops roll past in the distance.

"Their air-planes," said Moffis, "were worse yet."

"Then how did you ever win?"

"For one thing," said Moffis, "they weren't expecting it. For another, they wasted energy fighting each other. Then, too, our troops were in good order then. They were used to victory, and they were convinced they were superior. Then, too, we used the Fleet to cut the natives' communications lines."

Horsip looked through the telescopes for a while, then straightened up decisively.

"Well, Moffis," he said, "we're in a mess. We're like a man in an ice-block house when the spring thaw sets in. We don't dare step down hard anywhere lest the whole thing fall apart. We've got to walk easy, and just hope the cold wind gets here before it's too late ... But there *is* one thing we ought to do."

"What's that?" said Moffis.

"The reserves. They aren't committed anywhere. We've got to hold them in hand. And if we need them, we want them to be a club, not a length of rotten wood. We've got to train them so hard they don't have any time to get flabby."

"Truth," said Moffis. "There are so many leaks to patch, one forgets other things."

The occupation army got through twenty-four of the thirty days like a ship sinking slowly on a perfectly even keel.

On the twenty-fifth day, however, a procession of native military might passed by Horsip's mountain headquarters in such strength that the ground was felt to tremble steadily for three hours and a half.

On the twenty-sixth day, a native delegation called on Horsip and politely but firmly pointed out to him that this military occupation was disrupting business, and was causing all manner of trouble to everyone concerned; it should, therefore, end. Horsip was very agreeable.

On the twenty-seventh day, three hundred traveling forts blocked traffic on one of the main highways for more than two hours.

On the twenty-eighth day, a flying bomb came down a mile and a half from headquarters, and left a hole big enough to hide a space fleet. The ground shuddered and quaked with marching feet. That evening, the native delegation called again on Horsip and stated their position in short pithy sentences, and words of few syllables. Horsip pleaded that he

was tied up in red tape. The natives suggested the best way
to get rid of red tape was to cut it with a knife.

In the early morning of the twenty-ninth day, a flight of
Centran air-planes, trying to scout the strength and direction
of the native movements, was forced down by humanoid air-
craft that flew at and around them as if they were standing
still. Horsip ordered the rest of his air-planes grounded and
kept hidden till he gave the word. The observers of the
planes forced down straggled in to report massive enemy
concentrations flowing along the roads past the small forts
and splat-gun nests as if they did not exist. The troops in the
forts and nests were apparently afraid to fire for fear of
being obliterated.

Horsip received the reports while Moffis carried out a
last-minute inspection of the fortifications at and around
headquarters. Late that morning, a hot meal was given to all
the troops.

At noon a traveling fort of a size suitable to have trees
planted on it and take its place among the foothills was seen
approaching headquarters. It moved into range, came up
close, and swung its large gun to aim directly at the concrete
doorway heading down into the mountain. Horsip ordered his
gunners not to fire, his unexpressed reason being that he was
afraid it would have no effect. He then bade Moffis a private
farewell, walked out the concrete doorway in full regalia,
glanced at the huge fort, laughed, and remarked to a white-
faced man at a splat-gun that this would be something to tell
his children. He carried out a calm, careful inspection of the
fortifications, reprimanding one gunner mildly for flecks of
dirt in a gun barrel. He glanced confidently up the mountain-
side where ranks of cannon snouts centered on the huge fort.
The gunners around him followed his gaze. Horsip returned
the salute of the officer in charge and went back below.

On the plain before the mountain, hundreds of traveling
forts were grinding across country, clouds of dust raising up
behind them.

"We should open fire," said Moffis.

"No," said Horsip. "Remember, we're playing for time."

The traveling forts swerved and began approaching. Behind them, the hills were alive with troops and guns.

Horsip gave orders that a huge orange cloth be unrolled on
the far side of the mountain. A landing boat circling far
above did a series of dips and rolls and rose rapidly out of
sight.

The traveling forts came closer.

The monster fort just outside headquarters debouched one

native who came in under guard and demanded Horsip's surrender.

Horsip suggested they hold truce talks.

The native returned to his fort.

The troops in the distance began spreading out and crossing the plain.

The huge fort moved its gun a minute fraction of an inch, there was a blinding flash, a whirl of smoke. The tunnel entrance collapsed. There was a deafening clap and a duller boom. The ground shook. Tons of dirt slid down over the entrance. There was a fractional instant when the only sound was the last of the dirt sliding down. Then the earth leaped underfoot as the guns on the mountain opened up.

The traveling forts roared closer, their firing a bright winking of lights at first, the boom and roar coming later. The troops behind followed at a run.

Horsip ordered the planes up, to ignore the forts and attack the troops.

Humanoid planes swooped over a nearby hill.

Life settled into a continuous jar that rattled teeth, dulled thought, and undermined the sense of time. Things began to seem unreal and discontinuous.

Reality passed in streaks and fragments as Horsip ordered the movement of cannon by prepared roadways to replace those put out of action. There was a glaring interval where he seemed to live a whole lifetime while reports came in that enemy troops were swarming up the hillside to silence the guns by hand-to-hand fighting. When the attack slowed, he sent a body of reserves to drive the attackers back down and away. But more came on.

The enemy planes began a series of dives, unloosing rockets that bled his troops like long knives stabbed into flesh. Moffis ordered the highest guns to fire on the planes and the rest to carry on as they were. Horsip spent a precious second damning himself for not making that arrangement prior to the battle, and then a yell from the enemy sounded as they surged through the doorway Horsip had thought blocked. He sent a few troops with splat-guns to fire down the corridors, then had to turn his attention to a rush up the reverse side of the hill that had captured a number of the lower gun positions there. He sent in a picked body of the Headquarters Guard he had ordered concealed on the side of the hill for that very purpose.

Evening had at last come, and with it a steady rumbling from the near distance, where the sky was lit with a blue and yellow blaze. Centran ships were pounding the gun positions on the opposite ridge, and their screens were flaring almost continuously with the impact of missiles slammed against them.

The fighting had died out around the mountain, and Horsip and Moffis went out with a small guard to inspect the positions personally. The air was pungent and damp. Their ears felt as though they had layers of cloth over them. There was a thin moon, and here and there on the ground pale glimmerings could be seen as wounded men moved. There was an almost continuous low moan in the air. A soldier with his back against a gun feebly raised a hand as Horsip came near. "The Great One bless you, sir," he said. "We threw 'em back."

Horsip went back to his command post after ordering several guns moved and some spike-bar barriers set up. He felt dazed. He lay down on a cot for a few hours' sleep, and was wakened in the early morning to be told an important message had arrived.

On the thirtieth day, five million reinforcements landed.

❋ VII ❋

Argit Finds His Q-Mine

Horsip spent the day explaining the situation to Drasmon Argit, the Supreme Integrator.

Argit paced the floor, ate meals, lay down on a couch, stretched, pounded out questions, gave orders to hurrying subordinates, and listened, questioned, listened, as Horsip, in a desperate urgency to get the situation across, explained and expounded, using charts, maps, diagrams, and photographs. He tried to get across the sensation of struggling uphill through a river of glue, and was gratified to see that Argit seemed to be getting the idea faster than he—Horsip—had.

After the evening meal was eaten and the dishes cleared away in the privacy of a small office, Argit got up and said, "All right, I think I see your point. The natives are technologically more advanced than we are. By a freak, they don't have space travel. We beat them for this reason and because we caught them off guard and they attacked each other. There is also the possibility that they are more intelligent than we are.

"All these things are possible. In the course of occupying a million worlds—and there must be that many—who could hope we would not find beings more intelligent than we? Yet these intelligent beings had not yet succeeded in integrating their own planet, much less whole star systems, as we have done. On the contrary, they were about ready to blow their own planet apart when we landed. Why was that?

"You know the principle of the nuclear engines. There is a substance Q that flings out little particles. These little particles strike other atoms of Q, which fling out more particles. There is also a substance L, which absorbs these particles. Success depends on the correct proportioning of Q and L. There must not be too much L or the particles are absorbed

before things can get started. There must not be too much Q
or the particles build up so fast that suddenly the whole thing
flies apart.

"Now, consider these natives. What are they like? An engine with too much Q, is it not? And what are we like? To
speak frankly, Horsip, we have a little too much L, don't you
think?"

Horsip nodded reluctantly, then said, "I think I see your
point all right, but what are the flying particles in this comparison?"

Argit laughed. "Ideas. From what you tell me of these
people, they fairly flood each other with ideas. Horsip, you
and I and others in our position have had a difficult time. We
are like atoms of Q tearing ourselves apart to try and fling
enough particles—ideas—through the general mass so the
thing won't all grind to a stop. We only half succeed. At intervals these Mikerils come along and hurl us halfway back
into barbarism. We should be able merely to raise the speed
of reaction a little and burn them back into outer space. But
we haven't been able to. The machine was running as well as
it could already. . . . Not enough Q. Horsip, this planet is a
veritable mine! There are vast quantities of Q here. It is just
what we need!"

Horsip scowled. "Getting it out may be another matter."

Argit nodded. "We only arrived just in time. A little longer
and it might all have blown up. We have to fix that first."

"How?"

"Your idea, first. You intended to mix whole populations
up, because the language and customs difficulties would cause
much confusion and tie them in knots. That is very good.
That would act, you see, to slow up the spread of particles—ideas. But we want these people on our side. To that
end, we must first help remove their own difficulties—while
serving our own purposes, of course. We couldn't stand too
many eruptions like this.

"Horsip, with due consideration for their various levels of
civilization, we must transfer groups of young people, and
various professional groups, from one region of this planet to
others. We will not insist that they mix races or customs, but
chemicals react best when divided in small lumps, so—who
knows?—perhaps it will bring an end to some of these enmi-
ties.

"Meanwhile, they are bound to pick up our language. And
we will pick up such of their technological skills as we can
make use of. They need a universal language. We need new
discoveries. Both will profit.

"And then we will offer posts of importance, trade agreements, raw materials——"

"How do we know they are going to accept this?" said Horsip, remembering his own eagerness.

"Ha!" said Argit. "You showed me yourself. They are a born race of teachers and talkers. Every time they've been in here, what has it been? ... 'Let me show you how that should be done.' 'No, look, you have to do it this way.' 'Put a hole in the guard of that knife and you can slip it over the gun barrel.' " Argit laughed. "I will bet you the hairy arm of the first Mikeril that attacks us after we get this settled that half the trouble with these people is, they can't find anybody to listen to them."

Argit opened the door. A number of Centran troops were squatting in a circle outside, where a medical aide was bandaging a wounded native. The native was talking eagerly in the Centran tongue that appeared to seem simple to them compared to their own languages.

"Now," he was saying, "see here. Put a heavy bolt through this place where these bars come together, and you can vary the focus from here, with one simple motion. See? What's the advantage of having to swing each of these barrels around one at a time? It takes too long. You waste effort. But from *here*, you just loosen the nut, swing the barrels close, tighten it with the wrench, and you're all set. It'd be easier to carry, too."

The circle of Centrans looked at the native, looked at each other, and all nodded.

"Truth," said one of them somberly.

Argit closed the door.

"You see?" said Argit. "They're born Q material."

Horsip sadly shook his head. "It seems so. But what are our men? ... Damper rods."

The sound of tramping feet sounded outside in the corridor as the leading elements of more reinforcements marched past.

"That's all right," said Argit. "*We* need Q material."

The tramping rose to a heavy rumble. Horsip felt reassured and Argit nodded approvingly.

"And more than anything else I can think of," said Argit, speaking over the noise, "these people need damping rods.

"You have to have *both*."

❧ VIII ❧

Holding Down the Lid

Some days later, Horsip found himself studying the maps, where bright orange symbols showed the disposition of fifteen million fresh Centran reinforcements, with another five million standing by in their transports.

"I think," said Horsip, "that we can finally say that we have conquered this planet."

Moffis looked at the map skeptically. "That's what I thought, about a million and a half casualties ago."

"There's no armed resistance."

"There wasn't then, either."

Horsip nodded moodily. The effect of Argit's enthusiasm had worn off somewhat, and Horsip was again bothered by the natives' exasperating mental superiority. Horsip was now inclined to think that instead of merely mixing the natives up on their own planet, it might be a better idea to scatter them all over the universe—too much Q material in one spot could be dangerous.

Horsip, however, didn't want to make Moffis feel any more discouraged than he already did, and so, after a few comments recognizing the seriousness of the situation, Horsip shifted gears:

"However, thanks to numbers and surprise, we *have* conquered this batch, Moffis, and now we have to figure out what to do with them."

Moffis glanced at the maps.

"Let's just make sure they don't heave us right off the planet. I don't want to go through what we've just been through all over again. We need the rest of these reinforcements down here where we can get some use out of them. The longer we leave them in those transports, the more stale they're going to get."

45

"All right," said Horsip, "where do we put them?"

"Some place where the country is rugged, so we can defend it, and where the natives are scarce, so our men don't have too much contact with them, and get depressed by the comparison."

They pored over the maps, and Horsip said, "This Main-Base Defense Zone A looks as good as any—and we've already got it fortified. The main supply dumps are there, and the country couldn't be much more rugged. It's the least bad place to be if the enemy has any nuclear bombs left. But we can't cram *all* these reinforcements in there. Let's spread them around in these other main-base zones. The country there is fairly rugged, too, and the zones support each other."

Moffis looked relieved.

"Good. . . . Now, will Argit go along with it?"

Horsip thought a moment. Argit had understood the situation quickly, and even got along well with the tailless, furless inhabitants of the planet, who, in turn, appeared to forget that Argit was a Centran, the Chairman of the Supreme Staff, and the ultimate Centran military authority on the conquest of new planets.

"H'm," said Horsip. "That's the place where the troops will hurt the natives least, and help us most. I think Argit would be all in favor of it. But he's leaving these details to us. *His* problem is to figure out how to fit these lop-tails into the Integral Union without wrecking it, and I think he's busy enough with that. He's already mentioned some ideas to me."

Moffis grunted.

"Then let's get the troops down here. If we're going to keep this volcano from blowing up again, we need more weight to hold down the lid."

"Oh," said Horsip, glancing at the map, with all its reassuring orange symbols, "things aren't that bad, Moffis."

Moffis failed to look convinced.

The following days passed with great activity on everyone's part. Horsip's troops worked as if inspired—as they were, by Horsip, Moffis, and the other survivors of the first expedition. The natives, for their part, carried on an enormous trade. Argit, too, was busy.

One day Argit summoned Horsip to his office. Looking as if he had gone through several weeks of penance and fasting, Argit nevertheless spoke with satisfaction.

"When you want a stubborn, headstrong individual to do something," said Argit, "one way is to argue *against* it. Think up plausible reasons why you might want him *not* to do it, and act accordingly. The odds are good that he will end up doing what you tell him not to do, which, of course, is what you really want him *to* do."

Horsip thought it over. "You've persuaded the natives to—"

"They have persuaded me to open up the Integral Union to them. . . . Believe me, Horsip, there is all the difference in who persuades whom."

"Now it's *their* idea?"

"Exactly."

"But why *wouldn't* we want them to spread out?"

"Obviously—from their viewpoint—our supposed fear that they might take over the Integral Union. Of course, I never mentioned it. They deduced it."

Horsip thought of the number of star systems in the Integral Union, and his mind boggled.

Argit smiled. "Remember, Horsip, they have no real feeling yet for space. They've had no experience. They don't appreciate the order of magnitude involved. But they're moving in the direction we want. Now, for the first benefit of this policy, I will want your help, Horsip, in attending a meeting of the Supreme Staff, where we will evaluate a new military department, and the . . . ah . . . man in charge."

Horsip looked interested.

"Who is he?"

"His name is Towers. Let's see, *John* Towers."

"A lop-tail?"

Argit winced. "If we are going to get desirable results, Horsip, I think it would be just as well for us to call them 'Earthmen.' "

"He's one of the locals?"

"Yes. And as nearly as we can discover, his ideas, directly and indirectly, have cost us better than half a million casualties."

"He must be one of their highest officers."

"No. Ideas are not so rare with them as with us, so they don't value good ideas properly. This officer is appreciated only by a few loyal followers. He has the temporary rank of brigadier general, and the permanent rank of major. He is outspoken, and he has highly placed enemies. To get him out of their way, these enemies have cleverly decided to unload him on us. I think we can use him. We are going to have a special meeting of the Supreme Staff to consider the matter. We will need someone with firsthand experience of these Earthmen.

"And," added Argit, frowning, "we may run into opposition on the Staff itself. I'll appreciate your support."

Horsip considered what it would be like to have some Earthmen on *his* side for a change.

He nodded cheerfully. "I'll do my best."

❀ IX ❀

The High Command

Horsip, aboard the warship that served as their headquarters, looked on with awe as the generals of the Supreme Staff settled into their massive seats around the oval table. There was a creak of leather, the rustle of paper, the snap of lock-levers as the seats were adjusted. Then, halfway down the long side of the table, Argit, Chairman of the Supreme Staff, cleared his throat.

"The fourth meeting of the twentieth session of the present cycle is hereby opened. The meeting was called to consider a new military department. The secretary will note that all members are present, and will read the summary of the previous meeting."

A thin, nervous-looking individual at a small side table rose to his feet.

"Summary, third meeting, twentieth session. All members were present, two regional seats unfilled due to vacancies. Business at hand was to evaluate performance of General Klide Horsip, Planetary Integrator of Earth. Testimony of General Argit favorable. Records and reports examined. Exhibits: stitching-gun; stitching-gun, portable; several rolls four-tooth fang-wire; flying bomb with Q-metal warhead; disassembled warhead mechanism; scale models, traveling forts; other exhibits, listed in full minutes. Much discussion. Examination of casualty figures. Lively discussion. General Takkit moves for censure of General Horsip. Motion defeated. General Argit reprimands General Maklin for referring to General Takkit as a 'brainless molk.' General Argit reprimands General Roffis for correcting General Maklin, to say General Takkit is an 'addled molk.' General Maklin moves for approval of General Horsip's conduct. Motion passed. General Argit raises question of empty regional seats.

49

Lively discussion. General Roffis proposes General Horsip to
fill vacancy. Motion passed. General Argit raises question of
second vacancy. Much discussion, no agreement. General Argit closes meeting."

The secretary sat down.

Horsip, dazed, was escorted to a seat at the table. Argit
cleared his throat.

"We welcome our new regional member, and trust he will
add to the wisdom and harmony of these meetings. Horsip,
we need your experience on this next item of business. Now,
we have approved the plan, and the High Council has sanc-
tioned it, to give every opportunity to these Earthmen to disperse. We have now been offered use of an Earth military
unit—"

A bull-necked general seated to Argit's left cleared his
throat.

"Gride Maklin speaking. Let the secretary get it in the
minutes that I'm opposed to arming native troops. The Great
Records show we've already had two revolutions and an interstellar war out of that."

Argit said politely, "General, there's no need to interrupt.
You'll have full time, during the discussion."

"I want it in the minutes before you get us convinced in
spite of ourselves. We don't control a gun some native's got
in his hands. Our men get soft, and theirs get tough. Next
they jam our tail in the meat grinder. No, thanks. *We'll* keep
the guns, and *we'll* do the fighting. That's simpler."

Argit growled, "You've got it into the minutes now, General."

Maklin nodded. "It had to be said. Armed natives are poison."

A slender general near Horsip snarled, "Secretary, note
that Dorp Takkit opposes Maklin's giving the background
discussion."

A white-furred, steely-eyed general at the far end of the
table looked around.

"Sark Roffis. Note, secretary, that I back General Maklin's
opposition to native troops, and I back it to the hilt."

Takkit snarled, "We have one chairman. We don't need
three."

Another general growled approval.

A murmur arose like a hornet's nest when someone jars
the tree.

Argit said, very courteously, "The opposing viewpoints are
now on record. I hope that any further comment can wait
until we reach the discussion. Otherwise I will have to cen-

sure it, and the censure will go in the condensed summary. The High Council always reads the condensed summary."

There was a silence that bulged with unspoken comment, and Argit went on.

"These Earthmen have technological ability demonstrated in action, and shown in previous exhibits. They have been granted *full partnership* with Centra. 'Full partners' have to do their share of the fighting. The Earthmen are *not* going to be armed by us. Despite everything we can do to disarm them, they are still armed to the teeth, by their own efforts, and this unit in particular has a method of fighting that ought to be put to use for Centra's benefit.

"The question," said Argit, "is not of arming native troops, but of putting the prowess of this special unit to work for Centra. We have already suffered severely from the operations of this unit, and now, since the unit's commanding officer is unpopular with his short-sighted superiors, we can whisk this unit out from under the control of the Earthmen and put it to use ourselves. The general in charge of the unit is right outside, and we can call him in and evaluate the man and his methods."

There was a silence when Argit finished, and then the discussion began. General Maklin still opposed the idea, but he and everyone else wanted to see this native general. Argit turned to the guards.

"Show in General Towers."

The guards escorted into the room a trim Earthman, whose uniform bore a double row of ribbons, wings, and other emblems. The officer's bearing was quiet, but there was an indefinable something about him that made Horsip uneasy.

Around the table there were creaks, scrapes, and snaps as those with their backs to the door craned, shoved their chairs back, or pivoted around. Then came a grunt and murmur at the sight of the tailless, almost furless alien.

It came to Horsip that the indefinable something about this native was his quiet unimpressed look. There was no need to put him at his ease. He *was* at his ease.

Argit was saying, "Members of the Supreme Staff, this is Brigadier General John Towers. General Towers, we are considering the suggestion that you and your Special Effects Team serve as part of the Centran Armed Forces. What is your view of this?"

Towers said warily, "It's an idea."

Argit frowned. "Perhaps you'd care to give us your opinion?"

Towers looked stubborn.

"It all depends on who is over us, and how he operates." Towers, narrow-eyed, looked over the Supreme Staff, and, for an instant, Horsip seemed to see how he and the others must look to the Earthman:

Furry creatures, like some kind of blend of Earthmen and the furry animals they called *lions*.

Towers suddenly grinned.

"I don't know *how* it would work out. We've got some ideas we'd like to try out, but if I'm given orders what to do, and then when I start to do it some blockhead starts telling me I can't do it that way, or if I get orders to stick to my headquarters so I can fill out all the forms and be there when the phone rings, why, we're going to have trouble, and we might as well find it out right now. Give me a job—I'm not worried about how *hard* it is—but then leave me alone. Let me know what the problem is at the *beginning*. If I'm given to understand that the problem is such-and-such, and then every time I try to make a move some new condition is added, it isn't going to work. And there's something else. We might as well have this out in the open too. I figure there's no special break in the chain of command between top sergeant and second lieutenant. I don't see any unbridgeable gap there. If that's the wrong attitude, get somebody else for the job, because that's the attitude I'm going to have, whether I'm a buck private in the rear rank or the man in charge. What counts isn't rank, so far as I can see, but whether the man can and does do the work."

Towers looked at them, started to say more, then changed his mind, and waited attentively.

The clear impression came to Horsip that whether or not Towers was on trial before the Supreme Staff, the Supreme Staff was, in effect, on trial before Towers. Horsip, though agreeing with what Towers said, began to see why Towers was unpopular with his superiors.

Near Towers, the slender general named Takkit said, "You know, Towers, there are many unpleasant jobs in the Integral Union. An officer who failed to show a cooperative frame of mind could find himself with a succession of rather unpleasant assignments, with no advancement, and with—shall we say—a somewhat *tedious* life ahead of him. But life can be quite pleasant for those who are cooperative."

There was a sudden tense silence, with every eye on Towers.

Towers' eyes glinted, and then he smiled and faced Takkit. "Oh, I will cooperate, General."

Takkit said coolly, "I rather thought you would."

Towers added, "I just won't cooperate with a blockhead, General."

To Argit's left, the bull-necked general named Maklin suddenly grinned.

Takkit said coldly, "I trust—what is your actual rank?—Major, isn't it?—I trust, Major—line your hands up along the seams of your trousers, there—I trust that you understand the penalties for even the hint of discourtesy to superiors?"

Again there was silence, with every eye watching Towers, who clicked his heels, stood at stiff attention, and said, "Yes, sir."

Takkit said lazily, "Oh? Is that so? I'm surprised. I thought you had been in the lop-tail—pardon me, *Earth*—armed forces. How would *you* know *what* our regulations are?"

"Because, sir," said Towers, "when offered this opportunity to transfer to your armed forces, I naturally studied your regulations first."

"Is that so?" said Takkit, sounding somewhat foolish.

"Yes, sir," said Towers, without intonation.

At the far end of the table, the white-furred General Roffis looked at Takkit's expression and began to grin.

Towers remained at stiff attention.

Takkit said, "At any rate, *Major*, whatever order I directly give *you*, you *will* at once, and without hesitation or question, obey that order, *won't* you?"

"I will not, sir," said Towers matter-of-factly.

"WHY NOT?" roared Takkit.

"Because, sir," said Towers politely, "I am not yet a member of the Centran Armed Forces, and your authority over me is nonexistent."

At the far end of the table, General Roffis was beaming.

General Maklin, grinning, banged his fist on the table.

Takkit opened his mouth and shut it again.

Towers remained at stiff attention, waiting.

The silence stretched out, and Argit, with the urgent distracted look of someone groping for a way to cover up someone else's peculiarly stupid blunder, said, "Were there any more questions that you wanted to ask General Towers, General Takkit?"

Takkit let his breath out with a hiss.

"That will be all for now."

Towers turned to face Argit, and relaxed from his posture of stiff attention. He now looked alert and attentive, but at ease.

Argit said uneasily, "I think we understand, and are sympathetic with your ideas of command, General Towers . . ."

Horsip, watching, did not know how the Earthman's face could express, with scarcely a movement of the muscles, such a profound lack of agreement.

Argit studied Towers' face, cast an irritated glance at the fuming Takkit, and then suddenly glanced around at the other generals, a large number of whom were watching the scene with expressions of profound gratification. Argit seemed to come suddenly to a decision.

"General Towers, if you want the job, and are agreeable, we will, first, support your complete force, allow initially for recruitment to three times its current level, and give you a completely free hand in its organization."

"*That* part is more than satisfactory, sir," said Towers, plainly reserving judgment.

"Now," said Argit, "some of our men—even occasional general officers—are not always receptive until they get their minds on the track. Even highly able officers occasionally make errors. . . . We all do it. . . . And there are always clashes of personality amongst able men. You will need plenty of authority to get the proper cooperation. We cannot give you high rank in the beginning, until your method proves itself clearly. What I propose, to bridge the gap, is a device we have used occasionally in the past. This is the 'code name,' and its associated rank. If my colleagues agree, your regular rank with us will be that corresponding to the Earth rank of colonel. This rank is solid, not temporary, but it is insufficient to deal with a hard-headed general in a tight spot. We therefore offer, if the majority of my colleagues agree, a code name—say, 'Able Hunter'—together with the rank of general, grade III, and—again if the majority of my colleagues agree—a regional seat for Able Hunter on the Supreme Staff. You see, General Towers, we cannot give *you* this rank, but we can give it to the code name, and then, at our will, assign the code name to you. You can then use the code name whenever you find it advisable. As code names receive no pay, you will suffer a disadvantage in pay for every day you assert this rank. However, once your method proves its worth, there should be little difficulty."

Argit looked around. "What do you say, shall we give General Towers the rank and code name, with the particulars I've just mentioned? . . . Secretary, note the votes."

A rumble of Yes's followed, and Argit turned to Towers, who cheerfully accepted the offer.

Horsip, smiling, considered the situation. The Integral

Union was so big that there were always upheavals of some kind going on somewhere.

If Towers, code named "Hunter," needed a place to try out his special methods, the Integral Union could certainly use someone who could straighten out problems.

The question was: *Could Towers do it?*

As Horsip asked himself that, there came a rap at the door, and the guards let in an officer who bent by Argit's chair with an air of gloom.

Argit's face took on a special look of frustration that could mean only one thing.

Horsip braced himself.

Argit looked up.

"Another revolt on Centralis II. This time, they've managed a *total* surprise."

There was a groan, then Argit, and everyone else, turned to the Earthman.

"Towers," said Argit, "if you want to test your methods, here's your chance. Get your troops together. We are sending you to Centralis II as fast as we can get you there."

❋ X ❋

Pandora's Unlocked Box

After Towers' departure, Horsip remained on the warship that housed the Supreme Staff. He had his own room and his own office, but spent most of his time working on a special three-man committee formed to keep track of the Earthmen's activities.

General Maklin and General Roffis sat with Horsip amidst growing stacks of papers, which they read with profanity and bafflement.

Horsip exasperatedly read of one Q. Zoffit, who had illegally bartered a Class VI landing boat for a "classic Packard in mint condition."

General Roffis smoothed back the thick white fur of his head and neck.

"While you were on this planet, Horsip, did you happen to have any experience with a . . . ah . . ."—Roffis glanced at a document flattened onto his desk—" 'glorious sun-drenched quarter acre on the warm sandy shores of a hidden inlet on Florida's unspoiled west coast, all conveniences, golf course, pool, garbage pick-up, and exclusive clubhouse'?"

Horsip looked blank. "No, sir, I never ran into anything like that."

"XXth Rest and Recuperation Battalion," said Roffis, "purchased some of these 'sun-drenched quarter acres' for a rest and recuperation center for IInd Western Occupation Command."

Maklin scowled. " 'Purchased'? Why not requisition them?"

"According to this document, the commanding officer intended to do just that, but got into a conversation with the 'sales manager' of the HiDry Land Reclamation Corporation, and the result was that the battalion bought the land 'on time.' " Roffis glanced at Horsip. "What is 'on time'?"

"I suppose ... h'm ... 'on time' would mean 'without delay,' wouldn't it?"

"To get the 'down payment,' the commanding officer got talked into going to a 'loan company.' "

" 'Loan company,' " said Horsip, "that sounds like a usurer."

"This outfit," said Roffis, "charged 25 percent. The battalion pledged its space transport as 'collateral' for the loan."

Maklin growled, "*Then* what happened?"

"The battalion couldn't repay the loan—naturally, where would they get local currency, unless they stole it—so, the loan company claimed the transport. Then the HiDry Land Reclamation Corporation 'repossessed' the 'sun-drenched quarter acre.' The result is that the Earthmen have the space transport, and the XXth Rest and Recuperation Battalion has insect bites, sunburn, and three men 'presumed eaten up by alligators.' "

Horsip nodded moodily.

"That sounds familiar."

Roffis said, "When we have dealings with these Earthmen, we get carried off in a basket?"

"Yes, sir."

"How do they do it?"

"When they get through talking, everything looks different."

"How do they accomplish *that?*"

"They seem to emphasize one point, and slant everything to build up that point."

"Do they see what we overlook? Or do they take some unimportant aspect and puff it up out of proportion?"

"I think they emphasize whatever favors their argument."

"Then they have a weakness. If they restricted themselves to truth, they would be strong. With this procedure, they will take up false positions."

"Still, they pull our men off-base."

Maklin's eyes glinted. "They won't pull *all* of us off-base."

General Roffis said, "Nevertheless, we have a serious problem. They have gulled our men into giving up valuable space ships in return for—let's see—fancy ground-cars, cabin cruisers, vacation trailers, sauna baths, *The Collected Adventures of Sherlock Holmes,* air-planes, undeveloped real estate, a 'private ocean backyard swimming pool' ..." Roffis looked up. "This isn't very promising."

Maklin growled, "And all this is against regulations. Every one of these transactions is a capital offense. Yet the punishment is light. Here, for instance, is a report on an individual who traded a supply ship for a 'Complete Library of the Works of the Leaders of World Communism.' On going into this further, I find that 'communism' is a scheme for overthrowing one ruling class to install another. What did the fellow *want* with this collection anyway?"

Roffis tossed his list on the desk.

"What we have here is trouble, now and in the future, on a scale we never saw before."

"We could eliminate some of it," said Maklin. "Hang the offenders. Then we'll have an end to this business."

Roffis picked up a slip of light-blue paper, and read aloud:

" 'Secret Order Number Four, Earth Command: "All offenses relative to the providing of space transportation to the local inhabitants will be dealt with leniently, as it is High Policy to disperse the Earthmen as rapidly as possible throughout the Integral Union. . . .' "

Maklin said, "Argit is behind that. . . . All right, *disperse* them. But *this* means of doing it violates discipline!"

Horsip was again getting that sensation he'd first had on Earth—the feeling of struggling uphill through layers of glue.

Roffis looked as if he had a headache. He glanced at the stacks of unread reports.

"Horsip, you've had experience with these Earthmen. What do *you* think of our policy?"

"It won't work. I thought at first that it would, but I don't think so now."

"Why?"

"The Earthmen are too smart. Somehow they'll take over the Integral Union."

"But they'd have to get control of the High Council. The High Council hasn't got an Earthman on it."

"No, sir, but they may not do it that way."

Maklin snarled, "I've run into three separate reports here on how to overthrow governments. It looks to me as if they've had practice."

Roffis massaged his chin. "There must be some way to put the Council on guard—"

There was a rap on the door, and Maklin called, "Come in!"

Half a dozen armed guards came in, escorting an officer and a sergeant. The officer saluted, and put an envelope and receipt form on Horsip's desk.

Horsip signed, and officer and escort went out.

Horsip broke the heavy wax seal, and took out a sheet of thick paper, to read:

By Command
The High Council

Distribution: One (1) copy to Chairman, the Supreme Staff.
One (1) copy to Earth Surveillance Subcommittee of the Supreme Staff, through General Klide Horsip.
One (1) copy to the Commanding Officer, Special Group "B."

Circulation: All members present of the Supreme Staff; C.O. and C. of S., Special Group "B."

Disposition: Read and return, within the day of receipt.

A. Effective immediately, the Integral Union is divided into two zones:
   (1) Open Zone—That portion marked in red on the enclosed section charts.
      This zone will be open to penetration by the inhabitants of the planet Earth.
   (2) Sealed Zone—That portion left unmarked on the enclosed section charts. Earthmen will be discouraged from entering this zone. Any Earthman who enters this zone will be killed and his body and effects destroyed.

B. Effective immediately, all personnel of Information Facilities in the Open Zone will be withdrawn to the Sealed Zone, and replaced by new personnel.

C. Effective immediately, all Official Charts of the Integral Union in localities within the Open Zone will be delivered to representatives of the High Council, to be replaced by new charts issued by the High Council.

D. Effective immediately, Special Group "B," under the direct control of the High Council, will put in effect all measures necessary to detect and destroy any inhabitants of the planet Earth who penetrate the Sealed Zone.

E. Effective immediately, no member of the Supreme Staff will volunteer to any Earthman any information regarding the Sealed Zone, nor acknowledge its existence as an inhabited region.

The punishment for disobedience to any of the above commands will be death, preceded or not preceded at the discretion of the High Council by whatever degree of torture may be deemed to suit the offense.

The purpose of these commands is to restrict the influence of the inhabitants of the planet Earth to a limited, although vast, region, so that the nature of that influence may be determined before permitting it to extend over the whole of the Integral Union.

Any failure to obey the spirit as well as the substance of

these commands will be dealt with summarily, as the existence
of the race is at stake.

> By command of the High Council,
> J. Roggil
> Vice-Chairman

Horsip whistled.

Maklin, reading over Horsip's shoulder, grunted. Roffis
said approvingly, "They aren't asleep."

"But," said Maklin, "just how do we keep the Earthmen
from getting information that's so widespread?"

Horsip looked inside the envelope, and fished out a set of
charts on fine paper. As he leafed through the charts, gradually a picture began to form in his mind. The Council, in dividing the Integral Union, had *made* use of every hazard and
particularly large distance separating one part of the Union
from another, to pass a border between two regions in such a
way that passage from one region to another not only would
appear difficult and unattractive to one not used to space
travel, but also so that the loss of a ship on such a route
would seem understandable.

Roffis straightened. "Maybe it *is* possible."

Maklin nodded. "This is a masterpiece. This Open Zone
even has roughly the shape of the whole territory. It's only
the scale that's off."

Roffis reread the orders.

"If they've prepared everything this carefully, a trip to an
information center would probably convince an Earthman
that he had the facts. But what do we do about scholars who
know differently?"

Maklin said, "They must have thought of that. What *we*
have to do is to make sure our own arrangements don't give
us away. For instance, we've already got this Earthman,
Towers, on the Staff with us. He has a perfect right to see
our documents and charts."

Roffis said, "We'll have to split the Staff, one part for the
Open Zone, and one for the Sealed Zone. The Records Section will have to be split too."

"This could make trouble."

"These Earthmen could make more."

"Well, if Towers should fail, we'll dump him."

Some weeks later, Horsip, methodically working through
new reports, pulled out one titled:

Rebellion on Centralis II
Handy Methods and Devices
by
Able Hunter

Able Hunter, of course, was John Towers' code name. Horsip flipped pages, and nodded approval. The report gave the facts plainly and then stopped.

Horsip cleared his throat.

"Towers hasn't fallen on his face yet."

He handed the report to Roffis and Maklin.

As they read, Horsip had a vision of what cooperation with the Earthmen could mean.

While gripped with this enthusiasm, his gaze happened to fall on the upturned title of an unread report:

Entrapment Into Communist Cells—
A Serious and Growing Problem
What *Is* Communism?

The headache that had disappeared with Towers' report came back as Horsip looked over this document.

Then there came a sharp rap at the door.

Maklin barked, "Come in!"

Armed guards entered to present Horsip with a sealed envelope.

Horsip drew out a crisp slip of paper reading:

By Command
The High Council

The High Council requires the presence of General Klide Horsip, at once, to report his experiences on the planet Earth, and recent relations between the Integral Union and the inhabitants of the planet Earth.

J. Roggil
Vice-Chairman
The High Council

❋ XI ❋

The High Council

The High Council was on board a massive warship designed for their use, accompanied by a formidable fleet. Horsip walked down a corridor lined with guards, passed through a door emblazoned with the emblem of Centra in gold, and found himself suddenly in a small room in which sixteen men sat around an H-shaped table, hard at work. One of the men glanced up.

"Ah, General Horsip. Pull up a chair."

In a daze, Horsip heard himself introduced, replied to the brief comments, smiles, and intent glances, then he was seated at an end of the H, explaining Earth to the man who had greeted him, and whose name Horsip in his confusion had already forgotten.

"Then," the member of the High Council was saying, "you believe the Earthmen, on the average, are more intelligent than our own men?"

"No question of that, sir."

"You have no doubt of it?"

"None, sir."

"Now, *in what way* are they more intelligent?"

Horsip sat blankly, aware of his questioner's keen gaze, but unable to grasp the question. Then his experiences on Earth came back to him.

"You mean, sir, is it a question of some special skill—"

"Exactly. Intelligence is not an undifferentiated quality, any more than physical strength. If you feel that the Earthmen are the same as we are mentally, but stronger in every respect, why, say so. I want your impression of their strong and weak points mentally."

"They seem to have two strong points—but it may be that they boil down to one—their ability to make clever devices,

62

and their ability with words. Their weak point ..." Horsip groped around, and shook his head. "I can't think of any weak point."

"You feel that their strong point is a technical skill in handling words, and in handling tools and materials?"

"Yes, sir."

His questioner was intently still for a moment, then sat back.

"Now, Horsip, let's hear your experiences on their planet. I am familiar with your reports, but I'd like to hear it first-hand. Please be frank, and complete. I want your feelings, as well as what happened, and I don't care how long it takes. I want the full account."

Horsip, faltering at first, then gathering confidence as the memories came back, told of his first sight of the planet, and of his irritation with Moffis' description of the difficulties. He described the confident arrival of the Planetary Integration staff, their brisk plans for integrating the planet, and their troubles later on. He described the recovery of the Earth-men's military power, their revolt, and the struggle it took to put that down. At last he described the most recent reports, which fit in with past experience.

Now and then during the long account, Horsip was vaguely aware of continuing activity around him. But his listener, silent and intent, seemed to miss not a word as people came and went, as notes passed around the table, as at a far end of the H a huge map was unrolled and intently examined. A sense of harmony and singleness of purpose was gradually borne in on Horsip. Through the seeming confusion, there seemed to loom underlying order. Then at last he came to the end of his account.

"That," he said, "is all I can tell you, sir. It seems to me that the Earthmen cut deeper than we do, their people are smarter, and they tie us in knots." Horsip glanced around, and added wonderingly, "But I don't think they would tie many people in *this* room in knots."

For an instant Horsip saw the High Council as the Earth-men might see it, and even so, the Council looked formida-ble.

Some sense of nagging apprehension suddenly evaporated. The name of the man opposite him popped into his head: Jeron Roggil. The names of the people he had been introduced to came back. He had a sudden feeling of confidence.

Roggil said, "Earth may have a higher *average* intelligence, but Centra has a far greater population. In such a population, the number of outstanding intellects is greater, and we value such intellects. Moreover, from what you tell me, the Earthmen *do* have a weakness."

"What's that, sir?"

"A man who does not have much money, Horsip, but who is sensible, tries to use that money wisely. He learns to distinguish between what is truly useful and satisfying, and what rouses his desire but gives no real benefit. A person who has much money is in a different situation. If he is so inclined, he can spend freely, and acquire all manner of possessions. What is showy but worthless does not deprive him of something useful. He can have *both*. What's more, he may not realize, since he is not driven to analyze the situation, what it is that gives him satisfaction. A fool's money may surpass by a hundred or even a thousand times, at the beginning, the money at the disposal of a wise man. And yet—despite this difference—the difference in actual use and satisfaction is nowhere near so great, because a wise man in such a situation will use his money to the greatest effect, while the fool will waste his. Is this not so?"

"Truth," said Horsip, nodding.

"Well, Horsip, we should not be made overconfident by the fact, but from what you have said, it appears to me that these Earthmen are like rich men, in that they have much brainpower—more by far than they strictly need—and the larger part of them have not analyzed what they should spend this brainpower *on*. They do not use it methodically and consistently, as *we* are compelled by brute necessity to do. They *squander* it. Look at this General Towers you speak of. If he were a Centran, he would be on the High Council, never doubt it. We may put him there yet. Already his ability has been recognized, and he is a member of the Supreme Staff. But, with the Earthmen, rather than recognize such ability, his competitors use their mental skill to confuse the issue. We have obtained a good deal of information on the history of the Earthmen. Horsip, the recorded instances in which superior Earthmen, of no matter what degree of ability, have been beaten into the muck by jealous competitors would make you dizzy. The Earthmen squander their mental wealth. They do it as a group, and the bulk of them seem to do it as individuals."

"Nevertheless, sir, when they have as much as they have—"

Roggil nodded intently.

"True, Horsip. But we must bear in mind that there are, in effect, *two* mental levels—*two* different kinds of brainpower. One is what we ordinarily think of as brainpower—raw intelligence. The other is that directing faculty that guides the *use* of raw brainpower. Both levels must be considered, and we are not inferior on this second level. Moreover, very few contests are contests of intelligence alone. The elements of will, and of pure physical power, for instance, cannot be ignored."

Horsip thought it over. "Truth. But—having fought them—that does not give me as much comfort as it might."

Roggil smiled. "We must certainly do our best. One of the most important things is to keep close track of these Earthmen, and what they are doing. We want an organization devoted entirely to that job. I can think of no one better fitted to head it than you, and you will have a free hand in setting it up."

Roggil reached around to a set of pigeon holes against the wall behind him, and handed Horsip a slip of crisp white paper.

Horsip read:

By Command
The High Council

By command of the High Council, each and every person without exception in the Integral Union, whatever his rank may be, is required to assist General Klide Horsip in the gathering of information concerning the activities of new citizens of the Integral Union, that their activities be mutually beneficial to the Union and to themselves.

The High Council holds this commission to be of such importance that in carrying it out General Horsip is empowered to act with the inviolable authority of a Full Member of the High Council.

By command of the High Council,
J. Roggil
Vice-Chairman

Horsip swallowed, and looked up at Roggil.

Roggil said seriously, "What we are giving you, Horsip, is no perfumed hammock of sweet flowers, believe me. But the job is urgent, and we aim to see that you get cooperation. As you are a member of the Supreme Staff, few would dare block you. If you should run into opposition on the Staff itself, however, the work could be stopped. In such a case you have the authority to do whatever you choose. You need justify your actions to no one but us. And all *we* are interested in is results. We want a clear picture of what these Earthmen are doing, and we will have it, or the firing squads will go to work."

❈ XII ❈

General Takkit
Is Most Particular

On the way back in his ship, Horsip worked out the organization he wanted, and decided that what he needed more than
anything else was someone he could trust absolutely. At once
he thought of Moffis, his military deputy back on Earth.

Once back in his office, Horsip glanced over the bank of
phones on the wall, each connected to a different department,
and picked up the phone marked "Personnel."

A small voice said, "Personnel, Major Dratig."

"General Horsip speaking. I'd like to know the where-
abouts of General Brak Moffis, formerly Military Overseer of
the planet Earth."

"Just a moment, sir." There was a sound of file drawers
sliding out, and of paper being riffled. "General Moffis is now
assigned to the personal staff of General Dorp Takkit of the
Supreme Staff as a confidential adviser."

Horsip looked blank. "Confidential adviser?"

"That's what it says here, sir."

"What might that be?"

"I don't know, sir. I never heard of it before."

"How can I get in touch with General Moffis?"

"You'd have to ask General Takkit, sir."

"Is there," growled Horsip, "some reason why I can't
reach Moffis direct?"

"Well, sir . . . there's nothing listed here."

"I see. Thank you."

"Yes, sir."

Horsip's teeth bared in a snarl. He was taking down a second phone when there came a rap on the door.

Horsip looked around. "Come in!"

The bull-necked General Maklin stepped in, leather belt
and insignia shining.

"Sorry to bother you, Horsip. I can come back later."

"This can wait, sir."

"I'll take the molk by the horns, Horsip," said Maklin. "We're all curious to know what the Council had to say."

"The Council wanted me to set up an organization to keep an eye on the Earthmen."

Maklin looked approving.

"How did they seem?"

"All business, sir."

"Then, at least, there's no softness there. Well, Horsip, I won't take your time. I imagine you're setting things up already."

"Trying to, sir."

"What's wrong?"

"Someone has a man I need."

"*Who?*"

Horsip hesitated.

Maklin pinned him with his gaze.

Horsip explained the situation.

"Takkit?" Maklin's face darkened. "What does he want with a confidential adviser? What *he* needs is a brain." Then he shook his head. "Once they get on Takkit's personal staff, Horsip, you don't see them again. He gets them working on some private fantasy, and that's the end of them."

"Moffis is just the man I need."

"That won't bother Takkit."

Horsip reached around to his bank of phones, and took down one marked "Sup. St.—Takkit."

A voice spoke, cool and remote:

"Office of Colonel Noffel, Staff Secretary to General Takkit."

Horsip growled, "General Klide Horsip speaking. May I speak to General Takkit?"

"General Takkit is not available."

"Then may I speak to General Moffis?"

"Who?"

"General Brak Moffis."

"Just a moment . . . Now, just what is your name again?"

Across the desk, Maklin, overhearing this, snarled under his breath.

Horsip said shortly, "Who am I talking to?"

"I *beg* your pardon?"

"*Who are you?*" snarled Horsip.

There was a *click*, a *buzz*, and a new voice.

"Colonel Noffel speaking."

Horsip said evenly, "This is General Klide Horsip."

"Oh, yes, General Horsip. Congratulations on your appointment to the Staff. General Takkit is tied up, I'm afraid, and won't be free today. If there's anything I can do for you, General Horsip, please feel free to ask. Call me Radge."

Horsip opened his mouth and shut it. He took a fresh grip on the phone. "I want to speak to General Takkit about General Brak Moffis. Moffis is a confidential adviser, as I understand it, to General Takkit."

Noffel's voice became wary.

"What did you wish to speak to General Takkit about General Moffis for, General Horsip?"

"I'll make that clear to General Takkit."

"I'm afraid I may not have made the situation clear, myself, General Horsip. General Takkit is most particular regarding the protection of his personal staff from outside distractions. I'm afraid if you should raise this question with General Takkit, you might run into—there might be a good deal of—a certain *unpleasantness* which could all be avoided by simply mentioning the matter to me. . . . You see?"

Horsip said shortly, "I want to ask General Moffis to work with me in an organiza—"

"Quite out of the question, I'm afraid. General Moffis' time is fully taken up at present. . . . And for the foreseeable future, I might add."

"This organization is—"

"No. I'm *very* sorry, General Horsip. This is a matter of standing policy."

Horsip spoke very politely.

"The High Council has given direct orders to set up this organization. The matter is urgent."

"And *you* are to head this new organization?"

"That's right."

"You are certainly to be congratulated, General Horsip. Permit me to be the first to extend my felicitations to you on this auspicious assignment. But as a new member of the Supreme Staff, you are, of course, junior to General Takkit."

"That's beside the point."

"Not at all. This is quite central to the issue. You wish to—forgive the term—'raid' General Takkit's staff for personnel. General Takkit is your superior officer. Moreover, General Takkit has a prior claim on the individual in question. You wish to use this assignment you have been given by the High Council as a lever to—forgive me—'pry' General Moffis loose from General Takkit's personal staff, disregarding both General Takkit's superior rank and his prior claim on the man in question. We've experienced this sort of

thing before. General Takkit's policy is quite clear. Your request, if it is a request, is refused. Pardon me if I speak
frankly, General Horsip, but you see, it is much better that I
make this clear than that General Takkit be disturbed with
this matter. . . . Was there anything else?"

Inside Horsip, something wound tighter and tighter, and
then snapped.

Horsip suddenly felt very relaxed and at ease.

Horsip said, quietly, "Get Takkit on this line, Colonel."

"The general does not wish—"

"I don't care what he wishes. Get him."

"General Takkit is in confer—"

"Where?"

"In his conference room, and he left explicit—"

"Is he in easy reach?"

"Physically, I suppose, but—"

"Get Takkit on this phone."

"The general left specific ord—"

"I don't care what he left. I said get him, and you will get
him," said Horsip, pleased that he could be quiet and reasonable about this, "or I will step down the hall and get him myself."

Horsip took down another phone marked "Provost."

A brisk voice came out:

"Provost Marshal's office. Major Rokkis speaking."

Across the desk, General Maklin looked alarmed.

From General Takkit's phone, Colonel Noffel's voice said,
with a faint quaver, "I certainly can't carry out this request.
It is contrary to General Takkit's specific order."

Horsip spoke into the phone marked "Provost."

"Send a section of guards to my office, equipped to smash
down a door."

"Yes, sir! At *once!*"

From Takkit's phone, Noffel's voice cried, "What? What?"

Horsip hung up the phone marked "Provost," and spoke to
Noffel.

"You have now put General Takkit in the position of re-
fusing to cooperate with an order of the High Council. Just
incidentally, you are defying me by calling a direct order a
request. Get Takkit to that phone or face the consequences."

There was silence from Takkit's phone, and then a heavy
tramp of feet in the corridor. There was a rap on Horsip's
door.

"Captain Bokkil! Guard Section B, at your command, sir!"

Maklin said urgently, "Listen, Horsip, do you know what
you're doing?"

"Come in," called Horsip. He pulled open a drawer of his desk, and took out Roggil's order. As the burly captain saluted, Horsip held out the order. "Here's my authority. Now, just wait a minute, while I see if I have to use it."

"Yes, sir!" The captain read the order, saluted, leaned into the hall, and shouted, "Splat-gunners to the front! Hurry up with that ram!"

A grating voice spoke from Takkit's phone:

"This is Dorp Takkit speaking. I will say this only once. Your request is refused. That is final."

There was a *click*.

Horsip turned to the guard captain. "Knock on General Takkit's door. If they don't open, order it opened in the name of the High Council. If they refuse, smash it down. Ask General Takkit to get on the phone to me here, and if he refuses, put him under arrest, by authority of the High Council, and bring him down here."

A few minutes later, the guards smashed down the door, and dragged a furious Takkit into Horsip's office.

Horsip showed the struggling Takkit the order signed by Roggil, and Takkit knocked it from his hand. Horsip read it, and Takkit shouted so loudly that neither he nor anyone else could hear it. Takkit commanded the guards to release him, and one of them, awed by Takkit's rank and fury, let go. The guard captain himself pinned Takkit's arms, and Maklin, picking up the paper from where Horsip had set it on the desk, read it, his eyes widened, and his face suddenly lit with pleasure. He sucked in a deep breath, and faced Takkit.

"AT—TEN—*SHUNN*!"

Takkit looked blank, snapped to attention by reflex action, and Maklin said cheerfully, "Takkit, you are in disobedience to the High Council. In just a few minutes, I am going to be on the direct code to the High Council, to accuse you of actions contrary to an order of the High Council. That will mean an accusation before the Council. Now, read this paper."

Takkit, pale and trembling, stared at Roggil's order.

"I wasn't told this!"

"That certainly isn't my fault. All *I* know is what I've seen here, right before my eyes, and what I've heard over the phone. In this matter, General Horsip is clearly acting as a Full Member of the High Council. You have refused to cooperate, defied him, hung up on him, knocked the order of the High Council to the floor, and shouted it down when it was read to you. By so doing, you have defied the High Council.

You have also struggled with guards acting on authority of the High Council."

"But I didn't know!" screamed Takkit.

"Unfortunate," said Maklin. "If an ordinary soldier defies your order, can he defend himself by claiming that he kept his eyes squinted so he didn't see your insignia of rank, and shouted you down so you couldn't tell him who you were? Of course not. But you can explain all that later, in your defense, at the same time that you explain why it is so important to keep Moffis tied up on your staff when Full Member of the High Council Horsip needs him on the High Council's work."

Takkit said desperately, "He can have him!"

"Very generous," said Maklin. "You mean it's *not* so important that you keep him? In any case, Member of the High Council Horsip has only to give the command, and Moffis is reassigned to his organization regardless of *what* you choose to do. Each member of the High Council stands further above you than you stand above the lowest recruit in the rear rank of the punishment detail." Maklin turned respectfully to Horsip. "Sir, I am going to accuse this man, and request a full Council investigation while I am at it. I want to respectfully suggest that you release him now on his own recognizance, if he promises to end his defiance to the Council. He is going to be rearrested shortly, anyway, to face the accusation."

Horsip said, "Do you agree, General Takkit, to end your defiance of the High Council?"

Takkit swallowed. "Yes . . . I mean . . ." He looked blank.

Horsip nodded to the guards. "In that case, release him."

Takkit reeled out into the corridor. The guard captain saluted Horsip in awe, and stepped outside with his men. The door shut. Maklin turned to Horsip, but before Maklin could speak, Horsip said, "Sir, now that's out of the way, do you actually plan to accuse Takkit—"

"Don't *you* call *me* 'sir,'" said Maklin, smiling. "Yes, sir, of course I'm going to accuse him. I'd do more than that to get that walking disaster off the Supreme Staff. That cretin has done more damage by his absurdities than anyone else has ever dreamed of doing. Thanks to this, I've finally got the boob by the throat, and I won't let go till I drag him to the ground or the High Council itself pries me loose. At the very least, I'm going to get the lid off this special staff of his." Maklin beamed and stepped to the door.

"Good luck, General Horsip. I expect to be back once the investigation is over."

Maklin, smiling cheerfully, saluted, went out, and shut the door.

Horsip took a deep breath, and reached for the phone marked, "Sup. St.—Takkit."

A voice stammered, "C-Colonel Noffel, Staff Secretary to General Takkit."

In the background was an uproar like distracted animals loose in a barnyard.

Horsip cleared his throat.

"General Horsip speaking. Is General Moffis there?"

"I . . . He . . . General Takkit doesn't wish—"

"I think," said Horsip, "General Takkit might be willing. Ask him, why don't you?"

A moment later, Takkit's voice carried, "Yes! Yes! He can talk to him!"

Moffis' voice came over the line, weary and disgusted.

"Brak Moffis speaking."

"Klide Horsip. My office is just down the hall, Moffis. It has the number eleven on the door. I'd like to talk to you."

"I'll be right there, sir."

Moffis came in, wearing a uniform complete with loops of blue and green cord around the shoulders, purple lapels with golden sunbursts in the centers, and a large star-shaped emblem on the left side of the jacket below the decorations.

Horsip looked blank.

Moffis growled, "This wasn't my idea, sir."

"Is Takkit out of his head?"

"In my opinion, yes. But all I know is, I got orders to come here, and Takkit told me I was in charge of his 'liaison with the situation on Earth.' Aside from writing reports and giving my opinion on all kinds of questions about Earth, I might as well have been in cold storage."

"Questions like what?"

"What was the decisive battle that broke Earth's resistance? How did Earth recover? Would the Earthmen accept a Centran as leader if his rank were high enough? How would the strength of Earth compare with Centra if allowed to develop uninterrupted for five years? Ten years? Can Earthmen be hired as fighters? For how much?" Moffis shook his head in disgust.

Horsip considered it, frowning, then shrugged.

"How were things on Earth after I left?"

Moffis looked uncomfortable.

"On the *surface*, everything seemed all right."

"The Earthmen were busy, were they?"

"Yes, that and—the impression I got was that the ground was turning to quicksand under my feet."

"What do you think will result from letting the Earthmen loose in the Integral Union?"

"Trouble."

"Would you like to help me keep track of them?"

Moffis looked interested.

"How would we do that?"

Horsip described his talk with Roggil of the High Council.

"You see, Moffis, I need someone I know I can trust, who understands these Earthmen. . . . How about it?"

"Fine," said Moffis.

Horsip got out his rough draft of the organization, and began to explain it.

To get his organization set up took less time than Horsip had expected. Word got around that Takkit had gotten in Horsip's way—and look what happened to Takkit. Takkit's effects, meanwhile, were being sent to his family, which marvelously expedited the cooperation that Horsip received. Then General Maklin came back, strongly commended by the High Council, to add the blowtorch of his personality to the work. The organization was set up and functioning well ahead of schedule, housed in a special converted warship that accompanied the Supreme Staff.

Horsip glanced at Moffis.

"Well, Moffis, now let's take a firsthand look at what the Earthmen are doing. There's nothing like seeing for yourself, and I have just the planet for us. Look at the summary on this report."

Moffis looked over Horsip's shoulder, to read:

Summary: The situation on Adrok IV: In short, then, the situation on this planet since the arrival of the Earthmen is almost unbelievable. All over the planet there are Earthmen setting up what they call "dealerships." A dealership is an arrangement for selling things made by somebody else, and distributed by still other people. Since all of these people have to make a living from the sale of the thing, it is not clear how the price can be held down, but apparently this is done by making the most of the economies of production in bulk. A factory for Earth-type vehicles has already been set up, and is now going full-blast. No one can figure out what is happening, but the Earthmen with the dealerships are all getting rich.

At the same time, however, other Earthmen have made their way to the planet, and on arrival have been afflicted with ills never heard of here before. They are on poor relief already, and no matter how fast the relief is poured to them, they get poorer all the time.

Meanwhile, there are rumors of something called a "communist cell." What "communists" are is not clear yet. There is also a "revival movement" sweeping the rural parts of the planet, although what is being revived has never in the memory of any living individual ever existed here before.

In short, the situation on this planet is incomprehensible, and it is getting more incomprehensible fast.

Horsip glanced at Moffis.
Moffis nodded.
"That sounds like it, all right."
Horsip and Moffis headed for Adrok IV.

❈ XIII ❈

"Do Not Let Me Disturb
Your Righteous Work"

Horsip and Moffis intended to tour the planet by the iron
road, stopping at various places to look into the things mentioned in the reports. But they were rudely disillusioned
shortly after stepping off the space-liner.

"The iron road?" said the man behind the ticket agent's
window in the spaceport building. "Ah, la, the iron road. Yes,
we *did* used to have connections all over the planet linking all
the cities and even the towns, and connecting with Meridian
and Big Hook spaceports. But"—he glanced at Horsip's uniform thoughtfully; Horsip, as a disguise, was wearing a colonel's uniform, and Moffis a major's uniform, with regulation
sidearms—"but," he repeated, lowering his voice, and glancing around, "*that* was before the coming of the Earthmen—no criticism, you understand. But, from right here, I
could sell you a ticket to Big Hook or to some hamlet off in
back of Molk Junction. All you had to do was climb aboard,
then settle back and take her easy. Every now and then, you
might have to climb off of one rail-waggon and onto another—but where's the strain in that? Eh? Well, it's all different now. Just take a look out that window over there, and
you'll see what I mean."

Horsip and Moffis took a look out, to see through a cloud
of dust a number of traveling four-wheeled machines of various sizes and shapes. There went one like a waggon with no
loadbeast. Here came a thing like an overgrown shiny insect,
no more than four feet high at the top, and, as Horsip
watched, the front end dropped into a big pothole, and
despite new clouds of dust as the rear wheels spun, that was
where it stayed. Through the dust loomed a monster truck,
billowing clouds of black smoke from a vertical pipe, with
big, lighted searchlights mounted on the front and on both

running boards. The driver was leaning out and peering over a searchlight into the rolling murk as the truck headed straight for the little vehicle, whose driver leaned out the window, waved his arms, shouted, then, as a huge wheel loomed overhead, sprang out and ran. He had barely got started when he stopped to do a desperate dance out of the way of a long black vehicle that rumbled through the dust carrying what looked like a huge horizontal cylindrical tank. Once that was gone, a number of smaller vehicles rushed past, trailing clouds of gray smoke that mingled with the dust.

"H'm," said Horsip, going back to the ticket agent's window. "Do you mean to say that the iron road has been replaced by *that?*"

"Yes, sir. . . . Oh, you can still get a connection from Big Hook to Meridian if you want. But how do you get to Big Hook? Eh? You drive to Big Hook, that's how. And what that is like, you just saw from that window. Every time a passenger ship comes down or takes off, that is what we have out there, and on the big roadways it's worse."

"Is there at least the spur line from here to town?"

"No, sir. To get to town we have a—heh—'convenience-bus' that pulls up just outside the door where that crowd is waiting. Don't get on in back, sir. Get in up front with the driver. It costs a little more, but, believe me, it's worth it."

Horsip and Moffis carried their bags outside, and breathed through their handkerchiefs.

"Not a very happy start," snarled Horsip.

"No, sir," said Moffis. "What's *that?*"

A kind of monster ground-car loomed through the dust, headlights glaring. It bounced over a protruding rock in the road, and slammed to a stop in front of them. A large sign running the length of the top proclaimed: "One Way—50—Round Trip—95." The front of the vehicle was enclosed, and the rear was a long platform like a flat-bed waggon. Running lengthwise down the center of the platform was a long brass rail, about waist-high. Above this was a flat roof, and above the roof was the sign proclaiming the price.

There was a *"Blat! Blat!"* from the horn, and the engine roared.

The crowd swarmed aboard, and a head thrust out the side window.

"Not much room in back, gents. Double price up front."

With a shock, Horsip recognized that the driver was an Earthman.

Horsip glanced back at the crowd clinging to the brass rail

with one hand and their baggage with the other, and climbed in. Moffis got in after him and slammed the door. The driver bent over the controls, there was a roar, a rumble, and the vehicle jerked forward. He manipulated a long lever, there was a clash of metal, the vehicle picked up speed, slowed to avoid a big pothole, gathered speed with another adjustment of the lever, and bounded along the road with shouts and screams from behind.

The driver thrust a hand toward Horsip. "One-way, or round trip?"

"One-way," said Horsip.

"That's two, even. Plus thirty-five in advance for the tip, and then I'll help you off with your bags when we get there. I could see you were first-class gents when I pulled up. That's two thirty-five total, and I can't make no change. Any bill you got over two will do it."

Moffis growled under his breath. Horsip reached into an inside jacket pocket and took out a worn leather change purse. He undid the drawstring, and drew out two small twelve-side silver coins, which he put in the driver's hand.

"We'll carry out the bags," he said, pulled the drawstring tight, and put the purse back in his pocket. "What's wrong with the iron road?"

The driver slid the money into his pocket, and looked at Horsip sidewise.

"Price of progress."

"What's *wrong* with it?"

"Hard to say. That's out of my line." He studied Horsip's uniform. "Not many troops on this planet, are there? You just here for a little vacation?"

"Weapons procurement," said Horsip, vaguely.

"Oh? How's that?"

"In line of duty," growled Horsip.

"What's *that* mean?"

"Just what it says."

"You going to buy weapons here?"

"Do you have any to sell?"

"Well, now, that depends."

"On what?"

"Price you care to pay, and how much *red tape* there is."

For an instant Horsip didn't realize what had happened. Then it dawned on him that the driver had been talking Centran, practically without an accent, and then had used two words Horsip wasn't familiar with: "red tape." Those words must be in some Earth tongue.

Horsip took a guess at the meaning. "This would be an official sale, with all the necessary formalities."

The driver looked uncomfortable.

"Can't help you, then."

While talking they streaked past a stand of second-growth
trees and several farms, detoured a pugnacious-looking molk
with lowered horns, and now, looking up the road, Horsip
could see that they were approaching the outskirts of the
city. Smaller plots were becoming the rule, with the houses
closer together, and barns and outbuildings more rare. They
rounded a curve, to pass a tall narrow metal frame.

"Oil well," said the driver. "Want to get into that line myself, if I can scrape a stake together. . . . You gents interested
in a fast shot at a small bundle?" He nodded toward a large
gray wooden building with a sign out front:

THE DAILY TRUMPET
None Bigger—None Better
Top Circulation
All the News—*Fit or Unfit!*—
THE TRUMPET PRINTS IT!!

"Any place they sell that paper can fix you up."

"I see," said Horsip, who didn't see at all, but didn't want
to reveal his ignorance. Ignorance looked expensive on this
planet.

A pall of smoke now dimmed the view, and they passed a
number of huge buildings. Many tracks of the iron road led
through a high fence to the buildings, outside of which a
gigantic lot was filled with glittering new ground-cars.

The driver leaned over, and hissed, "Railroad from the
spaceport would have had to cross these lines. . . . *That's* what
happened to it."

"Oh."

"Can't get in the way of progress," said the driver. "You
can't lick 'em, join 'em. You change your mind on those
guns, let me know." He swerved around a corner, and soon
they were going down the main street of a considerable Centran city, past houses four and five stories high.

The vehicle slammed to a stop.

The driver leaned out. "Everybody off!" He glanced at
Horsip and Moffis. "Kind of keep your eyes open when you
get off here, gents."

Moffis shoved open the door, and Horsip followed, keeping
a tight grip on his bag. As they stepped to the sidewalk, a
uniformed individual with six rows of ribbons, straggly fur on

his face, and a hideous scar, stepped forward holding out a helmet with coins in it.

"Wounded on Earth and Centralis, sirs. Twenty years in the line. If you'll just give—"

Moffis gave a snarl, his left hand shot out, gripped the upper end of the "scar," and stripped it off like a length of flypaper. He knocked the imitation veteran back against the granite front of the nearest building.

Horsip caught a blur of motion, and turned to see someone start off with Moffis' bag.

Horsip jerked his service pistol from its holster. "Stop, thief!" The thief did not stop. Horsip fired one shot.

There was a scream, and then another movement caught Horsip's gaze.

Behind Moffis' back, a pickpocket expertly cut open Moffis' trouser pocket and removed the wallet. Horsip cracked the pickpocket over the head. As he stepped forward, Horsip's suitcase became light in his left hand.

He whirled, to find an individual directly behind him holding a piece of uniform in one hand, and a knife in the other; right beside this individual, a second put a pair of powerful snippers in his pocket as he bent to pick up Horsip's bag, the handle of which was still in Horsip's left hand.

Horsip muttered to himself, shot the pickpocket in the shoulder and the thief in the leg. He broke the gun open, reloaded it, and looked around.

The thieves he had shot were now on the ground. One was smearing blood on his face. Another was tearing his clothes to bits.

Moffis finished ripping combat badges and ribbons from the imitation veteran's uniform, looked around, and discovered that his suitcase was gone.

Horsip nodded toward the farthest of the thieves, who had now reduced himself to a ragged shambles, and was rolling around spitting out foam, and rubbing blood on his face.

Moffis stared.

Horsip said, "I shot him, Moffis. He was making off with your bag."

"What's he doing now?"

"Don't ask me."

As Moffis came back with his bag, a small man emerged from the crowd wearing a tag reading "Press," and bent beside the nearer thief. A second person, taller and carrying a camera, pushed through the crowd.

The man wearing the "Press" tag spoke sympathetically to the thief.

"What happened, fella?"

The thief said eagerly, "It was terrible. One of them held me while the other shot me and beat me up. I got a real wound. Do you suppose you could get a doctor?"

"Not now. What happened?"

"Will this come out with my name on it and everything?"

"Sure, don't worry."

"Can I sue?"

"Of course you can sue. Come on, come on, let's have it! I haven't got all day!"

"This hurts awful."

"It can wait. Here we go. What happened, fella? Did the beasts get you? Speak right into the mike."

"Yeah. They ... they shot me. They held me. They beat me. I ... I'm weak."

The Centran reporter raised the microphone, and spoke into it smoothly. "In the Integral Union, here in a main thoroughfare of a principal city on the planet, even here citizens are not safe from the attacks of the murderers. They learned to kill on foreign planets, and now they bring their blood-lust home with them. . . . Fella, I don't know what to say to you. I . . . I guess *all* of us are guilty. . . ."

Moffis glanced at Horsip.

"Which one is the thief?"

"The one on the ground."

Moffis looked baffled.

The Centran reporter gestured to the photographer, and rose from beside the thief.

"Yes, we all are guilty, for allowing *beasts* to walk among us like *men*. There!" He pointed dramatically at Horsip and Moffis.

"There they are!" cried the reporter. "The kill-crazed murderers! This time the people must rise against the cowards!"

There was a murmur from the crowd.

Moffis gave a start.

"*Cowards?*"

He dumped his bag on the sidewalk, and stepped forward. The Centran reporter backed up into the crowd.

The crowd looked interested, and shoved him forward.

"Wait a minute," said the reporter. He glanced at the photographer. "Help!"

The photographer eagerly raised his camera.

Moffis smashed the reporter on the jaw, knocking him back into the crowd. The crowd, cheering, heaved him forward, and Moffis knocked him flat.

Someone pushed past Horsip, and from his long brown robes, Horsip recognized a Centran monk.

The monk, tall and severe, loomed over Moffis, who gave a guilty start.

The monk looked at the outstretched reporter, then smiled benignly upon Moffis. "Son, do not let me disturb your righteous work."

He turned to Horsip. "I see you are both new here, my sons. If you will get your baggage together, perhaps I can be of assistance."

Horsip, who could use any assistance anyone could offer, nodded agreement. He and Moffis got their bags.

The monk looked grimly at the reporter, then glanced at the pickpocket and thieves.

"So, this is the latest benefit you have derived from the search after money without work? Put your ingenuity to use finding a way you can help someone, then sell your service to *him*. . . . And, why not pray a little now and then? What hurt can it do?"

The pickpocket and thieves looked embarrassed and muttered incoherently.

The monk nodded to Horsip and Moffis.

"This way, my sons. As you see, I have no truck with these new inventions, but use sensible transportation which should suffice for any man."

Horsip, carrying his bag under one arm, waited till the traffic let up, then followed across the street, with Moffis right behind him. On the far side waited a four-wheeled coach drawn by a creature whose long powerful body appeared built to deliver dazzling bursts of speed. Its large paws were armed with sharp, partially retracted claws, and, as it cleaned its short black fur, its blood-red tongue licked out past teeth like daggers.

The monk opened the door on the left side of the coach.

"After you, my sons."

Horsip uneasily climbed in, but Moffis paused. "Your ... ah ... loadbeast, Reverend Father—what breed is that?"

The monk beamed. "That, my son, is a man-eating gnath. Gnaths, you know, are said to be killers by nature. Their reflexes are so fast it is impossible to follow their motions. Their teeth are very strong, of a hardness which rivals diamond. The jaws have compound leverage, with an action similar to a ratchet, and can bring terrible pressure to bear on the prey. Few zoos can hold the gnath. It has been known to chew steel bars into bits to exercise its jaws. See the size of its head? It is highly intelligent, but much of that head is skull, of unusual thickness, armored with the substance that makes its teeth so tough. A single gnath has been known to slaughter almost a whole company of soldiers before one managed to hit the heart with a lucky shot. The ribs of the animal are flat, they overlap, and, like the rest of its bone, they are exceptionally hard and tough, so that the bullet must penetrate the abdomen at just the right angle to reach the heart. Since the gnath moves so fast, it is, of course, difficult to make this shot while being attacked by the beast."

Moffis uneasily put his hand to his holster, then let go with a dazed look.

The monk, beaming benignly, said, "I have raised this gnath from a cub, feeding it vegetables and milk, and radiating thoughts of universal love and brotherhood in its presence. By kind treatment, its manners have been transformed." He lowered his voice. "Get in, brother, or the bystanders over there—what are left of them—may think you do not trust the Great One to protect you."

The monk followed Moffis in, shut the door, and swung around a kind of semicircular latch that snicked into its rests like a bolt.

He seated himself, and took the reins, which went out two vertical slits under the thick front window. He gave the reins a light shake.

The gnath leaned forward.

The carriage jerked into motion.

The gnath lazily stretched out his legs. The carriage rolled briskly behind.

After traveling some time in silence, the monk said, "There are now those on this planet who would not hesitate to take advantage of the Brotherhood. . . . Look there."

Up ahead, the huge factory was coming into view. An elaborate ground-car, with a silver bird on the front end, was starting out onto the road.

The monk slapped the reins.

The gnath leaned into the harness. The carriage picked up speed.

Up ahead, the ground-car came to an abrupt stop, backed, turned, and headed for the factory, a cloud of dust stretching behind it.

The gnath sniffed and growled as he passed through the dust cloud from the car.

The monk slowed, to turn off onto a narrower road.

"That ground-car back there," he said, "belongs to the manager of the factory. Some weeks ago he tried to force me off the road." The monk gave a spare smile. "He was not yet acquainted with the nature of the gnath."

Horsip thought this over in silence. Such conduct, toward the Holy Brotherhood, was almost inconceivable.

"Is it only the factory manager who is responsible or—"

"It is anyone who submits to the teachings of the Earthmen."

"Perhaps there is some misunderst—"

"Bah! We understand each other well enough. Either the Earthmen's system or ours must break, and they well know it. Yet, bad as the Earthmen are, they are as nothing compared to our own people, once converted to their ways. That gossip-mongering 'reporter' is an example of it. We had an Earth reporter here not long ago, teaching how it was done. The fellow was unbearable. But not as unbearable as our own men when they do the same thing. The Earthmen have *some* restraint."

"Yet they break down our ways?"

"Their theories twist facts, present the doer of evil as a harmless fellow, and the honest man who does his duty as some kind of fiend. They make the average person uncertain where to turn. He is hag-ridden by all their conflicting subtleties and false guides. I tell you, these Earthmen—"

Moffis gripped Horsip by the arm.

"Look—behind us."

Horsip turned. Coming along the road behind, an armored ground-car trailed a cloud of dust, and gained steadily on them. Behind it, at an angle, as if to block the other side of the road, came a second armored ground-car.

Horsip looked around. The road was narrow, bordered on both sides by rows of trees.

The armored cars closed the distance fast.

From the nearest of the cars came the flat commanding blast of a horn.

Moffis drew his gun.

The monk smiled. "No, my son, trust that those who do evil will be punished."

There was a slight *bump,* and the carriage tilted. Through the carriage's rear windows, only the flat gray tops of the armored cars could be seen.

The ground-cars dropped back again, then surged forward.

The monk, watching, gripped the brake lever, drew it back with a loud ratcheting click, and shoved it over and back. He jerked a knotted cord on the dashboard, and gave a penetrating whistle.

With a loud scream from the wheels, the carriage slowed.

The gnath bounded free of the traces. There was a thud-*click* as padded metal shutters dropped over the windows.

The horn blast grew suddenly loud. There was a slam, a crash, and the carriage tipped heavily.

The world seemed to turn over as the carriage careened to a stop. There was the sound of smashing glass, screams and curses, and then a bloodthirsty roar that startled Horsip out of unconsciousness.

The carriage was bobbing slightly, the inside dark. Horsip unlatched a shutter and looked out.

Jammed between two trees was one of the armored ground-cars. The other was on its back, wheels up. The gnath, one end of a metal plate in his mouth, rivets sticking out like torn threads, muscles standing out on his big fore-limbs, slowly straightened up to a loud *ik-ik-ik* noise, and the scream of straining metal.

There was a loud snap, and the gnath tossed the massive plate into the air. Gears and shafts flew in all directions. Then the gnath worried the engine out of the wreckage, peeled back the firewall, crouched, lashed his long tail, and insinuated his head into the ground-car's passenger compartment. There was the banging of a pistol, then screams.

Horsip tried to get up, saw the whole world turn end-for-end, and everything went black.

Somewhere there was a murmur of voices, the slam of a door. Horsip opened his eyes, to find himself looking up at the lower limbs of a big tree. Propping himself on one elbow, he could see a shambles of metal plates, gears, axles, a shaft with steering wheel on one end, wiring harness with the generator still attached, fan belts, coolant hoses, bandoliers of ammunition, strewn over the road, or scattered in the grass. The largest piece he could see was a length of I-beam two feet long, with the sun glinting on a freshly sheared end.

A third ground-car, this one not armored, had stopped in the road, and Moffis was standing beside it talking to an individual with broad shoulders and brawny arms, who beamed expansively upon Moffis.

"Honored sir, I shall be happy to welcome you to my dwelling, and if your superior is hurt, we may summon a healer, as I have long-talker hooked up right in my own house. I am off work for the day, and will help you all I can. Let's see, you say there was a whole ground-car here—in one piece—when the wreck happened?"

Horsip looked around, to see the carriage still in good

shape, but with an outline in crushed wood at the rear. Looking at the carriage, Horsip became aware of a steely glint from underneath the splintered wood.

At the far end of the carriage, the gnath placidly cleaned itself, radiating contentment and well-being.

Horsip got to his feet, and saw the monk sitting up. Horsip helped him up. The monk's eyes glinted.

"There," he murmured, "is *more* work of the Earthmen. You see that fellow? Sark Rottik is a good honest workman, skilled at his craft. But if he has two brass halfpennies to scrape together, I will be surprised. . . . He has everything else, I'll grant."

The workman called, "Greetings, Reverend Father. What happened? It looks as if a junk waggon ran into you."

"The last I knew, there were two armored ground-cars behind us. Luckily, our workshops build strong."

"I see no one lying hurt from the other vehicle, at least," said Rottik.

"No?" The monk looked momentarily blank, glanced at the gnath, looked serious, and turned to Horsip and Moffis.

"I had intended to offer you hospitality. But . . . this situation requires attention. Perhaps . . ." He glanced questioningly at Sark Rottik, who beamed.

"I have already invited them. My ground-car is right here. We can go at once."

Horsip and Moffis said good-by to the preoccupied monk, and their new host ushered them to a ground-car with leather seats, folding top, and an impressive array of instruments. The ground-car gave a whine, then a howl, shoved them back in the seats, and was moving fast before Horsip could get the door shut. Rottik grinned.

"The Earthmen designed it, but I helped build it. Observe the floating action. The Earthmen are wonderful! . . . My house just up ahead is conveniently close to my work."

They rounded a curve, shot up a side road, braked, rounded another curve, and there loomed in front of them a kind of palace, administration building, or headquarters of the planetary governor, with flagpole, swimming pool, mansion of gray stone trimmed with yellow wood, neatly mowed lawn, graveled walks, and avenues of flowering trees.

Radiating pride, Rottik drove up the broad driveway, to stop under an overhanging roof supported by stone pillars and wrought-iron lattice up which vines of purple flowers climbed.

As Horsip and Moffis stared around, Rottik got out, beaming, felt through his pockets, pulled out a small gold key ring, and bent briefly at a massive paneled door. The door swung noiselessly open.

Rottik grinned, and bowed to the speechless Horsip and Moffis.

"I am as yet unmarried, so that my hospitality is limited. But you will find the stocks of foods and beverages complete, as they came with the house. Also the linens. Everything is included on the Revolving All-Payment Plan. Please make yourself at home, and if you want anything, just ask for it. I am sure I have got it here somewhere."

A few minutes later, in a palatial guest room on the second floor, Horsip and Moffis stood at a big window.

"If this is what comes of cooperating with the Earthmen," said Moffis, "I can see why anyone would cooperate with them."

Horsip looked out at the water sparkling against the pale-green tiles of the swimming pool.

"I have to admit, Moffis . . ." He paused, frowning. "On the other hand, I wonder what a 'Revolving All-Payment Plan' is?"

Moffis looked thoughtfully at the walks, pool, bathhouse, green lawns, and statue of a demure female with water spurting out of the top of her head.

"H'm," he said. "We will have to ask about that."

✤ XIV ✤

Contagious Earthitis

Horsip and Moffis, on returning from their trip, were a little dazed. Their heads whirled with details of installment loan contracts, franchises, interest compounded at 24 percent, inflation increasing an 8 percent, and riches for everyone, with poverty in lock step close behind. But before leaving, they had made arrangements with the Holy Brotherhood and others to transmit information on the planet; so that, at least, was accomplished. Their organization was now sending the High Council information on the numerous activities of the Earthmen. Horsip, however, was dissatisfied.

"Moffis, do you *understand* this stuff we're sending out?"

Moffis hesitated. "To tell the truth—no."

"Me either," said Horsip. "We have this report we sent back about our own visit. Consider the oil production information alone. By the time figures are on hand, it's obvious the Earthmen are increasing oil production at a fantastic rate. Despite an inflation of the planet, the price of oil has *dropped*. That benefits everyone who buys it. Despite big taxes on the oil, the drillers and refiners are getting rich. That's to *their* benefit. Apparently *everyone* benefits. But— meanwhile—there's this 'Society for a Livable Environment.' They claim that if something isn't done quick, the air will be unbreathable in twenty-six years and a half. They've got the facts to prove it. Then there's 'Concerned Citizens for Community Conservation.' They say the oil will run out in 24.7 years, unless rationing starts now, and they've got figures to prove *that*. Next there's the 'Oil Industry Research Council,' and they claim that if they're allowed to push their production to the limit, that will give them money for research, and they'll be able to make oil out of rock inside of twenty years. They've got the figures for *that*. Each one of these organizations is run by an Earthman, and they all disagree. Moreover, each one can prove he's right. But, at best, only one *can* be right, because they contradict each other."

Moffis looked harassed.

"It's even worse than it seems. I just got a batch of reports wherein our people disguised themselves as 'newsmen,' and questioned some of these Earthmen. The Earthmen were all glad enough to answer questions. . . . Listen to this."

Moffis separated a bulky sheaf of papers from a bulging stack of reports, leafed through the sheaf, and read aloud:

"Mr. Smith was checking over his company's figures as I came in. He was beaming with good nature. He motioned me to sit down while he totaled up a column of figures, and murmured, 'Sixty million two hundred eighty-six thousand four hundred seventy-two. *That* checks.' He looked up, smiled broadly, and said, 'What can I do for you, young fellow? You aren't here to tell me your government has come out with an income tax, I hope.' He looked worried, and said, 'You aren't, are you?' " Moffis paused, and scanned the pages rapidly. *"Here* we are. This is the part I wanted. . . . Mr. Smith stated, 'Our purpose, young fellow, is to press back the frontiers of poverty and the wilderness of despair. We can do this through sheer *productiveness.* Produce!—That's the answer to the problem! Make, build, produce, build, and produce again! Pile it up! Poverty can't stand up against it! That's the way to do it! With our methods of production, we can turn out ten, a hundred, a thousand items while the hand-laborer is working on one. Ours may not be quite as good as his, at first, but that's the next step. *Produce,* that's the first step. *Improve,* that's the second step. The more you make, the cheaper it gets to make it. Just let the forces of the market guide production into the right lines, and keep the producer unhampered, and the problem's solved. Nobody can be poor when he's got everything he needs. And he isn't likely to be despairing, either. As the stuff piles up, the price on it gets cheaper. It's bound to. Then everybody can afford it. This way, everybody gets rich. There's only one thing— keep the government out of it. Once they start sucking the profit out, all the prices go up. And they aren't subject to the laws of the market, either. They'll push production into the wrong lines. Then they've got a special bag of tricks to keep away any depression. A depression, you know, is when all the mistakes add up, and the something-for-nothing crowd gets taught what the truth is. A little depression puts everyone on his toes, after he's got fat and lazy from too much easy living. . . . So, you've got to keep the government out of it. And one other thing—you got to put some kind of limit on the number of college professors there are running around loose. You get a lot of funny things out of college professors. I don't understand it, but that's how it is.' "

Moffis put the report down, and Horsip frowned and massaged his chin.

Moffis said, "You see what I mean, he didn't hold anything back."

"But," said Horsip, "what does it mean?"

Moffis nodded. "That's it."

Horsip said, "Let's see that."

Moffis handed it to him.

Horsip sat back, scowling, and leafed through the report.

"It appears to me, Moffis, that Smith has already been through a lot of things we've never dreamed of."

"Yes, but with Smith putting his solution to our problems into action, maybe now we *will* experience these things."

"H'm. I wonder what a 'depression' is?"

"I don't know, but I don't like the sound of it. It may not bother Smith, but it doesn't sound good to *me*."

"Whoever made up this report should have had the sense to find out what the words he put in the report meant."

"A lot of these reports don't add up, even *with* explanations. Here, let's have that one. . . . Now, here in back—here we are. 'Depression: A state of acutely depressed business conditions. In a "depression," there is no money. Except for the urgent necessities, the means of production are idle. Nearly everyone is filled with gloom and despair. The future looks dismal. People kill themselves from lack of hope. Objects worth large sums of money can be had cheaply by anyone with the money to buy them. But nobody has any money.' " Moffis looked up. "That's a depression."

Horsip said fervently, "It doesn't sound good."

"No," said Moffis, "but how does the money disappear? Here, under 'Boom,' it says, 'Exuberant state of the economy. Everyone has money. Prices are high, but no one hesitates to buy, as everyone expects conditions to be even better in the future.' "

Horsip shook his head. "This is as hard to figure out as an 'installment loan contract.' "

"And it's only the beginning. Here, for instance, we have a report titled 'Hairwire Finetuning of Planetary Economic Systems.' I haven't found a complete sentence in it anywhere I can understand. My mind sort of slides over the surface, and can't get a grip."

"This is another interview with an Earthman?"

"Yes, this one is a famous economics professor. He even impresses the Earthmen."

Moffis reached into his stack of reports, and pulled out another sheaf. "Listen to this. 'Economic Systems—Their Sabotage and Overthrow. How to Do It.' Take a look at this."

After the first three sentences, Horsip had an attack of chills, but he read through to the end.

Moffis said, "How do you like that one?"

Horsip reread the summary, then looked up.

"Do you notice, Moffis, that when one of our men interviews an Earthman, he comes away talking like the Earthman? Here, for instance, our man is describing what's the best thing to blow up first. That's all right, because this interview was his job, and he's summarizing it. But listen to this. 'By this stage, the capitalists and their lackeys will lie awake nights drenched in sweat and shaking with fear. In their nightmare, they see the Revolution approach.' And so on. What's this?"

"Let's see that," said Moffis. He looked it over, frowning. "I didn't notice that when I was reading it. I suppose after reading that interview, this seemed mild by comparison. It's as if this Earthman had a bad case of something, and our man caught it from him."

"Let's see that first report again—the one on production. . . . Let's see now." Horsip settled back, and turned to the summary. "Here we are. 'In summary, then, the important thing is, *produce.* Turn out the goods so fast and in such quantity that poverty and need are overwhelmed, swamped. Then, if too much is produced, the price goes down so anyone can buy the goods, and there is no harm done. Produce! That's the important thing! From high production, *everybody* profits!' "

Moffis sat up.

"You're right! He caught it too!"

Horsip, scowling, weighed the reports in his hands.

"All these Earthmen, each with his special theory, are spread out through the Integral Union. That much we foresaw. But now—you remember, our men were supposed to make more fanatical 'reporters' than the Earth reporters who taught them. Apparently an Earthman can convince our men, and then our men are as strong believers as he was. Can that be?"

Moffis was thinking it over. He said, "But, in that case . . ." And that was as far as he got, because at this point he stared across the room and stopped talking.

Horsip said, "Well, whether it's so or not, there's nothing

we can do but improve the information network, hang on tight, and hope the High Council has some plan for taking care of this."

He became aware that Moffis was watching someone thread his way through the desks of busy workers and team supervisors, striding fast toward their slightly raised cubicle at the corner of the room. Horsip recognized Nokkel, the Security Chief.

Nokkel, looking as if he were suffering from a bad case of indigestion, opened the door of the cubicle, stepped in, and saluted.

Horsip studied Nokkel's expression, and returned the salute.

"Sir," said Nokkel, "we've turned up a communist cell in the Communications Section. And I—we—don't know what to ..."

Horsip glanced out at the room full of desks and apparently busy individuals, where an intense silence suddenly reigned.

Horsip smiled, and spoke so his voice would carry.

"Good news, Nokkel! That's fine work! Have a seat, and we'll work out the details."

The morbid interest on the faces turned to boredom, and the volume of noise in the room started to return to normal.

Horsip growled in a low voice, "Pull up a chair, Nokkel. Now, what's this? Let's have the details, and keep your voice down."

❋ XV ❋

Nokkel Develops
His Clinical Sense

Nokkel leaned forward on the edge of his chair.

"Sir, what happened is that we got a tip from one of the men in the Communications Section that something suspicious was going on. We've used a new ... ah ... 'bug' and we've got evidence against the assistant chief of the section, two of the shift supervisors, and three of the men. The six are members of a 'cell,' and the leader is one of the men. He reports to someone else, and we're trying to trace that down, but we haven't got it worked out yet. They use 'drops,' code words, transmitters, something called 'microdots,' and ciphers that have driven my best men half out of their heads—and, well, frankly, sir, it's a mess. Somewhere there's an Earthman giving them instructions, but we don't know how he gets the information to them. We can't leave them where they are, because they will eventually trace down our sources and expose them to their own people on other planets. Moreover, they're trying to recruit new members. So we've got to stop them. On the other hand, if we close in now, we won't find out who they're reporting to, and it may be someone high in our own organization. We'd shift them onto less important work, but if we do they'll know we've found out. Every minute they're where they are, they do damage. But we don't dare touch them, because they're our only link to someone who may be doing more damage yet."

Horsip glanced at Moffis, who looked serious, and said nothing.

"So," said Horsip, turning to Nokkel, "you need to know what to do about this 'communist cell,' is that it?"

"Yes, sir."

Horsip again had that melting-ice sensation he had had back on Earth.

92

Nokkel said jitterily, "I have the feeling that once I rip the cover off, there's no telling *what* we'll find. I'd have trusted these men anywhere. But they're all corrupt. My own assistants could be in on this. The whole organization could be . . ."

Horsip watched Nokkel alertly.

Nokkel gave a shuddering sigh. "No matter what you do, you can't beat the Earthmen. Some of those ciphers—I tried to show my men how to do it, but I got in a worse mess than they were in. You can't win. They're too smart. You—"

Horsip spoke confidently.

"You're overstrained, Nokkel. Now, don't worry about beating the Earthmen. It's true, they're clever, but they work against each other. Just bear in mind, there are a lot more of us, and we *don't* work against each other."

"But that's just it! Now we *do*. We—"

"Keep your voice down." Horsip looked intently into Nokkel's eyes. "All this is part of a great plan worked out by the *High Council*, Nokkel. It *looks* as if the Earthmen are making progress. But you know the High Council. The Earthmen see deep, but the Council sees deeper. Now, I can't tell you what the plan is. I don't claim to know more than a small part of it. But I can tell you the Earthmen are like a newly caught wild molk running around in a pasture. The molk looks ferocious. He *is* ferocious. But the herdsmen are watching him, and when the right time comes, they will throw out the tangle-ropes, and the molk will go down. Now, when I say *we* don't work against each other, naturally I mean our *top men*. Our top men are just like one man. But what of the leadership of the Earthmen? They are working in all directions. They are wasting their strength strangling each other. They *can't* win, Nokkel. Their strength is subtracted from each other. Not so with the High Council. Our strength is one, united, all working in the same direction. You and I may have a difficult time, but that doesn't matter. We will win in the end."

Nokkel's expression wavered through various shades of doubt and hope, but, as Horsip confidently approached the conclusion, Nokkel heaved a great sigh of relief.

"That's true," he said. "I've been so close to the details I've missed those points." His brow furrowed. "But now—on this business with this 'cell'—what do we—"

"Clean them out," said Horsip firmly. "Arrest them, and put them to the question."

"But we'll lose the only link to their superior!"

"True, but every moment we leave them where they are,

they do damage. And we can't move them without warning them, which would be worse. So, if we wait for them to give some lead to their superior, we may have a considerable wait, and the damage they do will offset what gain we make by capturing their superior, if we capture him."

"Truth," said Nokkel. He was silent a moment, his expression distracted and his lips working. Then he nodded again, and beamed. *"Truth,"* he said briskly. "I will take them in at once."

He came to his feet, saluted, and went out.

Horsip, watching him leave, saw one of his men study Nokkel alertly, then pick up a telephone. Horsip glanced over his staff. No less than three were speaking into phones while watching Nokkel.

Horsip noted their names on a slip of paper.

Moffis had watched Nokkel go out.

"I just wonder if we have the man for this job."

"He seemed all right when we were setting up the job."

"I'm talking about *now*."

"Who would you suggest?"

After a lengthy silence, Moffis nodded. "That's so. At least Nokkel does do the job *somehow*." Moffis picked up a slim report, and tossed it over to Horsip.

"Someone is doing his job right."

Horsip glanced at the title of the report: "The Planetary Mob, and Its Control," by John Towers. Scowling, Horsip opened up the report, to read of a planet populated by huge numbers of humanoids that could digest practically everything that grew on the planet, and hence created population problems such as he, Horsip, had never conceived. Towers had gotten the Centran expedition on the planet out of a very tight spot, and yet the report was straightforward and free of poses of superiority.

Moffis said, "Just as I give up hope, another report from Towers comes in."

"Well, let's hope Nokkel cleans out that 'cell.' Maybe then things will come back to normal—whatever *that* may be."

Several hours later, Nokkel came in, to tell Horsip the members of the "cell" had been caught, along with enough evidence to shoot the lot. Better yet, one of them had folded up under questioning, and revealed the name of their highly placed superior, who had also been seized.

"So, sir," said Nokkel, his face glowing, "this foreign influence is wiped out, and everything is now in good order."

"That's good," said Horsip. "Now, Nokkel, there is just

one thing that bothers me. This ... ah ... informant who uncovered the 'cell' ... ?"

"Yes, sir. He will be rewarded, sir. We will take him into our organization, and give him staff rank."

"H'm ... yes, but—how did he uncover this 'cell'?"

"By informing us, sir. He came right to us with the information. That broke the whole thing."

"Yes, but how did he *find out* about it,"

"He ... ah ..." Nokkel looked blank. "Let's see, now. He ... h'm ... it seems to me that what happened was that he came to us without anything specific, he just was worried and ... these people acted suspicious to him, and he ... well, he thought it was his patriotic duty, even though they *were* colleagues of his, and ... well ... it turned out he was right."

"I see," said Horsip, with no great air of conviction.

"Often these things depend on intuition," said Nokkel, looking wise. "It isn't the kind of thing you can lay your hand on, but there's just something that your ... ah ... clinical sense"—he tapped his head and smiled expansively—"fastens on and says to you, 'Nokkel, my boy, there's something about this fellow that isn't right.' And then there's nothing to do but keep an eye on him, and as often as not it's the dull unspectacular routine that gets him in the end."

Moffis cleared his throat coldly.

Horsip squinted at Nokkel, who was looking yet more expansive, and seemed about to let loose a new flood of wisdom. Gently, Horsip said, "Well, now, Nokkel, what does your intuition tell you about someone who comes to you and gives you a hint to watch someone else, and manages to get away without giving you any information at all as to how he knows what he knows?"

Nokkel, leaning back and twirling a little chain with some kind of watch charm that wound up on his finger, suddenly straightened up and looked awake. A hint of intelligence showed in his eyes.

"If you look at it *that* way ..." He frowned, then shoved his chair back. "I'll check on it, sir." He saluted, and went out in a hurry.

Horsip, looking out over his staff, saw three of his men pick up their phones as Nokkel went out.

Moffis said, "Nokkel's clinical sense must have got chloroformed sometime."

"Either that," said Horsip, "or it's getting so many signals it can't handle them all. Don't look too interested, but in the Correlation Section there are two people on the phone, and in the Abstracting Section there's another."

"I see them," murmured Moffis. "That bird in Abstracting was looking at Nokkel's back as he went by."

"It doesn't seem to make much sense," said Horsip, "but the same three did the same thing the last time Nokkel went out."

Moffis scowled. "It must mean something."

"Someone," said Horsip, "must want to know as soon as Nokkel is on his way back to his office."

"But why *three* of them?"

"I have an idea," said Horsip, "but it's going to have to wait until Nokkel takes care of this informant of his."

It didn't take long for that to happen.

Nokkel, looking haunted, settled into the chair opposite Horsip.

"You were right, sir. I sprang a surprise on him, told him I'd known all along, and he'd better come absolutely clean if he expected to get his sentence lightened. The shock jarred everything right out of him. *He* was working for MI-5."

Horsip felt queasy. " 'MI-5.' Let's see, that's—"

Nokkel said exasperatedly, "There's this island down there on Earth, it's just a little place, but we've got so much information on it no one actually knows anything about it. . . . Anyway, MI-5 operates out of there."

Moffis frowned. "If you've got so much information, how is it you don't know anything about it?"

"Because, sir, we can't digest it all. For one thing, we don't know for sure what's a fact and what's imagination. If we only had a tenth of the information, we'd be better off." He thought a moment. "A hundredth would be better yet. We could handle *that*."

Moffis suggested, "Maybe if you threw out some of this stuff . . ."

"How would we know what part to throw out? Besides, we get more of it all the time."

Horsip said, "At least you've discovered that this fellow who gave you the information about that 'cell' was an agent for MI-5? . . . That's settled, at least?"

Nokkel looked jarred. "Did I say that? No, that one was the agent for the CIA."

Moffis swore.

Horsip said, "I understood you to say you questioned him, and he was an agent for MI-5."

"Yes, sir . . . ah . . . I see what happened. There are so many of them, it's hard to keep track. He—the CIA agent— was the one that told me about the 'cell.' I got at him through this other fellow on our staff that I was suspicious of. *He* was working for MI-5."

Horsip squinted, started to ask a question, and thought better of it.

"*Anyway*," he said, "you got both of them?"

Nokkel said doggedly, "There were *three* of them by the time we got it all taken care of."

Moffis massaged his temples.

"At any rate," said Horsip, "they're all taken care of *now?*"

"It's like a weed with a taproot," said Nokkel. "I got the part I could get a grip on. But it looks to me like maybe it broke off further down."

"Just get all you can," said Horsip stubbornly. He had the impression that he was walking forward fast and nevertheless going slowly backward. "Now, while you're in here, Nokkel, is it possible that something could be taking place behind your back—something that would have to end when you leave—so someone would want to be warned *when* you leave?"

Nokkel said uneasily, "Well ... there are only three possibilities. But I'm sure each of them is well guarded against." He glanced from Horsip to Moffis. "Why, what ..."

"Three possibilities?" said Horsip.

"Yes, sir. First, there's my secret file. Second, there's my quarters. And third, there's the Master Control Center Surveillance Cubicle. But the file has a special lock, and I have the only key. My quarters can only be reached by a corridor that's always guarded by very trustworthy guards. And the Surveillance Cubicle has a special lock, extra trustworthy guards, and a secret camera and recorder that start as soon as anyone enters." Nokkel looked briefly smug, and then uneasy.

"Why?"

Horsip said, "Don't turn around, or give any sign, but each time you leave here, three of our men out there get on the phone."

Nokkel looked shocked, then mad.

"If I could borrow your phone for just a minute, sir? ... The one that connects up with Internal Security?"

Horsip reached out to the bank of phones, and handed it over.

Nokkel sat back.

"Hello, Groffis? Nokkel speaking. I want special details sent to surround and break into my quarters, the secret file room, and the Control Center Surveillance Cubicle. . . . I don't care what it makes us look like if there's no one there. You'll either carry out that order without delay, or I'll have you strung up by the heels, my boy, and what will people think of that, eh? . . . That's better. Now if no one is there, it was just an exercise, but if anyone *is* there, capture them, and if they resist, shoot them. The main thing is, *get* them one way or the other."

Nokkel's voice, instead of getting louder, stayed at the same level, but seemed to get more intense.

Horsip and Moffis looked approving, then Nokkel handed back the phone, and Horsip hung it up.

Nokkel gave a shuddering sigh.

"But I can't believe that anyone could be in any of those places!"

"Let's hope not," said Horsip. "But, in that case, we have the problem of why these three in here are on the phone when you leave."

"Well," said Nokkel grimly, "I've had plenty of practice lately shaking information out of people, and we can do the same to this bunch. The trouble is, I can get only so far. Even if they're willing to talk, there's a limit. These Earthmen apparently have more spies on that one little planet than we have in all the Integral Union. As nearly as I can figure it out, every dot of land down there has a spy system stealing information from everyone else. The result is, they know just how to do it. They've had so much practice the thought of it weighs me down. I feel outclassed."

"Luckily," said Horsip, "it's easy to tell the difference between one of them and one of us. Otherwise, they'd be all over the place. Now, as soon as we clear this up, there's another problem." Horsip was talking about this when there was a sharp ring, and he turned, to see the little metal flag raised beside the "Internal Security" phone. He took it off its hook, and handed it to Nokkel.

Nokkel listened intently to a voice that squawked excitedly as it ran words together. Finally, whoever was on the other end ran down, and Nokkel said, "All right, lock them all up separately, and get started on the questioning. . . . Yes, I'll be there, but not right away." Scowling, Nokkel handed the phone back to Horsip, who hung it up. "Sometimes," said Nokkel, "I wonder if I should trust *him*."

Horsip said, "Exactly my own feeling, Nokkel, about almost everybody in this room. I suggest you go back early, to just find out if you *can*. Now, here are the names of the three who watched when you went out. It might be a good idea to pick up the lot, as soon as possible. Then, since we've got things moving, I think we should search everybody's quarters while we're at it, and get a look at *anything* that seems suspicious."

"When, sir?"

"As soon as you can get things in order."

Nokkel shoved back his chair.

Horsip said, "Before you go—what did your men find in your three safe places?"

"Spies," said Nokkel.

As Nokkel went out, the same three members of Horsip's staff watched alertly, and picked up their phones. Looks of puzzlement, then horror, crossed their faces. Hastily, they hung up. Furtively, they glanced toward Horsip, then busied themselves at their work until Nokkel's men suddenly came in and dragged them all out.

By that same evening, Horsip was examining a collection of code books, miniature transmitters, propaganda leaflets, instructions for spies, false teeth with poison pellets inside, and numerous copies of *The Works of Mao Tse-Tung Translated Into the Centran.* Nokkel, obviously suffering from a headache, reported that he had so many prisoners he had run out of jail cells, and had put a lot of them in the same cell, whereupon a ferocious squabble had broken out, with prisoners accusing each other of being "imperialists," "commie goons," "revisionists," "lousy bloodsuckers," and other names that had so far proved impossible to translate.

The meaning of what was taking place suddenly dawned on Horsip.

The Integral Union was being turned into a battleground for all the conflicting opinions represented on the planet Earth.

And those conflicting opinions had come close to blowing Earth to bits.

That same day, Horsip put his conclusions into a report to the High Council, and grimly braced himself for the reply.

❊ XVI ❊

The Council Demurs

In the next few days, with a considerably smaller staff, Horsip got the routine moving again, and waited for the High Council to reply to his message. The High Council took its time about replying. Meanwhile, Horsip's system for gathering information had gotten into high gear, and the reports flooded in. The trend on the planets became glaringly plain, and the more Horsip saw of it, the less he liked it.

He tossed over to Moffis a report titled "The New Planetary Arms Race—Who's Ahead?" Moffis tossed back a report headed "Superneonazi Culture on Maphrik II—the Deification of a Racial Hero-Type."

Moffis groaned and Horsip snarled as he read:

"... thus in the launching of the first squadron of this formidable space fleet, the Warrior Hero of Ganfre's Cult of the Supreme is become the central *point d'appui* of the Total State. Vowing total conquest of the universe in twenty years, Guide Ganfre was cheered by a crowd of half a million as—"

Horsip looked up, to see a messenger salute, and present a sealed envelope and receipt. Horsip signed, the messenger went out, and Horsip read:

"You and your second-in-command are required to report at the earliest practicable moment, to give your personal assessment of the situation.... J. Roggil, Vice-Chairman, the High Council."

"At last," said Horsip. "Here, Moffis, read this."

Moffis growled, "One of these reports at a time is enough."

"No, Moffis. The message."

"What message?"

"Here."

"Ah, I thought it was another report. Let's see ... good! Good! Now maybe we can get some action!"

100

"Phew!" said Horsip. " 'Ganfre's Cult of the Supreme,' 'Moggil's Totalization of the State,' 'The Free Life on Qantros III,' 'The Dictatorship of the Proletariat on Gengrak IV,' 'Maximedimastercare Programs on Stulbos VI'—if I never see another of these things, that will be soon enough."

"Too soon," said Moffis. "I hope the Council is satisfied we have the Earthmen spread out enough by now."

"Moffis," said Horsip fervently, "when we get through describing this mess, I'll be surprised if the High Court doesn't squash some of these maniacs before the day is out."

The trip to report to the High Council took longer than Horsip or Moffis had expected. The High Council was in the far end of the Centran system, well beyond the line of demarcation of the Sealed Zone. In getting there, the contraction of time known to the Centrans by experience, and predicted in theory by the Earth mathematician Einstein, came strongly into effect. While the trip seemed long enough to them, from the viewpoint of a person back at their headquarters, far more time had passed. But, finally, the trip was over.

This time, the whole Council listened as Horsip and Moffis, in turn, gave their reports, and answered questions, and then Horsip summed up:

"The Earthmen have split up, as expected, but instead of quietly supplying a useful leavening for our own people, they have converted large numbers of them to *their* viewpoints. Now, this might not be too bad if only successful Earth viewpoints were put in action. Instead, every collection of fanatical believers has settled a planet of their own, and converted the populace to their own ideas. We now have all kinds of fanatics, all over the place. We're overrun with spies, dictators, weird philosophies, and little space fleets turning into big space fleets.

"These Earthmen are brilliant, but they have a capacity for being one-sided such as no Centran ever dreamed of. They can take a philosophy that's insane on the face of it, and make it work—for a while, anyway.

"I think we should straighten this out while there's still time to straighten it out.

"I respectfully submit that we should divide the planets taken over by the Earthmen into two categories—those anyone can see are the work of maniacs, and those that offer hopes of improvement. The first, we should take over by force."

Horsip became aware that the High Council was not being swept off its feet.

Roggil said thoughtfully, "An accurate presentation, General. But applying force right now won't work."

"Sir, we can't stand by while power-hungry madmen get started piling up space fleets. A lunatic is serious business once he's got a gun in his hand. As it is now, we can smash the lot of them."

"Whereupon, the trouble would spread. No, Horsip. It has to come to a head first."

Horsip felt a powerful impulse to disagree, but suppressed it.

Roggil studied Horsip's expression.

"There are some facts, General, known only to us and to the highest religious authorities. I can't say any more than that."

"Yes, sir."

"We are not necessarily unanimous. But many of us believe something very useful may come out of this situation. That, in fact, something useful is *bound* to come out of it. Accordingly, you are to continue to observe and report to us. When and if the time comes, we won't hesitate to use force in whatever way is necessary. Meanwhile, for your personal safety, we are assigning a unit of highly trained shock troops, and a reinforced squadron of the Fleet, to act under your direct command. You are answerable to no one but us for the way you use this force. We trust you to use it in strict accord with our expressed wishes."

Horsip, beginning to have visions of laying a few dictators by the heels, got control of his imagination, and said stoically, "Yes, sir."

And that was the end of the interview with the High Council, though some of them nodded in a friendly way as Horsip went out.

✻ XVII ✻

Snigglers and Wrettles

After the lengthy trip back, Horsip and Moffis found themselves once more at their desks, where things meanwhile had progressed. Although the trip had seemed long enough to Horsip, he hadn't realized how much more time had passed here.

The first report Horsip opened up suggested the change:

Summary: In summary, it appears safe to say that Premier Ganfre, in creating for himself (through his rubber-stamp cabinet) the post of Unified Planets' Guide, has solidified his absolute control over the six planets now subject to him. Guide Ganfre is thus well placed to protect himself from any attack by the comparatively split home planets of the Space Soviet. He can also, if he chooses, attack with the bulk of his forces any one of the planets of the Soviet. Intensive analysis of the situation suggests that either Ganfre or the Soviet can be expected to move soon against the various Free Planets, the Farmers Union planets, and the fantastic Free Life worlds. However, as all of these planets are under the control of various Earthmen, no certain prediction can be made, only estimates based on analysis of the relative military power of the various planets, and on intensive study of parallel situations on the Earthmen's home planet. No exact analogy to this present situation can be found, partly because of the control thought to be exercised over the Space Soviet from one nation on the planet Earth. But the apparent probabilities are those given above.

Horsip looked up dizzily. "Six planets." He turned to Moffis, who was studying a thick report he had doubled over, and which was threatening to spring shut at any moment.

Horsip started to speak, changed his mind, and looked sourly at the stack of reports on his desk. He told himself that, after all, he could consider that trip to the High Council as a kind of vacation. But the fact now had to be faced that, to write the overall summary of the situation at regular intervals, he had to keep track of what was happening. He took the top report, and looked at the title: "Agriculture in the Farmers Union."

Horsip opened it up, looked surprised, then began to relax. The report described friendly cooperation between farmers of various kinds from Earth and the Centran farmers. Photographs and sketches showed farm layouts, schemes for returning all the by-products to the soil, new breeds of molk and Earth cattle, ponds, orchards, descriptions of Earth fruits, vegetables, and grains, and Horsip, reading this, fell into a happy frame of mind.

And then he discovered that *this* planet was not armed.

Horsip sent for a copy of the Articles of Union between Earth and Centra, and discovered that Centran Armed Forces could be used to protect, attack, or otherwise regulate a planet only by approval of the Control Committee. The Control Committee was made up of three representatives from Centra, and three from Earth. The three from Earth were picked by the various power blocs on the planet. The three from Centra, in the last analysis, were appointed by the High Council. The decision of the Control Commission had to be unanimous to be effective. It any member voted against the others, the decision was nullified.

Checking the records of the Control Commission, Horsip found a long list of resolutions:

Resolved: That the Snard Soviet be warned against aggression . . . 5–1
Resolved: That Dictator Ganfre be seized and shot . . . 5–1
Resolved: That the Rogebar Soviet be occupied militarily . . . 5–1
Resolved: That Dictator Schmung be arrested . . . 5–1
Resolved: That the Snard Soviet be disarmed . . . 5–1
Resolved: That free elections be held on Snard . . . 5-1
Resolved: That Snard be warned against aggression . . . 5–1
Resolved: That Snard be forced to cease its military action . . . 5–1
Resolved: That help be dispatched to Lyrica against Snard . . . 5–1

Horsip looked up in disgust, All these resolutions were waste paper because they weren't unanimous. Checking further, he discovered that every time the vote was 5-1, it was some Earth representative who objected. When Centra objected, the vote was generally 3-3. Horsip nodded approvingly.

That was more like it. But the Earthmen, naturally, couldn't even agree with each other. He shook his head, sent the records back to the files, and reached for the next report. This proved to be about a planet renamed "Cheyenne" by the Earthmen:

> ... inhabitants all wear guns strapped around their waists, and excel in drawing the guns rapidly, in "horsemanship" (the horse is a beast imported from Earth—like a slender molk with no horns), and in games played with cards (like our Grab but more complicated), and by means of various contraptions intended to provide unpredictable chance. Exactly who set up this set of customs is not known, the first immigrants having long since been shot by later arrivals. While there is no visible reason for contentment, rough humor and good nature for some reason prevail. ...

Horsip scratched his head, sifted through the report, and read:

> ... somewhat over three thousand volunteers are believed to have gone to Lyrica during the Snard invasion. A resolution to punish Cheyenne was introduced in the Control Commission, but vetoed by the Euramerican representative. Upwards of ten thousand casualties are believed to have been inflicted on the Snard troops, who were baffled by the Cheyenne method of fighting. Survivors of the Cheyenne expedition are believed to have settled into rough broken country on Lyrica, from which they still raid the Snard troops. They are said to be led by an "Apache Indian." What that is, is not known, but it appears effective, as Snard is compelled to maintain a huge garrison. ...

Horsip skimmed farther, then picked up a paper headed "A Study of Conditions on the Planet Bibedebop."

He murmured the name to himself, weighed the report in his hand, told himself he would have to read it to report on it, flipped through it rapidly, and was not encouraged by the dense mass of print that looked up in one solid block of technicalities. Horsip turned to the summary:

> Summary: To summarize, in the simplest possible terms, the inhabitants of Bibedebop, believing in the vanity of any expectation of future reward or punishment, and the inapplicability of conventional mores to the human condition, strive to maximize the input of pleasurable sensation, while severely restricting the output of conventionally so-regarded productive effort. "Maximization of satisfaction with minimization of effort" might be regarded as the life-goal of the inhabitants. Indeed—

Horsip looked up angrily. From Moffis' desk came a
thump as he set down the massive report. Horsip tossed his
own report on the "Outgoing" heap. "Do you have one worth
reading?"

"Yes," said Moffis, "but it isn't pleasant."

"If you're through, let's see it."

Moffis handed it over. Horsip pried it open to read "Armament Rates on Earth-Dominated Planets."

Horsip felt a chill as he looked at charts marked "Weapons
Production, Overall," "Space Ship Production," "Growth of
Technological Production." Toward the edge of each chart,
the curves climbed like ships headed for outer space.

Absorbed, Horsip was only vaguely aware of exclamations
of astonishment from Moffis. When Horsip, skimming fast to
get the highlights, which fit together like a well-made gun, finally came to the end, Moffis was just looking up.

"Well, Moffis," said Horsip, "that *does* make unpleasant
reading."

"This is almost as bad. Would you believe that there is actually a planet where *everything* man-made is barred? And
they've made the rule hold!"

"What do they eat?"

"Nuts and berries. Roots. Snigglers and wrettles. Thou-
sand-bristled thread-spinners. Anything that's *natural*."

Horsip thought of the discipline that would have to be imposed to enforce such a rule. But the Earthmen had doubtless
accomplished it by putting across a *theory*.

Horsip shook his head.

"This is worse. All these dictators arm themselves at top
speed, while most of the other planets don't arm at all—"

"Of course," said Moffis, "the other planets shouldn't have
to arm. They have a right to look to the Fleet for protection."

"Yes, but with this Control Commission what use *is* the
Fleet?"

Moffis said thoughtfully, "If the Fleet would just blow up
the Control Commission . . ."

Horsip looked shocked.

"We couldn't have that. That would be a . . ."

He paused, considering it, then shook his head.

"That would be a breakdown of discipline. We couldn't
have that—unless higher authority *ordered* it."

Moffis nodded.

"Just let them order it *soon*."

❊ XVIII ❊

The Balance of Power

Before the eyes of Horsip and Moffis, the changes took place,
and if the High Council was disturbed by it, they gave no
sign. Day by day, the control of the Earthmen broadened
and tightened. More and more planets fell under their sway,
and instead of being slowed by the sheer bulk of Centrans
who had to be persuaded to new ways, their progress seemed
accelerated by the Centran respect for ideas. The Earthmen,
apparently used to more stubborn argument, seemed to orga-
nize whole planets overnight. Only where the Holy Brotherhood was exceptionally strong, or the Earthmen very weak,
were the Earthmen defeated. With these exceptions, the
peaceful conquest of Centra by Earth swept forward, with
the differences amongst the Earthmen extended to the Centrans. Horsip and Moffis, aching for action, varied their monotonous scrutiny of reports by occasional visits to planets.

"Ah, yes, my son," said a beaming priest, cracking his
knuckles as he stood overlooking a spaceport where large
numbers of dejected Earthmen were trooping out to waiting
space ships. "The Earthmen came, and the Earthmen went,
and the planet is still the same, and the Brotherhood remains.
Bad luck attended the Earthmen wherever they turned, dear
me! The design of the Great One, I think, was plain in the
way their factories burned down and their plans blew up,
whatever they did. Would you believe it, they had a usurious
scheme by which a person might squander money yet un-
earned on wasteful self-indulgence! They then aimed to sink
wells deep in the ground to suck out the lamp oil reserved to
future generations, and burn it up in a rush. If once they had
got started, there is no telling what deviltry they might have
brought to pass! But the Brethren were alert. We clung to
them close, and inflicted on them the Judgment of the Great

107

One. The loss the Earthmen suffered on this planet was fantastic! Look at the sorry crew! They may, of course, be back. We are busily spreading the tales of their evil designs so the people will be ready. If truth were told, there were one or two little ... er ... instances of excessive zeal amongst our own people. . . . But in a good cause."

"Phew," said Moffis, when they were on their way again, "did you notice the look in that priest's eye when he told about the Earthmen's factories burning down? By the way, the back of his robe, along the edge, looked scorched."

"It seemed to me," said Horsip, "that every one of the Brotherhood smelled of smoke—except the saintly High Priest, himself, of course."

"Yes, but what a crafty look his assistant had!"

Horsip nodded. "The Earthmen ran into it that time, all right."

Horsip and Moffis then went over the latest batch of reports, and had any sense of pity for the Earthmen knocked to bits.

"Look at this. The Snard Soviet has got *another* planet."

"So has Ganfry—and he's armed to the teeth."

Soon Horsip was reading a report of disasters and calamities that were hard to believe until he realized this was about that planet he had heard of before—where everything manmade was banned. Wide-eyed, he read:

... as no food has been stored, this frost in the Rradigg region was a disaster. Coming on top of the floods, which have occurred periodically throughout the planet's history, they aggravated the food shortage into a famine. Meanwhile, the planetary government issued assurances that all would be well. As the famine worsened, a delegation of leading citizens demanded a return to systematic *storage* of food, at least. The planetary government assured the delegation that the Bounty of Nature could be relied on, and that all man's troubles had come from eating artificial food, artificially raised by man. The tilling of the soil was unnatural, the government asserted, man having been meant to find his food in the field like other animals. If there was need, Nature would provide. If Nature did not seem to provide, then it was because the population was too high, and the thing to do was to let Nature *adjust the population downward*. The result of this pronouncement was revolution, and the planet, its population considerably shrunken, has returned to traditional Centran methods. Although it was only one particular kind of Earthmen who caused the trouble, the population now does not like Earthman, and in the past month two innocent tourists have been dipped in hot tar, while another was only barely rescued from being thrown headfirst into a volcano. The planet was a popular stop on the Nature-Lover's Tour before the food ran out, but . . .

There was the *whack* of paper on a desk top, and Horsip turned to see Moffis shake his head.

"No matter what you say, these Earthmen have increased production. They do it on the 'free-enterprise' planets. They do it on the dictator planets. They make a *fantastic* increase."

"But," said Horsip, "they aren't looking very far ahead. The waste is terrific."

"That isn't going to help us when we run into this concentration of spaceships."

"But they don't agree with each other."

"Let's hope they never do. They're going to be as big as the Fleet soon."

Horsip nodded moodily, and pulled a fresh report off the stack: "Disaster on Bibedebop."

"Ah," he murmured, "that's where they minimize work and maximize pleasure." He opened up the report, to read of whole sections of the population stupefied by drugs while others stole their possessions. He read of an arrangement whereby volunteers tried out new drugs without charge for a generous drug-manufacturing cartel operating out of Dictator Ganfre's home planet. There were so many volunteers that distillery owners and beer-parlor operators were virtuously trying to end the arrangement. Meanwhile, the cartel was testing a superhallucinant that provided the illusion of fulfilling the user's wants so vividly there seemed no need to *really* fulfill them. To get a satisfying banquet, it was only necessary to snort up the nose a quarter teaspoonful of a green powder. So why bother with food? As the population starved and the cartel's scientists methodically took notes, something else came along:

. . . wave after wave of Mikerils, without warning, each successive wave more powerful than the last, struck the main population centers . . .

Horsip, startled, read a grisly description that brought back the fears of childhood. But then he relaxed. . . . After all, this was the account given by the survivors of a tremendous overuse of hallucinants.

Horsip turned to the next report. This told of ". . . an amalgamation of these worlds that would have seemed un-

likely only a short time ago. The various varieties of plane-
tary Soviets, for instance, are now combining with the Snard
Soviet against the Free Planets Union, formed to resist the
National Racist Planetary Alliance dominated by Dictator
Ganfre. Ganfre, meanwhile, is successfully wooing more
planets that are alarmed by the conglomeration of Soviets.
Confronted by these gigantic combinations, the Free Planets
Union has formed an alliance with the agrarian planets still
uncommitted, but it is unknown how the balance of power
will be affected by . . ."

Horsip read on, report after report, and when he finished
he shook his head, pulled over a blank sheet of paper, and
began to write:

To the High Council:
Sirs:

I send herewith summaries of reports which describe typical
situations we are now facing.

I again urge the use of force in the greatest possible
strength, to smash the armed combinations now formed within the Integral Union.

I urge the use of the Fleet, reinforced to the maximum
possible extent regardless of dangers elsewhere, in a surprise
attack against either Ganfre or Snard. Immediately following
the elimination of this opponent, I urge that the Fleet at once
be placed in the most favorable position to attack with its full
remaining strength the other combination, whether headed by
Snard or Ganfre.

If this attack is made at the earliest possible moment, and if
all available force is used against each opponent singly, it may
still be possible to destroy these combinations.

Respectfully,
K. Horsip
Member, Supreme Staff
Director of Surveillance

Horsip handed the message to Moffis, who was moodily
eying a large chart headed:

Order of Battle, the Nationalist Racist Planetary
Alliance Compared with
Order of Battle, the United Socialist Planets Soviets

Moffis was grumbling to himself when Horsip handed the
message to him. He read in silence, then slammed his fist on
the table.

"*Good!* But there's no time to lose!"

Horsip nodded grimly, and sent the message.

❋ XIX ❋

The Mikeril

The rough idea of Horsip's recommendation found its way
into general knowledge among his staff, so there was a tense
silence as a messenger brought a sealed message to Horsip.

Horsip dismissed the messenger, ripped the envelope open,
and read:

> By Command
> The High Council
>
> The High Council believes that any interference in the
> situation at present would defeat its purposes.
> What is needed instead is fuller information.
> You are hereby requested to review the whole situation,
> basing your report as far as possible on *firsthand information*.
>
> J. Roggil
> Vice-Chairman

Horsip looked up in disgust.

Moffis read the message, sitting tense and alert as he started, and slumping as he read. He handed it back to Horsip.

"Now what?"

"Now we look over *more* planets."

"What would happen if instead of waiting for the Council,
the Supreme Staff ordered the attack?"

Horsip felt the electric jolt go through him. Then he found
himself mentally counting votes. Argit would be opposed.
Maklin would very possibly agree. Roffis would do what he
thought was right, but would he go against the High Council?
And what about the High Council itself? Horsip suddenly
laughed.

"It would be a disaster, Moffis. The High Council wouldn't

stand there with its tail wrapped around its ankles while we flouted its authority."

"But if we let this go on, *that* will be a disaster."

"I know it. But I know it wouldn't work to go against the High Council. . . . Besides, it would be wrong."

Moffis said unwillingly, "I know *that*. But something has to be done. This is almost out of control."

"Maybe the Council does know something we don't know."

Moffis showed a flicker of hope.

"In that case—if we keep looking, we should find it."

But no matter how they traveled, the situation was now developing so fast that the impression of its hopelessness had to be revised upward from day to day. They had traveled quietly on earlier visits, but now commerce raiders preyed on the shipping lanes, and terrorists amused themselves by planting bombs on passenger ships, and taking pot shots from the shrubbery around spaceports. This time Horsip brought along the guard allotted him by the High Council, along with the reinforced squadron of the Fleet that the Council had provided. Horsip had spent his spare time, while not reading reports and writing summaries, making sure his force was in good order; and the effect created by this show of strength brought home to Horsip how long it had been since the central authority of the Integral Union had made its will felt.

As his reinforced squadron, its guns and launchers bared for action against raiders, flashed past planets and space depots belonging to various authorities, its presence acted like a hot poker on tender hide. Through the big screens in the flagship's command center, Horsip could see the hasty departure of questionable ships, the scattering of convoys, and the hurried deployment of warships off the planets of dictatorships. Occasionally a challenge flashed in:

From:
Supreme High Command
National Racist Planetary Alliance
Supreme Commander
Region of Snarlebat II
Shock Combat Legion of Space
To:
Unknown Fleet
Message:
Identify yourself at once, or withdraw from NRPA territory, subject to attack by NRPA combat forces at full condition of readiness. Your reply is demanded immediately.

Signed:
Q. Drekkil
Supreme Commander
Shock Combat Legion of Space
Region of Snarlebat II

"What do we do about that, sir?" inquired the squadron's communications officer, as Horsip looked up from the message.

Horsip, itching to flatten Q. Drekkil, and sling the Shock Combat Legion of Space into the nearest sun, reminded himself of the High Council's instructions, and asked himself whether Drekkil could be induced to attack. Whereupon Horsip, of course, could defend himself.

"H'm," said Horsip. "This is an important matter. It will require some time to think of a suitable reply."

"Yes, sir. But ... ah ... beg pardon, sir, it says here an *immediate* answer is necessary."

"It does, doesn't it? Possibly I'll have it ready after the evening meal."

The communications officer blinked, and pulled out his watch. He looked up at Horsip, and just at that moment the squadron commander stepped in.

"Sir, we've got two squadrons of warships closing in on us. I've just had a point-blank warning to stop at once."

Horsip considered coldly what would happen if he were now attacked and he and the squadron wiped out while he was attempting to get information for the High Council. What would the Council do?

Horsip glanced at the communications officer.

"Send: 'This is General Klide Horsip of the Supreme Staff. These are Fleet ships of the Integral Union. We will neither stop, alter course, nor answer questions. You are required to stand aside and cover your guns in the presence of the Fleet.' "

The communications officer blinked, scribbled on his pad, and rushed out. The squadron commander stared at Horsip a moment.

"If they open fire—"

"We'll see how many we can take with us."

The squadron commander bared his teeth in a grin, saluted, and stepped out.

The big screen showed the onrush of the two squadrons of the Shock Combat Legion. From the angle of view and comparative velocities, it was evident that Horsip's squadron had not altered course or speed in the slightest. The Shock Combat Legion continued to close in. Then the view in the viewscreen turned into chaos as the ships of the oncoming squadrons clawed to get out of the way, broke formation, gun covers sliding over the turrets, the still uncovered guns and launchers deflecting in any direction to avoid aiming at Horsip's ships. The long-range detector apparatus of the scattered ships swung in all directions, obviously seeking what might be coming along behind Horsip.

Horsip shook his head. The ships of the Shock Combat Legion were now straining to form a guard of honor.

The communications officer came in, looking dazed.

"Sir, we've got a reply."

He held out a slip of flimsy paper. Horsip skimmed the heading, and came to the business part of the message:

High Admiral Querk Drekkil, Supreme Commander of the Shock Combat Legion of Space in the Region of Snarlebat II, extends respectful greetings to General Horsip of the Integral Union. High Admiral Drekkil wishes to assure General Horsip of the kind regard in which the Integral Union is held by the National Racist Planetary Alliance. If High Admiral Drekkil may assist General Horsip in action against any common enemy, General Horsip has only to request assistance, and High Admiral Drekkil will give the request his most careful consideration.

Horsip scowled, glanced at the screen, where the two squadrons had formed a guard of honor and were falling behind as they altered course to align themselves with Horsip's ships. The speed with which they maneuvered showed good discipline and good ships.

All the weapons of Drekkil's squadrons, as the individual ships were picked out under high magnification, were covered. Drekkil had obeyed Horsip's demand, but the message showed that he regarded the Integral Union as a foreign power, not a central government. The precision of handling of Drekkil's ships demonstrated the force supporting his position. Drekkil, however, had no way to know what might be coming along after Horsip. Possibly that was his reason for being so agreeable.

Horsip growled, "Let's have a message blank."

The communications officer handed over his pad.

Horsip wrote:

General Klide Horsip expresses his thanks for the offer of that assistance which is required of every citizen of the Integral

Union, to whatever planetary group or association he may belong.

As this is not the advance element of a punitive expedition, but merely General Horsip's personal guard, no such assistance is required.

Horsip considered the message narrowly, then handed it to the communications officer. The communications officer looked nervous and went out.

The squadron commander passed him on the way in.

"I don't like to say it, sir, but they handle their ships very well."

"Better than our own?"

"There isn't much to choose."

"You'd say they have the advantage?"

"Absolutely. We're outnumbered almost two to one."

"We may have a fight with them shortly."

"We won't come out of it alive, sir."

"But it's important that we give the best account of ourselves we can."

"Yes, sir."

The communications officer stepped in, looking bemused, and held out a slip of message paper.

Horsip read:

High Admiral Querk Drekkil of course recognizes the superior position of General Horsip in the hierarchy of the Integral Union, and respectfully offers salute as the Fleet passes.

Horsip's lips drew back from his teeth. A crawling sensation traveled up and down his spine.

The squadron commander looked uneasy.

The large-scale magnification on the screen showed the long-range detection apparatus of Drekkil's ships searching in every direction.

Horsip shrugged in disgust, reached out for the message pad, and wrote:

The Fleet returns the salute.

The communications officer hurried out.

Horsip handed Drekkil's latest message to the squadron commander, who said, "In case they change their tune, the gunnery officers have their targets selected."

Horsip nodded, but had given up hope of any such result.

Drekkil had sensed Horsip wanted a fight, and Drekkil was having nothing to do with it.

Drekkil's next message wished Horsip a fine journey, and Horsip could only return the good wishes. But while Horsip was disappointed, everyone else in the squadron seemed exhilarated. The substance of the messages leaked out, and was duly distorted, the resulting version being that Drekkil had warned Horsip he was outnumbered, and must stop, and Horsip had replied, "This is the Fleet, and the Fleet stops for no one. Stand aside or be destroyed." Instantly, Horsip's squadron was transformed into a crack unit that drilled continuously, willingly, with no hint of complaint.

And then, ships and men in perfect order, they began to see what the Integral Union had been transformed into, as one by one they visited the planets.

Looming through smoke and fumes, Horsip, at the bridge of the flagship, could see a thing like eighteen roads crisscrossing one atop the other. Vehicles of weird design careened around the numerous curves, while in the background loomed a giant city. Beyond the towers of the city there rose up, slightly to one side, a cone-shaped mound of peculiar reddish tinge mingled with all sorts of other colors in a vertical patchwork.

"Ah, that," said the planetary governor, perspiring freely, "that, now, is a . . . well . . . that's where we put the vehicles when they are . . . ah . . . used up. Yes, sir."

"I see," said Horsip, frowning. He had invited the governor aboard on a courtesy visit, according to hallowed custom of the Centran Fleet. The arrival of the Centran squadron had produced a sensation, as if a rug made out of some defunct wild animal had stood up and roared.

The governor, turning to Horsip, said hesitantly, "But that . . . ah . . . dump you refer to is just a by-product. There, you see, rising over the city, is the great tower where Mr. Schmidt rules over the planet through his gigantic enterprises. And that tower to the left, a little lower—that is the Consolidated Credit Building. Off there in the distance is Monopoly Motors. You see, it is not quite so high, but it is a very impressive building. And over there is the Intercontinental Construction Cartel. . . . They built this multilevel here—one of the biggest on the planet." The governor peered around the control room furtively, and lowered his voice:

"Ah, General Horsip, if I might ask . . . who . . . ah . . . who is your Earthman?"

"My what?" said Horsip, looking blank.

"Your Earthman, sir. Who gives *you* your orders?"

"The High Council gives me my orders."

"Ah, of course. Are they still in existence, then?"

"Of *course* they are in existence! Why not?"

"But what purpose do they serve, *Earthwise?*"

Horsip grappled with the word "Earthwise."

"*No* purpose," said Horsip, flatly.

The governor looked nervous. "Have you *no* Earthman, sir?"

Horsip said shortly, "I take my orders from the High Council, and I am a member of the Supreme Staff. There is no Earthman on the High Council, and only one on the Supreme Staff."

The governor blinked, then suddenly looked relieved. "Ah, then it's all right. . . . Well, well, that's *fine.*"

Horsip eyed the governor with great affection.

"And just who do you take *your* orders from?"

The governor thrust out his chest.

"From Mr. Schmidt. *Personally.*"

"Earthmen run this planet, then?"

"Definitely, sir. How else?"

"What are all these fumes?"

"Ah ... well ... you see those factory chimneys down there, and all these ground-cars too. I suppose, plus ... well, there's that dump over there, at the edge of the city. All those gas tanks are draining slowly, and ... well I imagine that's where it comes from. Yes, sir. . . . Most of it, anyway."

"Isn't it hard to breathe down there?"

"Incidence of respiratory diseases was up 2 percent last year."

"What is the advantage of all that smoke?"

"We are making more ground-cars. Mr. Schmidt has announced that this year, for the first time, everyone, on the average, will have a new ground-car before the year is out."

The governor beamed. "A new ground-car a year for everyone on the planet, on the average. *Think* of it!"

Horsip's mind boggled.

The governor banged his fist into his hand.

"And soon we may have a new ground-car twice a year! I have it from Mr. Schmidt—*himself.*"

"I see," said Horsip. "But what will you do with two of them a year? And what about the old ones?"

"Why, we will put them on that pile there that you just asked me about. What else?"

Horsip glanced back at the odd-looking mound.

"That is a heap of *used-up ground-cars?*"

"Yes, sir."

"Well, now, look here. . . . You mean to say these things *wear out in a year?*"

"Certainly. We have to use them very hard to get back and forth over the roads to work and still live in the country and at the sea shore."

"In order to get out of the smoke, eh?"

"Well, that's *one* reason, yes."

"Certainly they don't wear out all at once. Why not just replace the parts that wear out, and save all that work?"

The governor looked at him fishily.

"That would be *very* bad for business."

"To make these things so you have to throw them away every year is wasteful. They should be made so you could hand them down from generation to generation. *That* way a man could save a little money. As for using them to go back and forth from home to work—that is ridiculous! You should use iron roads—"

The governor muttered, "Mr. Schmidt would not approve of *this.* . . . Sir, we do not have iron roads. They do not exist."

"Then," said Horsip, "you are progressing backward. All this murk is created, you say, by these factories and ground-cars. There's the answer to your problem. Make the ground-cars so they last, put in iron roads, and you can shut down the factories except for making replacements and spare parts. Then you will be able to breathe again. See, the answer is right in front of you."

"We could *not* do that," said the governor angrily. *"Everybody's* work and income is connected with the making of ground-cars. That was Mr. Schmidt's first stroke of genius when he first came to this planet. No, General Horsip. You would create *unemployment* if you closed down the factories. If people received no pay, they could not only buy no ground-cars, but they could buy no other improvements, and they could even buy no food. It would be a disaster. Mr. Schmidt would never allow it."

Horsip angrily began to speak, but then shrugged.

The governor said tolerantly, "Ask your Earthman about it sometime, General Horsip. He will explain it to you."

Horsip's next visit took him to a planet where the air was relatively pure, but hosts of iron-helmeted troops marched by as a beaming trio returned the salutes from a reviewing stand. Guns and armored ground-cars rumbled past in such profusion as to bring back memories of the invasion of Earth. Clouds of air-planes swooped overhead, to be followed by a formidable fleet of space ships. The dictator himself, an Earthman, kindly explained to Horsip, "You see, Jack, I got the idea out of this book I read when I was a kid. *My Battle,* or something like that. But I'd of never had a chance to try it out if you hadn't come down on Earth, and given us a chance to spread out, like, and get a little elbow-room. Our people are kind of stubborn. These people here, though, they lap it up. Can't say I'm as big as Ganfre, but I'm doing all right."

When Horsip got back to his flagship, he found Moffis going through the latest batch of reports in silence. Horsip groped for a chair and sat down. Moffis reached out with the look of a punch-drunk fighter for another report, turned the pages automatically, put the report in another pile, and reached out for a fresh report, turned the pages automatically, and set the report in another pile. He reached out for another report, turned the pages automatically, set the report in another pile, and reached out for a fresh report. He turned the pages automatically, and—

Horsip said, "Moffis."

Moffis set the report in another pile, reached out for a fresh report, turned the pages automatically, put the report in a separate pile, and—

Horsip said, *"Moffis!"*

Moffis looked up, and his eyes came to a focus.

"It's too late," he said.

Horsip said, *"What's* too late?"

"We'll never stop them now."

Horsip leaned forward and said sharply, "Stop *who?"*

Moffis shoved the reports back.

"We now have planets run by communists, planets run by capitalists, planets run by lunatics, planets converted entirely into factories—that's what it boils down to—for some one specialty or to follow some one fad of the Earthmen. They could never have done it on their own. They're too quarrelsome. We would never have done it ourselves. We don't have that many ideas to try out. Argit thought the two of us would make a good combination and supply each other's lacks. It has worked exactly the other way around. We have given the Earthmen the opportunity to bring into existence every kind of one-sided stroke of genius that occurs to them.

Do you realize that we now have *one* whole planet devoted to nothing but *horse races?* The thing is inconceivable, insane! Worse yet, there's even a planet—a whole planet—devoted to what *they* call 'higher education.' I tell you, it's ruinous! But it's too late now. We can't stop it. It's gone too far. We might as well—"

Horsip said, angrily, "Stop that! There's no use moaning over it! What's done is done!" He paused, frowning. "Wait a minute, now. What was that again? A whole planet devoted to *what?*"

"Higher education," said Moffis wryly. "That's what they *call* it. As a matter of fact, it's a pesthole of subversion. The students are complaining because of the 'monotonous quality of life,' and the 'repressive narrowness of Centran institutions.' *Narrowness! Repressive!* They're running wild, like a molk with the bloat! And they don't know it! The professors on this planet are all terrorized. They teach what they think the students want to hear. I tell you, the thing to do is to land about six divisions of the Suicide Corps, and . . ." Then he shook his head. "But it's too late. There's no hope now. The damage is done. We might as well—"

Horsip said impatiently, "Wait a minute, Moffis. Back up. You said there was some planet devoted entirely to *what?* There was something else you mentioned."

Moffis said dully, "Horse racing. The horse is like a molk, only skinnier, and with no horns. The Earthmen used to ride around on them before they had ground-cars. Now they race them for fun, and to bet on which one is going to win."

"How could they possibly use a whole planet for a thing like that?"

"It's a small planet, and the gravity is low. These horses can go fast because of the low gravity. The Earthmen have figured out a way to get oxygen to the horse even though the atmosphere is thin. Any kind of special training, special drugs, special apparatus is all right, as long as the animal is a horse. There are special farms on the planet where they acclimate the horses to the low gravity. There are stud farms there, where they breed horses with bigger lungs. There's a gigantic rolling casino—"

Horsip said blankly, "A *what?*"

"The track—the race course—is enormous. These horses travel at terrific speed. There are cameras spaced along the track to bring the race, in three dimensions, to people who watch it at 'horse parlors'—central places on other planets where they show the race for a fee. For people who come to watch the race on the spot, the whole central building travels around a track set inside the curve of the race course itself. The building is on wheels with some kind of frictionless bearings. When they aren't watching the race, the patrons gamble in this casino, or ..." Moffis shook his head. "Maybe what *you see* is encouraging, but not what I get from these reports."

Horsip wavered, thinking of the possibility of raising Moffis' spirits. Then moodily he shook his head. "It's a mess, Moffis. I know what you think of those reports, and I've thought of trying to find someone else I can trust to work up the summaries while we're visiting these planets, but I can't, and the reality is no improvement, believe me."

Moffis nodded. "From what I've seen of it, that's what I thought."

"It's almost a relief to get on our way again, so I can go back to reading reports. It was a dream to think we could get away from this mess. It's everywhere you go."

Moffis nodded moodily. "I had the idea of getting a little relaxation after I read that report on the 'planetary university.' One of the ship's officers had bought an omnivision set on one of the planets we've visited. He wasn't using it, so I borrowed it." Moffis shook his head. "That was worse than either the reality *or* the reports."

Horsip looked around blankly, and saw a sizable grayish cube with crackle finish and a row of knobs under two small lenses thrust out on shiny stalks.

"Is that the thing, Moffis?"

"That's it."

Horsip said, "I've never used one."

"Try it if you want to. You put the eyepieces up to your eyes, and there are little plugs that come out and fit in your ears. There's another thing like a cup that fits over your nose. Naturally, that model is outdated already."

"What are those knobs for?"

"Don't touch them. I bumped one by accident, and thought the ship had run into a planetoid. Just work this knob off to the side. That makes the sound louder or fainter. And this rim that sticks out this slot and has numbers on it—that selects the signal you receive. You turn that to pick up different signals."

Horsip nodded, pulled over a chair, and sat down. He adjusted the eyepieces, found the earplugs, and swung up the little cup that fit over his nostrils. Nothing happened.

Moffis' voice reached him dimly. "I forgot. You have to push this switch."

Horsip heard a faint click. Then chaos sprang into existence around him.

A screaming mob armed with clubs and torches hurtled straight at him. The smell of hot metal and burning rubber filled his nostrils. An unkempt maniac with blazing eyes gave a piercing yell, and sprang for Horsip with hands outstretched like claws.

Horsip lashed out, his fist exploded in pain, the maniac dwindled and vanished, and there was a violent yank at his ears, as his head was pulled forward.

Horsip looked around blankly.

The omnivision set was leaning over on its little table, held from smashing to the floor by the cords of the earplugs.

Horsip glanced around furtively, and saw that Moffis was again going through reports like an automaton. Horsip massaged his fist, and hauled the set back up onto its table. No damage appeared to have been done. The sound was loud and clear. A wisp of smoke was drifting out of the nosepiece. A whining voice came across, and Horsip peered into the eyepieces.

Instead of a mob, there was a desk, with individuals hurrying in and out to lay message blanks on the desk. Behind the desk an unprepossessing-looking individual talked earnestly:

"Despite Planetary Premier Grakkil's speech, the disturbance still has not quieted, and it is feared that the Mekklinites will accept no accommodation short of unconditional surrender to their demands. Already the Mekklinites have razed the western portion of the city. Injuries have occurred, and this has angered the Mekklinites further. The mayor and other hostages, who were shot earlier by the Mekklinites, have been found buried under a cement wall. Panic rules this planet as the Mekklinites turn, no one knows in what direction, to avenge injuries to their people, to destroy the capital city as they have vowed to do if their demands are not met, and there can be no doubt now but that Premier Grakkil miscalculated badly when he failed to accede at once to their demands. Don't you think so, Sike?"

Horsip was suddenly looking at an individual with large eye-correctors and a look as if he had just been awakened out of a sound sleep.

"Yes, Snok, I believe implicitly in the law of instant acquiescence to the stronger force, and that's what we've got here. The Mekklinites obviously believe in death and destruction, and will stop at nothing to get their way. That's pretty plain by now, don't you think so, Snok?"

Horsip found himself looking at the first man, who perspired and nodded.

"It certainly is, Sike, it certainly is. And this should have been obvious to the premier, don't you think?"

Now the second individual was back again.

"It is to *us,* after seeing this precise thing happen so many times before. But the political animal doesn't learn except through kicks administered to his hide. That's a quote from Gek Kon, the Mekklinite leader, by the way, Snok."

"I know it is, Sike. But now, the question is, what's going to happen here? The mayor and the rest of the hostages are dead, of course. This in itself isn't surprising, because of course the Mekklinites are believers in violence. But couldn't it cause the premier to take the advice of the more warlike of his advisers and . . . say . . . use sleepy gas on the mob?"

"I *hope* not, Snok. But the premier might lose his head and attempt to do some such thing. Of course, since the passage of the No-Violence Act as an attempt to appease the Mekklinites, this would involve the immediate fall of the government."

"Yes. The premier is in a situation, Sike, that calls for the utmost political finesse, and I'm just afraid that he doesn't have that magical presence or *zeerema* or whatever it is that would enable him to pull it off. We'll be back with you again later, Sike. Thank you for a truly impressive analysis of the situation."

Horsip muttered to himself, groped for the signal-change switch, and was at once treated to a smell like dead fish.

Before he could get at the signal-change switch again, an impressive voice intoned in his ear: "This is the smell—or 'bouquet' in the words of the *aficionados*—of the drug garazal, or 'green drops.' Those of you who have the latest Constituex sets with full panoply of newsworthy scents will feel the actual effects of this drug as the room begins to rotate around you. We are now in an actual 'green-drop heaven' where the *aficionados* gather to experience what is said to be an elevation of the sense of awareness—far superior to ordinary experience, because the green-drop experience is 'genetically coded on the tissues of the brain.' This superiority of dream experience to the real world is said to enable the *aficionado* to 'block out' the real world and its experiences, which become irrelevant as he withdraws into green-drop heaven and its far more attractive—"

Horsip connected with the controls, switched to another signal, and was rewarded by the sight of an individual with large teeth, bared in a smirk, who was saying ". . . superiority of the immoral tridem to the moral tridem is that the immoral tridem simply *immerses* the viewer in a world he might otherwise never have known, and he can't—simply *can't*—get out of it if it's really well done. This gives the tridemist a real lift—a real *boot*—I simply can't describe it. It's a sense of power"—the recording camera zoomed in to enlarge his face until it filled the field of view—"a really *godlike* sensation, to use an antique term—"

Horsip's groping hand found the signal-change switch, and now he was looking at three people seated on three sides of a table, facing each other as Horsip viewed the scene as if sitting slightly back from the table on the fourth side. Two of the faces showed expressions of cynical disbelief, and one had a defiant, somewhat maniacal air. The two with the cynical expressions were seated to right and left. The defiant one was now saying, "In this year of indecision, I have been visited by a vision of the way things have been and the way things shall be." His eyes seemed to drill into Horsip's head. "Today I have a special message—"

Horsip located the signal-change switch.

Through the earplugs, like some voice of doom, came a monologue in which one word followed fast on the heels of another:

". . . situation has deteriorated badly in the last several days. Brog Grokig, new member of the Board of Control, suggests that in future it may be necessary to allow criminals to determine their own punishment. 'They will not accept it from anyone else,' Grokig warned. . . . Mroggis New College has found a way to cope with the dissatisfaction of its students in today's changing universe and maladjusted environmental situation. Mroggis now offers Certificates of Achievement Specializing in Revolution, in addition to the more traditional subjects. 'We do not prejudge the situation,' said Administrator Gurnik. 'One specialty is as specialized as another. Merely a different viewpoint is involved. Everything is relative.' . . . On Darg III, it is reported that the planetary president has been impeached for suggesting that weapons be supplied to the planetary constabulary. . . . Occupation of Dione IV by forces of the Snard Soviet is now reported to be complete. . . . Dictator Ganfre has warned against further aggression by Snard, and has also issued an ultimatum to the president of the planet of Columbia, warning that Columbia must join with Ganfre or be subject to precautionary occupation to prevent seizure by Snard.... A force of unknown size, but said to be powerful, and bearing the emblems of the defunct empire known as the Integral Union, is reported in the vicinity of the planet Hinkel. This force is under the control of a general named Orsip, who is believed to have drawn together the last shreds of the dying empire, and is now rumored seeking alliance with Dictator Hinkle.... Those of you who missed 'Makers of the Problems' today will be interested to know that Sedak Goplin, the religious so-called prophet, had a seizure during the show, but was revived promptly by administration of oxygen.... On Atrinx III, the agricultural planet, where 90 percent of all grain for this region of space is produced, the new outbreak of green army-weevils has been contained, under the super-powerful spray Arsoxychlorphosthicide. However, it is reported that the action of the spray has shriveled up the grain, and caused the soil to break up into little lumps of clay and water.... On Moxis II, where the weather-control satellites are now in action, a new series of disastrous floods has been followed by a plague which—"

At what point it happened, Horsip didn't know, but suddenly he felt like shooting himself. Even when things had been at their worst in the invasion of Earth, he hadn't felt like this. Dazed, he shoved back the eyepieces, pushed down the nosepiece, and pulled out the earplugs, through which came the words, "... and that's the news. Stay locked to this signal from morning to night. An informed citizen is a ..."

Horsip staggered to his feet, passed Moffis, still working like an automaton on the reports, shoved open a hatch, and stepped out on a kind of balcony, rigged for the occasion, that looked out over the spaceport where the ship had set down.

Horsip had scarcely pushed the hatch half-shut behind him when a movement in the brush at the edge of the spaceport caught his attention.

His mind a maze of hopelessness, Horsip watched a hideous hairy creature emerge from the brush, crouch, and spring directly for him, claws outstretched.

Horsip watched it loom larger, knew it meant the end, and didn't care. What was the use? Why bother?

His hand happened to brush the holster of his service pistol, and through tortuous channels of his mind, the sensation operated to rouse his stunned faculties. Abruptly, he whipped open his holster flap and yanked out the gun, to fire point-blank.

There was a high-pitched squeal, then a clutching of claws all around him.

Horsip fired again and again, discharging one barrel after another.

There was a hideous chattering sound.

The gun was empty, but Horsip, suddenly furious, raised a booted leg and rammed the creature in the midsection, knocking it off the balcony.

Moffis, gun in hand, was suddenly beside Horsip, and took aim as the thing streaked for the brush. He missed it three times in succession, then hit it as it dove into the bushes.

Horsip said, "That was a *Mikeril,* Moffis!"

"I saw it! But it *can't* be!"

Nevertheless," said Horsip, "it was. *Mikerils!* That's all we need! All right, let's go back in before another one shows up. We've seen all we need to here, anyway."

❋ XX ❋

The Accomplished Fact

Once back at his headquarters, Horsip found it impossible to believe what he had seen with his own eyes. But his staff assured him that, as a matter of fact, Mikeril attacks were becoming common.

Moffis said moodily, "The only bright spot in this mess is that Earth general we took on the Supreme Staff. Here's a report from Sark Glossip, on the teleports."

Horsip looked around blankly. "On the *what?*"

"Teleports. Glossip and his expedition were trapped by them, but Towers got them loose."

"What are *teleports?*"

Moffis handed him the report, and pointed out a line. Horsip read:

"... although obviously impossible, we were driven to the conclusion that these natives are teleports, and can go from one place to another *instantaneously*, regardless of intervening bars, walls, armor plate, or, as far as we could find out, anything else ..."

Horsip looked up.

"Towers solved a thing like that?"

Moffis nodded. "He found a weak point in their abilities."

Horsip gave a low murmur.

"What is Towers doing *now*, Moffis?"

"The last report I read, he was enlarging his organization. He has it up to six divisions now, I think. Of course, using his theories of war, these are small divisions."

"Is he ... ah ... way off at the other end of the system?"

"No."

"This outfit is all Earthmen?"

"As far as I know. But they seem to be a special kind of Earthman."

"They're *loyal?*"

"Absolutely."

"But would they fight against *Earth?*"

"I don't know."

Horsip thought a moment. All over his desk lay reports, and as he glanced at them, stray words and phrases sprang out at him:

> . . . chaos on this planet . . . upheaval . . . Snard landed another twenty divisions this morning . . . Control Commission voted 5–1 . . . another Snard army corps has been formed . . . now identified three flying-bomb squadrons of the Earthquake class . . . hopeless . . . ultimatum was delivered by Dictator Schmung . . . combined strength of Snard and Rogebar Soviets exceeds by a factor of four available Fleet strength in this region . . . NRPA appears to have a somewhat stronger central control, despite the still unexplained postponement of the attack on Columbia . . . local disorders continue to increase . . . Morality Index published by the Brotherhood now has reached (minus) —19.2, which is lowest recorded since catastrophe of . . .

Horsip's head whirled. He shoved back the reports.

"Send for Towers. We can use his whole six divisions right here."

"Wouldn't it be better to get the Supreme Staff to issue the order?"

"You're right, Moffis. And if they won't issue the order after I read them a few extracts from this mess, I'll be surprised."

The Supreme Staff, assembled at Horsip's request, listened in glum silence to the catalog of disasters. When Horsip got through, there was a lengthy silence. Then General Maklin looked sourly at General Argit, who looked stubbornly defiant, and then Maklin turned to Horsip.

"This is what comes of that plan that was to be of such great mutual benefit, and that was incidentally supposed to split up the Earthmen so they would be *harmless.*"

Horsip nodded, but said nothing.

General Roffis glanced at Horsip.

"Well, General, you must have something in mind. What is it?"

Horsip said, "It's too late to end this mess by force. These dictators are stronger than we are. But they're divided. If we concentrate our full strength, we are still strong enough to be a factor in the situation. Moreover, there are planets that are loyal to us, or at least independent of *them*. I suggest that we send out the warning signal to the Fleet, bring in Able Hunter and his Special Effects Team, make as great a show of strength as possible, and try to work these two sides against each other."

General Roffis nodded. "We might salvage something, at least."

"If," said General Maklin, "the High council doesn't countermand the order."

"Well, let's *do* it, and see what happens."

"All right. Let's put it to the vote."

There was at once a unanimous vote in favor of the suggestion.

"All right," said Roffis. "Now, we've got a sword. Who wields it?"

Maklin said, "Horsip has experience fighting these Earthmen."

Horsip said, "At getting beat by them, sir. No, the most capable man should be in charge."

Maklin bared his teeth in a grin, "You're more capable than you think, Horsip." Maklin looked around. "Put it to the vote. I nominate Horsip for Commander of the Fleet."

The motion passed, with Horsip abstaining and no one against it.

"Now," said Roffis, "let's not waste any time. Secretary, draw up the warning order at once, and also the designation of General Horsip as Supreme Commander of the Fleet, and—What's the phrase?—of the United Arms of Centra. Note in the body of the designation that the vote of the Supreme Staff was unanimous."

The secretary looked unhappy.

"General Horsip didn't vote for himself, sir, so ... ah ... the vote *wasn't* unanimous."

Roffis said in a no-nonsense voice, "I now ask General Horsip to so state if he wishes to *not* cast his vote for himself for Fleet Commander. The vote not being unanimous would convince our enemies there was disunion among us."

Horsip kept his mouth shut. The secretary began to write.

Ten minutes later, the warning signal went out to the Centran Fleet.

Fifteen minutes after that, Horsip was officially placed in command of all the armed forces of the Integral Union, exception being made for certain minor forces such as the guard forces for the Supreme Staff and the High Council.

Horsip's ship had apparently served many purposes in the past, and was now speedily made over as a "combined-fleets command ship," rooms being opened up that Horsip hadn't known were there. Meanwhile, he kept his information-gathering agency hard at work, and awaited a possible veto from the High Council.

Horsip soon was startled to receive a message reading:

By Command
The High Council

The High Council, by unanimous vote, *approves* the selection of General Klide Horsip to command the United Arms of Centra, including the Fleet of the Integral Union.

The High Council warns every Centran by race and birth to obey the commands of the supreme Commander, General Klide Horsip, on pain of death. So long as General Klide Horsip's command shall last, his word is the word of the High Council, and his decision is the decision of the High Council, and from this word and this decision there is no appeal within the Integral Union.

J. Roggil
Chairman
The High Council

Horsip, slightly dazed, looked up to see a trim Earthman, with quiet, businesslike manner, wearing the uniform of a Centran general, grade III, and the insignia of the Supreme Staff, cross the room amidst the electrified staff. Horsip recognized John Towers, and got up at once. He handed Moffis the message from the High Council, and then saw, coming behind the Earthman, a well-built member of the Holy Brotherhood in black robes with purple collar. The Earthman, realizing from the stares of those nearby that someone was behind him, stepped aside to let the Brother pass ahead.

The Brother halted before Horsip's desk to raise his hands and bow his head in an awesome gesture toward Horsip.

"By the word of the Council of Brothers," he intoned, some resonant quality making the words seem to ring in the head after they were spoken, "the cause of the Brotherhood is placed in your hands. Use the trust wisely, nor fear that ye may not succeed. The word of the Brothers is behind you and the Legions of the Brothers are rising, to consume the unrighteous in a flame that will burn them utterly and to the last. Until the task is complete, your authority is the authority of the Brothers, so long as your command shall last . . .

that there be no division in the ranks of the Union, the authority of the Council of Brothers is vested in you alone. This is the message which I am commanded to give, and to ask the blessing of the Great One on our united cause. I bow in reverent homage to the authority of the Council of Brothers, vested in you."

The Brother bowed deeply, and in a humble voice said, "I beg the permission of Your Excellency to report that my task is done, and the message delivered."

Horsip, with an effort, recovered the use of his voice.

"Thank you." The words came out with an echo of the brother's ringing tones. Horsip cleared his throat, and said in a carefully low voice, "Please give the Council of Brothers my thanks, and tell them that their message was delivered."

That time, he sounded more like himself, but he still had a disembodied sensation.

The Brother bowed low, backed away several paces facing Horsip, bowed again, backed another pace or two, then turned and strode with steady, measured pace to the door.

Moffis, with trembling hand, returned the message from the High Council to Horsip's desk.

Able Hunter watched the proceedings with a politely expressionless gaze.

Horsip sucked in a deep breath, and observed that his staff was looking on wide-eyed as if waiting for some spectacular manifestation.

Horsip cleared his throat.

"Back to work, men. Turn up the fans, there. Let's get a little air in here."

The trance seemed to evaporate, and a semblance of normality returned.

Horsip loosened his collar and sat down. He still didn't feel like himself, but he didn't know what to do about it.

Able Hunter now saluted. Horsip returned the salute, and cleared his throat.

"Pull up a chair—that pivot chair is comfortable—and tell me what you know about this mess."

Hunter eyed the pivot chair without enthusiasm, and pulled over a straight chair.

"I'll take this one, sir, if you don't mind. If I bump that lever, the whole works will go over backward."

"Nonsense," said Horsip, absently bracing his tail against the floor as he adjusted his own chair. "All you do ..." He paused abruptly.

Hunter said, "It takes *two* Earthmen to adjust one of these chairs. . . . As for the situation, no one has told me anything. Obviously, there's a mess of some kind. Some bird calling himself the commander of the 'Shock Combat Legion of Space' tried to hold us up on the way here. I identified myself as a member of the Supreme Staff, and that didn't even slow him down. We had to slice his outfit into giblets to get through. . . . The stars matched our charts, but a lot of the political units seemed new."

"You don't know *anything* about the situation?"

"Only what I've told you."

Horsip nodded. "Make yourself comfortable. This will take a while."

When Horsip finished describing the situation, Hunter looked bemused.

"This explains some comments made to me at different times. But I had no idea a thing like this was going on."

"We never thought it would turn out like this, either."

"What do you want me to do?"

"The first question," said Horsip, "is whether you are prepared to fight Earthmen."

One corner of Hunter's mouth curled slightly upward.

"This crew I'd cheerfully fight, whatever race they belonged to. *Most* Earthmen are either on Earth, or on planets like Columbia. This bunch that you're up against is the same kind that has always made trouble for us. Yes, I'll fight them."

"Would you take part in an invasion of Earth?"

"No. But we'll take on this gang you describe anytime."

"You have to bear in mind," said Horsip, "these dictators are powerful."

"Our opponents are *always* powerful. There's just one thing that puzzles me. What are these Mikerils you've mentioned?"

"I'll have to refer you to the records. What they *are* is beyond me. What they *do* is clear enough. Whenever we make progress enough to think we can settle back a little and take things easy, they turn up, and knock us halfway back into barbarism. But it's impossible to believe it until you see it, so half the time we're under the impression they're a myth."

"Where do they come from?"

"If we knew that, we'd blow the place up."

"Do they attack in one spot at a time, or on a large front?"

"It depends. Sometimes, they hit only one planet. At other times, the records show they've hit many planets at once."

"How does it look this time?"

"Worse than anything recorded since what's called 'The Year of the Horde.' The experts have charted the outbreaks and their projected curves go up off the top of the charts. It takes extra sheets of paper to show where these curves go to and they haven't found the peak yet."

"H'm," Hunter shook his head. "I'll have to examine these records." He shoved back his chair. "Is there anything else, sir?"

"As far as I know, that's all of it."

As Hunter headed for the records section, Moffis said hesitantly, "Sir . . ."

Moffis' tone reminded Horsip of the awesome authority he had been given, now that the opposition was so strong, and the Integral Union so weak. . . . Well, he told himself, at least the Fleet was warned. Now, the thing to do was to keep every element of strength the Integral Union possessed lined up in mutual support of every other element of strength, and the first step was clear.

"Yes, Moffis?" said Horsip briskly.

"I . . . sir, I . . ."

Moffis appeared dazzled by Horsip's presence.

Horsip cleared his throat, to make sure no trace of that reverberating tone was left over.

"Now, Moffis," said Horsip, feeling his way cautiously, "we have to remember there was just one purpose to that message from the High Council, and that visit by the Holy Brother. The idea is to unite any wavering Centrans, and make it clear they have just one choice—obey or be condemned. Since you were never a waverer, Moffis, all that wasn't meant for you. And it has no effect on the situation, either. We are still in the same pickle we were in before. So, the thing to do is to forget these things among ourselves, and keep our minds strictly on the job."

Moffis intently followed this argument to the end, then nodded.

"Truth."

"Now," said Horsip, "what is it, Moffis?"

"I . . . ah . . . was looking at these reports while you were talking to Hunter, and there are several I thought you should look at."

Horsip was by now allergic to reports, but he nodded gamely. "If you think so, Moffis."

Moffis picked up two reports that each bulked as thick as
the Centran casualty list after the invasion of Earth, and one
considerably thinner than the average report.

Horsip glanced at the titles:

"The Peace Wagers on Earth-Controlled Planets"

"Statistical Analysis of Armaments and Production, Fif-
teenth Revision"

"The Masked Planet: Columbia"

Horsip skimmed through the statistical analysis of armaments, and unconsciously hunched in his chair. The dictator
planets loomed up off the pages like giants. The Integral
Union dwindled and shrank to a pathetic shadow.

Angrily, Horsip straightened up. The Fleet, regardless of
its relative weakness, was still a factor. *Everything,* however
small, was a factor until destroyed. He slapped the massive
document on the desk, and settled back to read about the
"peace movement."

This report turned out to have been written by someone
with an exasperating turn of phrase. Horsip found himself be-
musedly reading the summary:

These individuals detest the possibility of the dictator planets
taking over their own planets, and hence they—the wagers
of peace—violently attack their governments for not yielding
faster to the dictators, in order to avoid angering the dictators,
since anger might lead the dictators to take over noncoo-
perative planets. This is certainly a very reasonable argument. If a man gives the robber everything he has before the
robber gets a chance to make his demands, then there can be
no robbery. It is always possible to prevent murder, provided
the victim can commit suicide fast enough. . . . The situation
is extremely dangerous and uncertain. The Peace Wagers, brilliant, ignorant, unwearied by the heaviest responsibility that
anyone else may bear, are not bought traitors, but a phenom-
enon brought on by the Earthmen's creation of plenty beyond
previous dreams of wealth, and their simultaneous minute
dividing of experience into numerous parts, so that one man
knows only the right paw of the animal, while another spends
his life studying the root of its upper left long tooth—this,
and the withholding of responsibility for long periods of time,
act as a rot on the sources of judgment, and here we see the
result. . . . These people are no part of any plot; but the
plotters rely on the unwitting help of these brave cowards,
these moronic geniuses. . . .

Horsip became vaguely conscious of the sound of workmen
in the background, but his attempt to unravel the meaning of
the summary held his attention riveted. Momentarily, he

would think he had it, then some new phrase would snap the thing into a different shape. Horsip scratched his head, reached out, and got hold of the thinnest of the three reports—the one titled "The Masked Planet: Columbia."

He opened this up with no great enthusiasm, read the first page, turned to the second, sat up, read on, and arrived at the summary:

Summary: The planet named "Columbia" has received little attention until recently, owing to its independent foreign policy and lack of aggressive designs on other planets. Also, it is a planet of a star somewhat removed from the usual routes, and even with the latest refinements to the stellar drive, distance remains a factor. Thus Columbia was largely ignored until the recent attempt by Dictator Ganfre to "protect" the planet against Snard by taking it over himself.

Ganfre's take-over began with a warning to Snard. Four hours later, an ultimatum was delivered to Columbia, giving the choice of "voluntarily" joining with Ganfre, or experiencing "precautionary occupation." Columbia at once rejected the ultimatum, and issued a general warning placing its solar system off-bounds to any ship without Columbian permission.

Ganfre's fleet was already approaching, and leading elements entered the Columbian System. From decoding of intercepted messages, what seems to have happened is as follows:

After passing the formal limits of the Columbian system, the leading ships of Ganfre's fleet began to accelerate. The fleet commander sent a signal ordering deceleration. The ships reported that they *couldn't* decelerate. They continued to speed up, headed directly for the Columbian sun. As following elements of Ganfre's fleet passed the formal boundary, they, too, accelerated. The fleet commander turned the main body of the fleet and notified Ganfre. Ganfre at once signaled Columbia, withdrawing the ultimatum, on the basis that he was now satisfied Columbia could protect itself against Snard. He requested permission for his scout ships to leave Columbian territory. The Columbians granted permission. The scout ships slowed, and simultaneously began to spin, tumble end-for-end, and overheat. Their courses changed into an arc which carried them out of Columbian territory.

Ganfre now suggested an alliance with Columbia. Columbia declined, pointing out that it was important to have uncommitted neutrals in any war, to help provide food and supplies in case the combatants wrecked each other, and also to give political refugees some place to go in case the worst happened. Ganfre accepted this reasoning.

Since this experience, Columbia has received a great deal of study, and it develops that all that is definitely known is that the planet was first settled by Centrans, and received a large influx of "Americans" after the treaty with Earth. These

Earthmen claimed they were going to "rebuild the planet on basic American principles," avoiding errors made on Earth. But since the planet aroused no interest earlier, no one knows what this means, and because of the off-limits decree, it is now impossible to visit the planet to find out.

Columbia therefore is indeed the "masked planet," formidable, aloof, and powerful, a mystery to adversaries who discounted her power until too late.

Horsip looked up exasperatedly.

"Moffis, what do we have on Columbia?"

Moffis had a few thin reports opened out on his desk.

"I've got it right here—what thers is of it."

"Let's see the ones you're not using. We're going to have to give that place some thought. It seems to me—" He looked around then, a pounding noise catching his attention.

Across the room, workmen were carrying off a bulkhead. This disclosed a room on the far side, where they were carrying in big spools of cable that ended in a maze of many-colored wires bearing fastening attachments. Other workmen were carrying in odd-shaped sections of some kind of furniture that fitted into recessed parts of the floor, the various wires from the cables being snapped, clipped, screwed, or bolted to mating parts of corresponding colors in the sections themselves. Meanwhile, other workmen were stuffing the cables into channels in the floor or walls of the room, and putting metal covers in place over the channels. Since there were cables and wires being unwound all over the room at the same time, and sections of all sizes and shapes being carried in simultaneously, this room suddenly exposed to view gave the impression of a look through the wall into a madhouse.

Moffis looked up and stared speechlessly. Horsip got to his feet. An officer with colonel's insignia, wearing coveralls, and carrying a sheet of yellow paper in one hand, looked around, and suddenly spotted Horsip. He crossed the room briskly, and saluted. "At the command of the High Council, sir, we are activating the command ship's Master Control Center. The equipment has been thoroughly checked, parts replaced where needed, oiled, and refinished. It's all in first-grade condition, but if you have any trouble, just let us know, and—"

Horsip glanced from the colonel to the tangle of wires and dismantled sections of unrecognizable objects. He groped mentally for the meaning of the words "Master Control Center." Nothing came to him but vague associations.

Horsip cleared his throat.

"Colonel . . . ah . . . what *is* the Master Control Center?"

The colonel looked blank.

"Well, sir, *that's* the Master Control Center. It's Sealed Section A-1. This room here is Open Section A-1. This work sheet says, 'Open communication between Sealed Section A-1 and Open Section A-1.' According to the work code, 'open communication between two sections' means, 'knock out the wall between them.' That's what we're doing. Now, farther back, it says, 'Recondition all equipment and reconstitute full panoply of representation and control units.' Now, according to code—"

Horsip said, "But what does this Master Control Center *do?*"

The colonel shook his head.

"Sir, that's not in my department. If we stopped to try to figure out what all this stuff *does,* we'd never get the sequence checks finished." He brightened, and shouted to a workman holding a clipboard in one thickly furred hand. The workman cupped a hand to his ear, and the colonel bellowed across the room.

Horsip glanced around, to observe that work had come to a stop among almost all his own staff. He picked up a pad, and duly noted who was still working. Then he waited until one of those not working glanced in his direction. Horsip fixed a ferocious glower on his face. The offender fairly sprang out of his skin. At once he began to bustle around. This hurricane of activity startled his neighbors, one or two of whom glanced at Horsip. In a flash, everyone was attending to business.

The colonel nodded to his workman, and turned back to Horsip.

"Sir, the manual is in the right upper drawer in front of the Master Control Seat—that's that thing they're setting up now."

Horsip looked at a thing like a big pivot chair just being lugged in, and nodded.

The colonel saluted, and hurried back to work.

Horsip turned to Moffis. "Where were we?"

"Talking about Columbia," said Moffis. "Do you want the reports I've finished?"

Horsip nodded, and glanced again at the chaos in the next room.

"I wonder if the Earthmen ever have a thing like this? I suppose not."

He took the first report Moffis handed over, and sat back to read about Columbia. From time to time, he reached out for others, and at last he had read them all. He sat back, baffled. These told him that the Columbians "rely on a highly developed system of rail transportation, with great care paid to the road grade, and continuous improvement of their unusually wide-gauge system. . . . Highway transportation on this planet is restricted to the original Centran road network, traveled by animal-drawn transportation, plus a limited network of roads elevated above the ground surface, and requiring little winter maintenance, as the wind ordinarily sweeps these roads clear of snow. . . . Production of ground-cars is limited, but the ground-cars are exceptionally well made and durable, as are nearly all Columbian manufactures. . . ."

Horsip looked up. What did all this tell him? ". . . rumors are that the Columbian electrical underground rail transport system is to be further extended, but little is known about this development, as the Columbians rarely talk about their plans in advance. . . ."

Exasperatedly, he skimmed through reports he had already read once, trying to piece together some picture that would explain the planet to him. He read, ". . . raising of farm crops has not been interfered with as on other planets. The Earthmen apparently do nothing except to introduce some of their own farmers, these being unusual only for their manner of dress and their exceptional skill. Like Centran farmers, they do not use complicated highly powered equipment, but rely on animals to draw the equipment. . . . The Earthmen, apart from their heavily equipped factories, seem to have a great number of research facilities. . . . Notable is the fact that schooling, by Earthmen's standards, is finished quickly, formal education usually being completed by the eighteenth year. . . . There is said to be a large armed force. All the Earthmen serve without complaint, certain picked Centran volunteers also being allowed to serve, it is rumored. . . ."

Horsip shook his head, and sent for a list of the uncommitted planets, and those still loyal to Centra. The lists showed that there were still a considerable number of planets loyal to Centra; but they were all either awkwardly located, barren, small, or otherwise undesirable, with the sole exception of Centra itself, the Centran solar system, from its experience of numerous attacks, remaining a fortress. Here the Holy Brotherhood was so strong, and the sense of imperial loyalty so great, that the Earthmen had made no noticeable dent at all. Examining the list of uncommitted planets, Horsip found that here the Holy Brotherhood again had been active, and some of these planets were even armed. But nearly all suffered from some degree of the dictator's influence or intimidation.

Looking over these lists, Horsip wondered if it might prove possible to make anything out of this wreck. He longed for the ancient days, when in times of trouble the central authority imposed the *clokal detonak*, and wielded its invincible Fleet like a sword. Studying the lists and charts, Horsip searched for a reasonable strategy—and found that the Earthmen had been there before him. Without a powerful fleet, it was impossible to piece together anything out of this scatter of bits and pieces—unless he could get the Columbians to cooperate.

Horsip glanced up at the Master Control Center, where some kind of order was starting to show through the chaos, then he turned to Moffis.

Moffis, with an expression of moody hopelessness, was skimming through reports, and shifting them from one pile to another.

Horsip cleared his throat.

"Moffis, what do you know about diplomacy?"

Moffis looked blank.

"About what?"

"Diplomacy."

"Sir, I don't know anything about it. Why?"

"That's what I know about it, too," said Horsip. "But that's what we're going to have to rely on. We can't rely on force. We *have* to use diplomacy."

To begin with, Horsip sent envoys to the wavering planets, to urge their leaders to stand by the Integral Union. It quickly developed that most of the leaders could not have cared less for the Integral Union, it being only the power of the Holy Brotherhood and popular sentiment that kept the planets from joining the dictators.

Horsip quietly initiated military training on a number of the planets most loyal to the Integral Union. He at once ran into shortages of all kinds. While Horsip had squads practicing with pitchforks, the dictators stood with upraised arms on reviewing platforms while troops thundered past forty and fifty abreast.

Horsip scraped together all of the Fleet that had yet trickled in, reinforced it with his own crack squadron, and sent it as a quiet show of strength to planets wavering on the edge of submission to the dictators. The dictators got word of this, and sent their own fleets around, creating unfavorable comparisons.

Horsip quietly hinted to the Columbians that they would find a warm welcome in the Integral Union. The Columbians politely explained that they preferred independence.

Horsip labored to solve the aggravating problems of infant or decrepit armaments industries on the few industrial planets under his control. Meanwhile, the dictators turned out battle fleets by mass production, and had the crews ready to board the ships as they came off the production lines.

Horsip struggled to create the impression of a quiet powerful force that might at its choice intervene decisively in the situation. The impression that came across was of a collection of antique relics manned by a team of amateur cheerleaders.

As one day succeeded the next, Horsip could sense that the tide, so far from turning, was gathering momentum in the other direction.

Meanwhile, the reports came in, more and more frequently, of Mikeril raids, and the raids were growing larger.

And now the swaggering envoys of the dictators began dropping in on diplomatic "courtesy calls," to urge Horsip with none too subtle arguments to stop trying to kid anybody, and pick out which side could do him the most good. Horsip was very polite. Next, the representatives of half-lunatic revolutionary organizations started coming around, to put forth grandiose plans that Horsip, trying to get enough straws together to make a raft, was in no position to reject. On the other hand, when he tried to combine these tiny organizations, to make something useful, he at once ran into a little difficulty: Each revolutionary wanted only his *own* revolution.

As time went on, the revolutionaries grew shriller, the Mikerils more numerous and bolder, and the dictators' envoys more smilingly suggestive.

As his position wavered on the edge of disaster, with his weakness daily more plain for all to see, the governing body of Horsip's largest industrial planet met to decide which dictators to join. Horsip examined the latest reports from the Holy Brotherhood on the planet, sent iron-clad instructions on his authority from the Council of Brothers, then sent an order on his authority from the High Council, stripping the planet's governing body of all authority, and placing its troops under command of a loyal Centran officer. Horsip's ships, approaching the planet on a courtesy call, received new orders. As dawn broke over the capital, the Brotherhood, with threats of fire and damnation, sent mobs of the faithful surging through the streets, the warships of the Integral Union appeared in the skies, and Horsip's crack bodyguard massed on the steps of the government buildings, to raise the Centran flag to the roll of drums and the delirious roar of the crowd.

As the shock from this event momentarily immobilized the dictators, Horsip summoned their envoys to a specially built audience chamber. Here, seated in an elaborate chair with the Supreme Staff in a curving row behind and above him, and with sixteen of Able Hunter's men seated in a curving row behind and above the Staff, Horsip met the envoys.

The envoys, incredulous and angry, glanced from Horsip to the Staff, sneered, and then saw the Earthmen.

Horsip spoke quietly. "Gentlemen, the situation is not what you may think. The basis of power has changed fundamentally, and I request that you notify your principals that any attempt to interfere with the proper exercise of Centran authority may lead to serious consequences. This is all that I am free to say. I ask that you consider it carefully."

As Horsip spoke, more of Able Hunter's Earthmen came and went, conferring briefly with this or that impressively uniformed Earthman in the top row of the dais, looking down coldly on the perspiring envoys.

Swallowing nervously, the envoys bowed low to Horsip, and left the room.

No one interfered with Horsip's occupation of the planet.

No one said a public word against it.

No one was at all disrespectful.

And when Horsip moved his command ship forward, to set it down in the planetary capital and make the planet the formal site of his headquarters, no one objected to that, either. The dictators said nothing at all. Only Moffis had his doubts.

"Look," said Moffis, "what happened is that the sight of Hunter's Earthmen, dressed in those uniforms, convinced the envoys that we were being backed by *Earth*, isn't that right?"

"Moffis," Horsip protested, "I didn't say that. All I said was that the basis of power had changed fundamentally—and it had, hadn't it? And I suggested that the situation was not what they might think. How can I be blamed if they jumped to the wrong conclusion?"

"What happens if they reach the *right* conclusion?"

"Let's hope," said Horsip, "that they don't."

❄ XXI ❄

The Last Bluff

In the days following Horsip's forward move, there followed a momentary suspension of action on the part of the dictators, as if they were waiting cautiously to see what might happen next.

Horsip used this pause to renew his offer to Columbia, to strengthen his grip on the planets that were loyal, and to bring as many of the waverers as possible into line. To reinforce the bluff, Able Hunter's Special Effects Team labored overtime to create a fleet of imitation warships realistic to the last welded seam. As the dictators, cautiously probing Horsip's position, sent little unmarked scout ships to check on what Horsip might have, this fleet was briefly exposed, lurking in the asteroid belt that ringed the planet's sun.

Moffis objected, "But they will be able to find out, from the Earthmen, that we aren't allied with Earth."

"Truth. We never said we were."

"The idea is to make them uncertain *what* we have?"

"Yes," said Horsip, "because anything they might imagine is better than what we *do* have."

Moffis looked serious, but said nothing.

Horsip, however, stayed determinedly optimistic.

The dictators, baffled by Horsip's arrangements, avoided any direct clash, but went to work to undermine him indirectly, each side bringing over to it those planets that were the most subject to coercion or bribery. Each time, they took pains to have heavy forces on hand as the planet "voluntarily" proclaimed its change of loyalty.

Each time, Horsip, seeing the hopelessness of intervening, did nothing, but continued to study his charts and maps, and the reports of his agents on planets in and out of the dictators' worlds. Particularly, he studied the reports from one small planet where popular dissastisfaction with the local Snard ruler was combined with relative closeness to Horsip's worlds, and where the Holy Brotherhood had gone underground but remained powerful.

As the dictators' power surged ahead, and their confidence revived, one fine day Able Hunter's Special Effects Team swamped the planet's primitive detection system, the populace rose in wrath and raised the Centran flag, the new president, elected on the spot, appealed to Centra for protection, and Horsip's elite guard came down on the planet to overawe the local soldiery. Officers in the local detection center reported a gigantic fleet standing off the planet, with monster transports ready to land hundreds of thousands of troops. The local subdictator blasted off in his escape ship, and poured on the fuel for far places.

The news of this event was broadcast and rebroadcast on the Centran planets, and combined in various ways with Horsip's take-over of the first planet, one report emphasizing the huge fleet, another bearing down hard on the weakness of dictators under stress, another pointing out the popular rejoicing at the event, in such a way that suddenly the Integral Union appeared the new force in the universe, and the dictators seemed almost feeble by comparison. As ringing sermons proclaimed the victory of the Old Ways, there was an outburst of popular enthusiasm for the new rise of the almost forgotten power. Abruptly, the reports from Horsip's agents began to turn optimistic, while the agents of the gigantic dictatorships began reporting a disastrous shift in public opinion.

As cheering events occupied the public eye, however, Horsip was just starting to replace new recruits' pitchforks with rifles, waves of Mikeril attacks were devastating the planet he had made his headquarters, and the latest confidential comparison of fleet strengths put him a tenth of the way up from the bottom of the page, while Snard and Ganfre were off the top of the chart.

The Columbians now again replied to Horsip, this time stating their sympathy with certain standards of the Integral Union, but again stating that they preferred to remain independent, and would not join the Integral Union under the present circumstances; but they would join no one else, either, under the present circumstances.

Moffis looked impressed. "They are more friendly than they were."

Horsip nodded, and looked confident.

Moffis said, "But the Fleet still isn't here. . . . Whatever there may be of it."

Horsip looked quietly cheerful.

"It will be, Moffis. Don't worry. Remember, the High Council itself is behind us."

Moffis said uneasily, "But I wonder if—"

Horsip cleared his throat.

"No need to be concerned, Moffis. After all—"

From the corridor came a muffled tramp of feet, then a heavy rap on the door. As Horsip and Moffis looked up, a scared junior officer reported, "Sir, there's a . . . a bunch of officers and *Earthmen,* and some guards in strange uniforms. They want to see you right away. They're from Snard, sir!"

Horsip told himself this could not be an invasion; it could be the local Snard ambassador, who had a guard like a small army.

"How many guards?" said Horsip.

"A lot of them, sir. The corridor is full of them."

Horsip turned to Moffis, but Moffis already had the phone marked "Provost" off its hook. ". . . every guard you can lay your hands on down here on the run, and bring them in through the Master Control Center. Shut the automatic doors between here and the corridors, and be ready to flood the corridors with dead-gas. But don't sound any alarm— notify the sections by phone."

Horsip loosened his service pistol in its holster, and turned to his frightened junior officer.

"Tell them to leave the guards outside—but the officers can come in."

The officers of Snard came in like a conquering host, thrust Horsip's people out of the way, brushed the papers off the desks as they passed, and reached out to shove over a cooler of mineral water, which smashed to bits on the floor. Right behind them came the armed guards. Horsip, watching them stream in the door, felt a wave of relief as the last one came in.

Horsip eyed them alertly. They all had a well-drilled look.

Horsip adjusted his uniform, stood up behind his desk, and looked directly into the eyes of the leading Snard officer, a broad-chested general whose muscles stretched the cloth of his bemedaled jacket as he strode down the aisle. This general's eyes were fixed in contempt on Horsip, and looked Horsip over like some peculiar form of insect.

Moffis, bent over back of his desk, was getting something out of a crate, but Horsip had no time for that. He watched the Snard officers approach, waited until they were almost at the end of the aisle, then abruptly inflated his chest to the limit, and intoned at the top of his lungs:

"Detaaiil *HALT!!!*"

The entire Snard military contingent, generals, officers, and guards, looked blank and came to an abrupt stop. Half a dozen civilians, trailing along behind, slammed into the backs of the soldiers and were knocked off their feet.

Horsip, unhesitating, stepped in front of the burly Snard general, and bellowed:

"Abouut *FACE!!!*"

"Forwaaard *MARCH!!!*"

Knocking the civilians out of the way, the Snard armed guards leading, the whole outfit, with the exception of three or four Earthmen, who looked around blankly, started for the door.

Horsip judged the moment, sucked in a deep breath, and intoned:

"Column riiight *MARCH!!!*"

The Snard guards, feet striking in unison, trailed out into the hall, turned the corner with precision, and disappeared.

The Earthmen from Snard looked incredulously at them, grabbed at the glassy-eyed Snard officers going past, and got them headed back toward Horsip.

Horsip drew his gun and aimed it at the officers.

The officers stopped, and glanced in confusion at the Earthmen, themselves speechless.

Horsip, listening for the arrival of his own guards, had yet to hear anything. The door to the hall was still open, and there was nothing to prevent anyone from coming in.

Horsip spotted a young Snard lieutenant, who looked more confused than anyone else in sight. Horsip snapped, "Lieutenant!"

The lieutenant swallowed at the tone of command and snapped to attention.

"Sir?"

"What the devil are you *standing* there for? Get out in that hall, and get those guards turned around. Lead them back this way, and halt them outside that door. They aren't to come in. They are to halt *outside*. Now, get out there, turn them around, and halt them outside that door! *Move!*"

The lieutenant saluted, and ran out. His bawled orders echoed down the hall.

The Earthmen looked at Horsip, then at the Snard officers as if they had never seen them before.

Horsip ignored the Earthmen, and focused on the burly general in front of him. From the stupefied expression on the general's face, it was clear to Horsip that the general's assurance had been momentarily pulverized. Horsip spoke in kindly tones.

"Stand at attention, General. I am the Supreme Commander of the Integral Union, and you are inside my staff headquarters. I have only to say one word, and you and all your party will be struck dead where you stand. Protocol requires that you salute."

The burly general glanced around, looked toward Moffis, and beads of sweat took form on his forehead. He glanced back at Horsip, stood straighter, and his hand came up in salute.

A quick glance showed Moffis behind a well-oiled stitching-gun, the snout aimed at the general's stomach.

Horsip returned the general's salute.

From somewhere came the sound of running feet, and the snap of safeties clicking off on a considerable number of guns.

The Snard general shook his head, and appeared to come out of some kind of trance. His jaw set.

"All right. You're the Supreme Head of the Integral Union, but the Integral Union amounts to nothing. Your so-called fleet, hidden in the asteroid belt, has been checked by these *Earth experts,* with the latest equipment, and we know it's *no fleet at all.* It's a set of dummies, with just a few real ships mixed in. We aren't certain what you used in this latest attack, but we've checked all the likely routes, and no such fleet passed any of them. We formally checked with Earth itself, and they acknowledge no alliance with you at all. Your whole position is hollow. I doubt that you have over a thousand armed men of your own on this planet, which is your capital. Our fleet is on the way. Nothing will stop us. We'll wipe you up, and after you the whole Integral Union, which is nothing but a memory propped up with cardboard. *I* call on you to surrender!"

From the corridor came the low rumble of automatic doors sliding shut. Horsip, in a quick glance, saw that where the open door to the room had been, there was now a solid sheet of polished steel, which reflected the room like a slightly wavy mirror. That was a relief, but he still had the general to contend with.

Horsip said, still gently, "If what you say were true, General, would I ever have taken a planet belonging to Snard?"

"You had to, to pull your own people together."

"To pull *your* people off-balance."

"What does that mean?"

"Think it over," said Horsip, with quiet confidence. "You are sending a fleet *here*, where in your own words I don't have a thousand men committed."

Horsip looked at the general quietly, as, inside his own mind, Horsip called up charts of space.

The Snard general was staring at him. "You mean this is *bait?*"

"What do you suppose will happen to Snard while it throws its weight against shadows?"

The general stared at the corner of the room, then shook his head. "We aren't that weak. Yes, if you cut in behind—if you had the strength—but we can shift the reserve fleets to block you. You could never get all the way in."

Horsip looked disappointed. *"Think."*

The general looked baffled.

Horsip nodded. "It's as I thought. You *don't* have the information."

"What information?"

"It's a question of *timing,* General. The Integral Union has long experience with timing. We have had to let Snard and Ganfre become large, because of the difficulty with—but you don't know about that. Well, I certainly won't explain it. But we don't need you or Ganfre any longer, to defend this region. One or the other of you is bound to attack first, and make the necessary opening. It's immaterial to us which one we clean up. It's only reasonable that we ally ourselves with one side to finish the other.... You see, General, you still don't realize who is with us, *do* you?"

The Snard general's eyes darted this way and that, as if trying to follow elusive objects that flitted just out of his range of vision. He swallowed, and took a hard look at Horsip, who looked back at him with quiet confidence. For an instant, the general looked shocked, said, "Ganfre wouldn't ..." then stared at Horsip in horror.

Horsip smiled, and said, "General, I don't need you any longer." He glanced around, to see a line of his own armed guards, with General Maklin beside them. The guards looked all business. Maklin had a look of wondering awe on his face.

Horsip stepped aside, to give the guards a clear line of fire,
if necessary. The Snard general thrust out his jaw and faced
the guards.

Horsip shook his head. "Relax, General, I need good men.
It should be possible to find quite a few after Snard is
smashed up."

"Ganfre will turn on you afterward!"

"If Snard attacks here, the chain of events can't be stopped."

"You can't trust Ganfre! He has no principles!"

Horsip shrugged. "It's too bad it has worked out this way,
but you don't think we can permit an attack without striking
back? You can understand this. It is exactly what you would
do, isn't it?"

Horsip glanced at Moffis.

"There is no reason for us to hold the general prisoner."

Moffis looked agreeable.

Horsip looked back at the Snard officer.

"How many armed men do you have with you here, all
told?"

The general was staring straight ahead, beyond the line of
Centran guards, at the big screens of the Master Control
Center. He had a look of fascinated attention, but turned
with a shake of the head to face Horsip.

"How many? About two hundred and fifty—the staff of
our embassy, plus the guards." He looked apologetic. "It
seemed like enough."

Horsip nodded. "Just get them all together, and get them
back to your embassy." His manner was open and generous.
"We will overlook all this." Horsip glanced at Moffis. "Instruct the provost to open up the doors one at a time, to let
the general and his men out." Horsip glanced at the general.
"You agree, of course, to get all your men back to your embassy, without delay?"

"Yes, as soon as I can. I thank Your Excellency for your
kindness."

Moffis got busy on the phone, the automatic door at the
end of the room slid open, the Snard general saluted, and
marched out with his officers.

There was a silence in the room.

Horsip let his breath out slowly.

He groped around, felt the edge of his desk, and found his
chair. He sat down slowly.

Moffis said soberly, "What happens when the Snard fleet
gets here?"

Horsip took a deep breath. "If he can get a message off

fast enough, maybe it won't. When does Hunter get back here with his Special Effects Team?"

"He was due the day after tomorrow. I sent a message through the Communications Section as soon as this started, to speed him up. He *should* be here tomorrow."

"Good." Horsip glanced at the stitching-gun beside Moffis' desk. "I appreciate your forethought, Moffis."

Moffis nodded, but he had the expression of someone adding up figures and not liking the total.

"What happens," he said, "if there *is* an attack? Hunter can't stop them. We don't have time to get our own guard back here soon enough. And practically every man we've got *here* is in the next room. We can no more stop Snard than tissue paper can stop an avalanche."

Horsip tried to think. The trouble was, he had next to nothing to work with. It was reaching the point where it took strokes of genius and special dispensations to keep going from day to day. The only sensible thing to do was to assemble the strength he *did* have in one place, so that he could at least act there with decision. But, as soon as he did that, the dictators would take over the rest of the Integral Union. The only place Horsip could hope to hold was the planet of Centra itself. But once let the dictators know his real weakness, and even Centra wouldn't be able to hold out for long.

Moffis was saying, "At least we could go down fighting. This way—"

"Sir," said the lieutenant who had announced the arrival of the Snard general, "the emissary from the NRPA is outside, and demands to see you. He says he has orders from Guide Ganfre himself."

Horsip sucked in a deep breath. "How many guards does *he* have with him?"

"None, sir. He has three officers."

"Send him in."

Moffis said, "What do you want me to do?"

"Ignore the whole thing. It's beneath your notice."

"I suppose I should put this gun away? But with Ganfre . . ."

Horsip looked at the stitching-gun, its ugly snout pointing at the spot where Ganfre's emissary would have to stand.

"Leave it there, Moffis. I hope you have the safety off?"

Moffis reached over, and there was a dull click.

"It's ready to fire. You only have to touch the trigger."

Horsip nodded, pulled out a report at random, and a chart showing the strength of Ganfre's fleet looked up at him.

As he shoved this back into the pile, he heard the rap of

heels striking the floor in unison. He glanced up to see four gray-uniformed officers, their caps at jaunty angles, approaching down the long aisle. Their uniforms were pressed into knife-like creases. Small emblems glittered on their chests. Their heads were tilted back, their expressions arrogant. Horsip ignored them.

With a click of the heels, they halted before his desk.

Horsip swiveled his chair, and bumped the gun.

There was a little gasp. Horsip looked up.

One of the lesser officers was eying the gun nervously. The other three ignored it.

Ganfre's emissary stood radiating contempt, then raised his hand in a formally correct salute.

Horsip looked him over without enthusiasm, then returned the salute.

Ganfre's emissary took one step forward, slapped an envelope on Horsip's desk, stepped back, and snapped his hand up again to salute, as if about to leave the room, his whole manner contemptuous.

Horsip rested his left hand on the gun, and said coldly, "I'd appreciate it if you would stay here while I read this. There may be an answer."

The emissary glanced from the gun to Horsip, and snapped his arm down. When he spoke, his voice carried:

"For that, I will have you hanged by your feet in the market place, to be ripped to pieces by wild dogs."

Horsip had a sheet of crisp paper out of the envelope, and had got it pried open enough to see what it was—an ultimatum with a half-day limit. He was balancing how to convert this colossal disaster into something useful when there was a harsh rap of heels. General Maklin, his uniform spotless, leather and medals glittering, stepped out, jerked the NRPA emissary around, and smashed him across the face. As the emissary went down, Maklin yanked him to his feet again.

Maklin's voice rang with confident good cheer:

"You piece of stinking garbage! *You* will have the elect of Centra hanged! That statement gives me the pleasure of doing what I've wanted to do since the first time I saw you! General Horsip, by your leave . . ."

Horsip, still absently trying to calculate what to make out of this mess, said, "Do anything you want with him, General, it's all the same to me."

Maklin booted the emissary down the aisle. Then he threw him out the door.

Horsip dropped the ultimatum in the waste basket, and

looked up at the three paralyzed officers, still standing opposite the desk.

From the corridor, Maklin's voice carried loud and clear:

"Guards! Take this subhuman garbage, carry it outside,
and dump it beside the main steps. Careful, or you'll soil
your uniforms."

The three NRPA officers stirred, as if struggling to come
out of shock.

Horsip, still trying to make something out of the mess,
concluded it was so far beyond hopelessness that maybe he
could do something with it, after all. He spoke irritably.

"Well, what are you standing there for? Isn't there any
sense in the whole NRPA? Get out there and help your molk
of a commanding officer back to his quarters before I change
my mind and have the lot of you shot."

The highest ranking of the three drew himself up stiffly,
and tried to speak. But the shock of this treatment caused his
words to get jammed up in a general congestion:

"You cannot . . . we . . . the insult . . . our mighty fleet . . ."

"Does it ever occur to you," said Horsip irritably, "that
we can get tired of trying to save you from yourselves? We
could smash your fleet anytime. Unfortunately, things are not
that simple. Now, we have had about enough for one day.
Get out there, and take care of your emissary. Believe me,
he is in better shape than your fleet will be in if we attack it.
Now get out. *Move!*"

The officers, shocked and incredulous, saluted and started
out, the highest ranking one first, the other two behind.
Though they walked stiffly, there was a jerking quality to
their stride so that they appeared to be tiptoeing.

Meanwhile, General Maklin came back in. Maklin did not
move an inch out of his path, so that the NRPA officers had
to jump aside.

Moffis watched their departure with pursed lips, then put
the safety on his stitching-gun. He aimed the snout of the gun
steeply upward, but kept it handy.

Horsip settled back in his chair, and tried to sort things
out. There were now two fleets on the way. Ganfre and the
Snard Soviet were *both* coming to wipe him out. All he had
was a handful of troops, his own command ship, an imitation
fleet that was already known to be imitation—plus the Earthman Hunter, and *his* imitation fleet, which was already suspected to be imitation. That should get here sometime tomorrow. Horsip shook his head.

General Maklin, with a look of grim satisfaction, strode up the aisle.

Maklin beamed.

"A great day, General Horsip."

Horsip looked around to see who might be in hearing distance that Maklin might want to bluff, turned back, and thought again of the approaching enemy fleets, which for all he knew might be acting together.

Horsip said politely, "Why?"

Maklin looked intently at Horsip. Suddenly Maklin burst out, "Great hairy master of sin! Was that all bluff?"

"Would you tell me what else there is around here to work with?"

Maklin clapped Horsip on the shoulder, and pointed toward the Master Control Center.

"The Fleet's coming in!"

Horsip crossed quickly to the screens of the Master Control Center, and stopped in his tracks. Staring down at him was a huge array of ships stretching across the screen, with enigmatic symbols above and beside the screen, to give details of distance, fleet strength, and direction.

Horsip dazedly feasted his eyes on the mighty ships, emblazoned with the emblems of Centra. The array seemed endless. The symbols detailing the numbers of the Fleet staggered the imagination.

For an instant, Horsip was carried back to the days of his youth, when Centra ruled the universe, when the Old Ways were backed by unyielding might, when the power had all been taken for granted, because it was always there. Tears came to his eyes. An instant later, he was alert, sentiment blasted like pretty flowers in a frost. He glanced at the figures beside the screen, then at Maklin.

"Do I read this correctly? These ships will get here *tomorrow?*"

"That's right, General Horsip." Tears were streaming down Maklin's cheeks. He banged one fist into the other. *"No one beats the High Council! That's where the corruption stops!"*

Horsip glanced around at Moffis. Moffis was carefully oiling his stitching-gun.

Horsip took a deep breath, went back to his desk, and sat down. In a low voice, he murmured, "What do you think, Moffis?"

"About what?"

"That fleet on that screen."

Moffis kept his voice quiet.

"*Able Hunter* is supposed to get here tomorrow."

Horsip nodded.

"At least, it *looks* convincing."

"So did the fleet in the asteroid belt—until the Earth experts went to work on it."

Horsip tried to think of some way to back up Hunter's bluff. Unfortunately, he could find nothing to work with.

Maklin spoke from the Control Center.

"General Horsip, the Fleet Commander wishes to talk to you."

Horsip got up. The "Fleet Commander," under whatever guise he appeared on the screen, would almost certainly be Able Hunter. And very possibly the conversation might be intercepted and monitored by Snard or Ganfre. That might even be the purpose of the call.

Horsip straightened his uniform, and strode to the screen, where a tough-looking Centran general in battle dress snapped to attention, and brought his arm up in a stiff salute, after the fashion of years gone by.

Horsip, impressed with Hunter's realism, returned the salute stiffly.

The Centran on the screen barked, "Nock Sarlin, Commander Battle Fleet V, reporting to United Forces Command Headquarters. Where is the enemy?"

Horsip thought fast. This must be a request for information.

Horsip gave a quick résumé of what had taken place that day, with his best opinion of the likely location of the approaching fleets of Snard and Ganfre, and their probable strength.

"Sarlin" saluted, made a quarter turn, and barked, "Fleet course: lock-on Target B. Close at maximum fleet maneuver acceleration, opening out by divisions to depth 3 plus 1. Heavy bombardment squadrons numbers 1 through 40 to the right wing, angular concentration plus 20 to minus 20; heavy bombardment squadrons numbers 40 through 50 to the left wing by groups; numbers 51 through 100 to Fleet Reserve. Fleet conform by squadrons. Number 99 heavy bombardment squadron will detach from Fleet Reserve with accompanying medium and light squadrons as escort for Landing Force Ships, which will remain in this system under direct control of the Supreme Commander. Numbers 1 through 4 ships of the guard will land near the United Forces Command Headquarters subject to approval of the Supreme

Commander, to act as the Supreme Commander's guard. *Execute!*"

Horsip, dazed as "Sarlin" turned to face him, returned his salute. Horsip's imagination was still catching up with the "Fleet Commander's" orders. Everything seemed technically correct, but it implied an even more gigantic force than appeared on the screen. Snard or Ganfre might easily have concentrated such a force. But would they believe he, Horsip, could do it?

With "Sarlin's" salute, the screen went blank, and before Horsip had time to recover, there flashed on the screen the image of a young officer, who saluted briskly.

"Nar Doppig, Guard Force Commander, reporting to the Supreme Commander for landing permission."

"Granted," said Horsip automatically, and an instant later, while returning Doppig's salute, it occurred to Horsip that he should have refused. . . . How could Hunter land nonexistent troops?

Horsip stood looking blankly at the screen, then, there being nothing else he could do, went back to work. He seemed hardly to have gotten started when Moffis' voice reached him.

"Sir," said Moffis dryly, "the emissaries from Snard and Ganfre want to see you again. Now they're here *together.*"

"Send them in," snarled Horsip.

"One at a time?"

"However they want to come."

Moffis spoke into the phone.

A minute or two later, there was a sound of heels and the two emissaries, one broad and burly, the other tall, haughty, and heavily bandaged, started down the aisle toward Horsip's desk. They halted before the desk, glanced at Moffis' stitching-gun, which Moffis had again lowered, so that they were looking down its muzzle. They cleared their throats, looked at Horsip, and, as if remembering something, saluted.

Horsip returned the salute.

They stood looking at him, but said nothing.

Horsip said, "Gentlemen, if you have something to say, I am listening."

The burly Snard emissary looked faintly regretful.

"You can't get away with it."

Horsip smiled.

The emissary from Ganfre spoke almost reluctantly.

"After what you had done to me, I should hate you. But, I

have to admit, you almost convinced me. Let me extend to you the compliment of my professional admiration. I never saw nothing made into such a convincing appearance of might."

The Snard emissary spoke almost sadly.

"You overdid it."

Horsip shook his head regretfully. His voice was assured.

"You have been warned. There is nothing else I can do for you."

"It is impossible," said the Snard emissary, "for the Integral Union to have such strength. It is therefore obviously a clever trick. With a third or a half of the number, you *might* have convinced us."

Horsip sat back and looked confident. There must have been *some* reason for Hunter to use that number of decoys.

Horsip said, "And what do your trained Earth specialists have to say *this* time?"

"Only that your technique of mass production of dummy ships is highly advanced, and that this batch might have fooled them, except for the excessive and uneconomical use of what reads out on the detectors as belt armor on the ships."

Horsip looked blank.

Belt armor was one of those things that the Centran Fleet had always made abundant use of—until the Earth specialists had proved by statistics that it was not economical.

But Hunter was as familiar with the present lack of armor belts as Horsip was.

Horsip spoke carefully.

"Let me be sure of what you just said. Except for the belt armor—"

"The *appearance* of belt armor—as our detectors, and data analysis, show it."

Horsip nodded. "Except for this appearance, you would now be here offering peace instead of threats?"

Ganfre's emissary said condescendingly, "And the numbers, General. But the point is, we are separately prepared to offer you considerable benefits if you join us willingly."

"Why?"

The emissary cleared his throat.

"We have agreed to unite with each other—our leaders, that is, have so agreed—in order to finish off ... ah ... Columbia—in an economical way. We are stronger even than you realize, but in dealing with the Columbians—who have peculiar weapons—our wise leaders choose to apply the maximum force. With your realistic dummy fleets, General, we believe we can deceive the Columbians as to our actual intentions. We propose to open the psychological attack against Columbia by the total defeat of the Integral Union. We will not reveal your actual weakness, but will give out reports of a great battle, which we have won by better leadership, in order . . ."

Horsip could feel the loathing rise up inside him, but kept his face expressionless until the emissary was through. As the emissary went into rapturous detail over the particulars, it took him some time to finish. Then he looked expectantly at Horsip.

"Well, General, you see you have no choice, and Columbia has no chance, correct?"

Horsip's voice came out in an ugly tone.

"If my fleets were made of tinfoil, I would fight." He smiled, and the smile was such that the emissaries looked jarred. "But," said Horsip, "they aren't." He leaned forward. "I advise you to get in touch with your leaders, and explain that the true fleets of the Integral Union *have always used heavy armor,* and have crushed their enemy in every war throughout recorded history. That you should be outnumbered is exactly what you should expect. You have challenged the *Integral Union!* Now, get out of here. There's work to be done."

For a moment, the emissaries stood paralyzed, but then they relaxed. They glanced at each other with tolerant smiles.

The emissary from Snard said, "You will hear from us again, General. Soon."

On the way out, Horsip could hear Ganfre's emissary say wonderingly, "Amazing. He almost did it again!"

As the door shut behind them, Moffis said, frowning, "Could it be?"

Horsip said stubbornly, "We *always* used armor belts until these Earthmen proved it was a waste. But it wasn't a waste! I never saw a ship yet where the men weren't happier behind a good solid shield. And if you have to go down into the atmosphere to get somebody out of a pickle, that armor backs up the meteor guards when they go to work on you with the artillery."

"But the *numbers!*"

"Maybe it is *part* bluff. But . . ." Horsip shook his head.

Moffis said, "Could we use the Control Center to get in touch with them?"

"And what if it is all bluff, and the transmission is picked up?"

"Truth," said Moffis.

Horsip said exasperatedly, "There's nothing to do but hang on tight and hope for the best. But if that fleet is fake, and these dictators punch right through it, then there isn't any good we can do here. We'll have to get out."

"At least, we can do *that* without too much trouble."

Horsip, who had had the command ship set down in the big courtyard of the planet's main administration building, said, "All we have to do is blast loose the connecting corridor, cut the auxiliary power cables, and leave." He paused, thinking that over.

Moffis said, "And ... if the enemy fleet is closing in when we leave?"

"That's not good."

"Suppose we left now? Then, if the dictators turn away, we can come back."

"If we leave, that news will be broadcast to them, so they will see through the bluff. We have to stay here until we're sure, one way or another."

Horsip, none too hopeful as to what the morning would bring, took a hot bath, and went to bed early. During the first part of the night, he was awakened by the provost marshal, who explained that there was rioting in the streets, and the local police were calling for help, but the provost marshal was afraid that, if he sent any of the few men he had, the command ship couldn't be protected.

"Tell them," said Horsip, "that there will be all the troops on the planet tomorrow that they can ask for. But they will have to get through the night on their own."

The provost marshal beamed. "I *heard* the Fleet was coming in."

Horsip grunted noncommittally. "Meanwhile, double the guard in the connecting corridor, disconnect the auxiliary power cables, and be ready to get your men into the ship on a moment's notice."

"Yes, sir. Ah ... sir, if the Fleet is coming in ... ah ... why would we want to get out of here?"

"Because," snarled Horsip, "we don't know *whose fleet it is.*"

The provost marshal looked startled, then nervous, saluted, and went out.

Horsip fell asleep, was awakened by the sound of shouting

and the rattle of stitching-guns, then fell back into a fitful doze interspersed with nightmares in which various dictators, ten times normal size, swaggered around a room in which Horsip had to jump and run to avoid getting squashed underfoot. The dictators were arguing over who was to get this or that piece out of what was left of the Integral Union. By morning, Horsip, who had gone to bed early to get a good rest, was worn out. He got up, washed all over in cold water, and was just rubbing himself dry when a thundering roar passed overhead.

Feeling that the day could not be worse than the night had been, Horsip buckled himself into his uniform, and went into his office.

Moffis was already there, cleaning and oiling his gun. The provost marshal, a portable stitching-gun under one arm, was directing Horsip's staff as they turned their desks into a barricade. Wounded men were lying on folded blankets, with medical aides taking care of them. In the corner, behind a white cloth, a surgeon was working.

Horsip paused by each of the wounded to say a few words, turned his holster flap under his belt so he could get his gun out in a hurry, opened up the locker behind his desk, got out a thick emergency ration bar, sat down, and spoke on the phone to the officers in charge of the ship's engines and navigation. They could leave anytime, but space off the planet was filled with ships, and one of them had just landed. As Horsip was talking, there was a roar overhead, and another one came down.

Moffis said, "We might as well fight it out on the ground. If we take off, we'll never get past them. But suppose we started out as if we were taking off, then landed and dispersed in rough country? They could have trouble getting us out of there."

Horsip shook his head. "We can't abandon the command ship. Centra needs every ship."

"We couldn't get through."

"Some way may turn up."

The provost marshal came over.

"Sir, request permission to abandon the administration building, down to the connecting corridor."

"Granted. Who are we fighting?"

"Up to the second watch it was vandals, then the Mikerils took over till halfway through the third watch, and we got three men out with pretty bad bites. Since then, it's been something called the Ahaj Revolutionary Army."

"What side are they on?"

"I don't know, sir, but it isn't ours."

Horsip nodded, and the provost marshal went off to direct his men.

Horsip glanced at Moffis, who was talking on the phone. Moffis glanced up inquiringly, and Horsip said, "Moffis, is there an armor belt on this pot, or isn't there?"

Moffis put his hand over the mouthpiece. "I think there is. I think it was made over from one of the old Warrior class. Sir, there's the Snard emissary on the wire. He wants to speak to you."

Horsip got out of the way of two men carrying a flame-thrower from an exhibition case of weapons used in the war with Earth, held the phone to his mouth, looked confident, and said cheerfully, "Good morning, General."

"Good morning, General. I call on you to surrender. Our troopships are landing in the capital. Our fleet is overhead."

"I've warned you of the consequences, General."

"Are you insane? I am calling on you to surrender."

Horsip put his hand over the mouthpiece. "Has anyone seen the markings on these ships?"

"No, sir. The men had to be taken off the detectors to hold the corridors."

Horsip spoke confidently into the phone.

"I advise you to pass my message on to your rulers. You are in grave danger."

Two more wounded were set down gently across from the white sheet in the corner of the room.

There was a harsh rasp from the phone. "Have you taken leave of your senses? Your situation is hopeless!"

"Nonsense. We are in no trouble here."

"I hear the firing in the background."

"Reinforcements have arrived."

A large black creature bristling with hair burst in the doorway. There was no one in sight there, and Horsip's staff were still heaving desks into place. Horsip held the phone in one hand, his palm covering the mouthpiece, and aimed with his other hand. The Mikeril jumped over the desks. The gun leaped in Horsip's hand. The Mikeril went down, then staggered up. Horsip fired again.

Just then, half a dozen grim-looking guards came out from the direction of the display case of Earth weapons, wheeling a squat gray object on a heavy cart. Across the room, the Mikeril was getting up. The phone was shrill:

"I call on you to surrender! You have no chance! My troops are marching on you at this moment!"

Horsip hung up, eyed the lettering on a placard stuck at an angle to the thing on the card, tilted his head, and the lettering suddenly was clear:

A-Bomb, circa 1955 (Earth-style) U.S.A. manufacture.

Across the room, the Mikeril got up and headed for the wounded.

Horsip swore, fired again, the Mikeril went down, and Horsip jumped over the desk, grabbed the arm of the nearest soldier, and pointed across the room.

"Get that thing out of here. How the devil would you like to be over there by the butcher's tent and have *that* take a bite out of you?"

"Sir, we want to blow up the Glops with this."

"You can't use it on the Glops. It's too strong. It will blow us all up. *Get that Mikeril.* ... Who's guarding that door? *There's another one!*"

Moffis put that one down with a short burst from his stitching-gun.

Horsip got a phone down, but at once a little flag on a different phone popped up. He took it off its hook, and the voice of the Snard emissary sprang out. Just then, Horsip spotted another Mikeril and hung up.

The provost marshal appeared in the doorway, looked around incredulously as the soldiers chased the Mikeril around the room, stepped back into the corridor, looked up, and roared, "Who left that hatch open?" He aimed his portable stitching-gun straight up, and opened fire.

Horsip heard a thud from the direction of the Master Control Center.

A Mikeril appeared in the doorway.

Horsip shot it, then shook the empty shells out of the gun, and worked in fresh bullets. The provost marshal approached.

"Sir," said the provost marshal, "request permission to arm the staff and put them on guard duty."

"Granted."

The Mikeril, red eyes glaring, black fur weirdly on end, rose to its feet, clawed hands lifting out.

Horsip aimed carefully, and shot it between the eyes.

The provost marshal glanced around, put a short burst into its neck, looked back, and said, "When they disconnected the power cables, they didn't lock the hatch. All that saved us is, a bunch of them tried to come through all at once, and got jammed in the hole."

The Mikeril struggled to its feet.

Another appeared in the doorway.

Horsip shot the first Mikeril in the head, and the provost marshal stepped aside to get a shot at the next without hitting the Control Center.

Horsip reloaded, scooped some bullets out of the top drawer of his desk, and looked around.

Across the room, weapons were being issued to the staff. Smoke was drifting in from the corridor. Several guards ran in, holding cloths to their faces, and set up a stitching-gun just inside the doorway.

Another Mikeril appeared in the Master Control Center.

Horsip aimed carefully, and shot it.

Moffis was speaking into one of the phones: ". . . the last automatic doors. Get ready to pull in the boom of the communications and control cables. Don't go out after them—it's thick with Mikerils out there. Be ready to start the take-off as soon as I give the word."

More guards came in, dragged out the Mikerils, then there was a rumble and the smoke from the corridor abruptly stopped coming in. Horsip looked around, saw no immediate trouble, crossed the room to the Master Control Center, to work the viewer controls.

In quick succession, there sprang onto the screen a view of an empty control room, then a gangway crowded with troops, then a view down a broad avenue that Horsip at once recognized as the capital's main thoroughfare. The scene shifted.

Now Horsip was looking at big grayish-brown traveling forts, even larger than those he had seen on Earth, moving slowly down the wide avenue. Behind them came full-tracked armored troop carriers with troops in battle dress standing on the tops of the vehicles holding small microphones, and glancing watchfully around. Abruptly there came into view several soldiers carrying automatic rifles, then a solitary drummer whose steady, slow, monotonous beat suddenly filled the room, then an officer in battle dress with a trumpeter to his right and a sergeant carrying a portable communicator to his left.

Immediately behind these three came a soldier carrying the flag of Centra.

Behind the flag, strictly aligned in rank and file, twelve abreast, moving in unison to the beat of the solitary drum, marched six ranks of silent drummers, drumsticks turned back under their arms.

Abruptly, there was the piercing blast of a Centran trumpet. The tone changed swiftly, to end on a single high note.

The massed drummers brought down their drumsticks. The crash of the drums filled the room.

Horsip snapped off the volume control.

From outside came the roll of massed drums.

On the screen, dense formations of heavily armed Centran troops filled the avenue, sunlight glinting on their guns, helmets, and the interlocked plates of their battle tunics. Overhead flew small ships, similar to spacecraft in appearance, but apparently built around one large gun or rocket-launcher that protruded from the front of the ships like the tip of a sword thrust out from behind a shield. In the background, at the far end of the avenue, out in the distance beyond the limits of the city itself, could be seen a looming tower, and behind it another and another, lined up at the city's spaceport. Climbing steeply from this distant spaceport came slim needle shapes that glinted in the morning sun.

From overhead came the roar of another huge ship passing over toward the spaceport.

There was a flashing yellow light to Horsip's right. Horsip snapped on the communications screen.

The same general who had reported to Horsip the day before saluted.

"Nock Sarlin, Commander Battle Fleet V, reporting to United Forces Command Headquarters. Sir, the enemy is destroyed as a fleet. Isolated enemy units are drawing away from us with acceleration slightly superior to our fleet maximum. Our detectors show the second fleet on our plot yesterday is withdrawing at high speed on a diverging course. A third fleet, approximately 20 percent superior in numbers to our own, is appearing on our remote pick-ups, approaching at high superlight velocities, beaming the command code of Able Hunter, and the identification of a Battle Fleet 46. We have Able Hunter on our books, but no Battle Fleet 46. These ships show characteristics contrary to Centran standard construction, but have beamed the correct recognition signal. Shall we maintain concentration and block Fleet 46? Or shall we continue the pursuit?"

From outside came muted sounds of a tramp and rumble, and of the shrill blast of whistles signaling orders.

Horsip fought his way out of his daze.

"Fleet 46 is a special unit and their ships are of nonstandard construction. This is normal for this unit. Continue the pursuit, but don't get too spread out."

On the screen, Sarlin saluted, made a quarter turn, and spoke briskly, "Slow units form on the axis of flight. Pursuit units to the front by flotillas, wings, and squadrons. Unit star with wreath to the outfit that brings down the most ships!"

The screen went blank. Horsip turned to find Moffis listening wide-eyed and staring at the screen.

"Those are our men?"

Horsip said warily, "If not, Able Hunter has tricks I never heard of. But we'd better take a look before we count on it."

Surrounded by guards, they reopened the door to the corridor.

Amidst dead Mikerils and corpses of the Ahaj Revolutionary Army, heavily armed Centran troops saluted. From outside came the deafening roll of drums.

From a window of the building, Horsip looked out on massive columns marching through heavy clouds of dust, followed by traveling forts, launchers, troop transports, and motorized cannon.

Moffis looked down in choked silence, then turned to Horsip.

"The High Council *has* come through!"

Horsip nodded. The High Council must have drawn on the resources of the huge Sealed Zone, and now put forth its concealed strength.

But Horsip, thinking of the charts he had seen of the two monster dictatorships, drew a mental comparison. Although victorious here, the Integral Union was in fact still not the equal of either of the two dictatorships.

Moffis said, "This will change things."

"Not enough. They're still stronger."

"What about Hunter's fleet?"

"*If* that were real, we'd be stronger than either alone, but not both together."

"As far as they know, it *is* real."

"And that gives us our chance. Well, Moffis, let's see if we can dig these dictators a hole and shove them into it."

❀ XXII ❀

Clokal Detonak

During the next few days, Horsip, like an accident victim after a gigantic transfusion and the most expert treatment, found himself in better shape than he would have dared believe possible. The loyal planets were swept by waves of enthusiasm. The uncertain hastened to his banner. The disloyal trembled. Dictator Ganfre earnestly talked peace, while the Snard Soviet and its allies were gushingly friendly.

Horsip, calculating the odds, and observing that Ganfre was now noticeably diminished by the outcome of the battle, was very agreeable to the heavily bandaged and crestfallen NRPA emissary. Horsip explained that the Integral Union had *had* to protect itself, that everything he could have done to warn of the danger had been done, that really it wasn't Ganfre that he wanted to fight, but certain "degenerate elements." The emissary, listening alertly, at once identified Snard. If, Horsip suggested, Ganfre and the Integral Union could get together, it might be possible to do something about these degenerates. The emissary swallowed the bait, and at once went off to get in touch with his master.

"Ganfre," Moffis objected, "is as bad as Snard—and Ganfre attacked us!"

"Yes," said Horsip, "but if Ganfre will go along with the idea, we should be able to beat Snard. With Snard out of the way, the threat that holds Ganfre's pack together will vanish. Then if we can get a few of Ganfre's people to go along, we can eliminate Ganfre."

Moffis intently followed this line of reasoning.

"Truth."

"Meanwhile," said Horsip, "we have to get Columbia allied with us. Somehow, Moffis, we have to get more of these Earth-controlled planets on our side. We aren't strong enough to win by ourselves, and the worst of it is, while we have a good-sized fleet *now*, these dictators have a big production to fall back on. We need to beat them quick."

Unfortunately, Ganfre sent a new emissary to make a pact with Horsip, by which Ganfre and Horsip would finish Snard *after* Snard and Ganfre, now secretely allied, polished off Columbia.

Horsip hid his disappointment. "Columbia is a minor power. We should finish the source of the trouble first. Columbia would be easy later."

"I am inclined to agree with Your Excellency," said the emissary, looking sincere. "If only your offer of alliance had arrived sooner! But the end of hostilities left us in temporary disarray, and it seemed wise to unite momentarily with the common enemy of both of us. We did not at that time realize, of course, how you felt. . . . Now"—he looked pious—"we must honor our commitment?"

"How," asked Horsip politely, "does this attack on Columbia enter into the commitment?"

"It was Snard's price for agreeing to hit you from behind if . . . ah . . . that is, for agreeing to stand by us in our hour of crisis."

"I see."

"But once we have fulfilled that sacred pledge, *then* your forces and mine may combine to eliminate the common enemy." The emissary looked earnest.

Horsip looked agreeable, but regretful.

"It may be that there will be nothing left for us to be allied with."

"But I thought Your Excellency was of the opinion that Columbia is a minor, if somewhat dangerous, power?"

"It is not your *enemy* that gives me concern, but your ally. In such an attack, there could be many opportunities for"— he searched for the word—"*errors.*"

The emissary looked moody.

"I think we have thought of all of them. But, it is true— with such friends as that, there is no telling."

Horsip said, "If you come out of it with a whole hide, *then* offer us this agreement."

After the emissary had left, Moffis said, "Once they finish Columbia, then what?"

"Then," he said, "they finish *us.* After that, they eat each other up."

"Then we should help Columbia."

Horsip nodded, and sent for Hunter, who had come in after sending the bulk of his mysterious fleet on "maneuvers."

Hunter entered the room looking faintly dazed.

Horsip, who had never seen Hunter like this, sat up in alarm.

"What's wrong?"

"I've just been in your Records Section, studying reports on Mikerils."

"Bad as they are, we have a worse problem. If we don't help Columbia, Snard is likely to win the war."

"Not Snard. The Centrans will win."

Horsip, knowing the way Earthmen used the word "Centrans" to mean anyone of Centran descent, considered the various dictatorships, revolutionaries, maniac faddists of all manner of cults, and said, *"Which* Centrans?"

Hunter glanced toward a rugged guardsman recently arrived with the Fleet.

"That's the kind. It won't be long before there won't be any other kind."

"Why?"

Hunter started to speak, then shook his head.

"To explain *that* would be complicated, sir."

Horsip shrugged. "Snard and Ganfre have ganged up against Columbia. Unless we help, I think Columbia will get beaten. But we aren't strong enough to intervene openly."

"If we waited until they are in the middle of the attack—"

Horsip shook his head.

"The commander of Fleet V tells me that there are other 'fleets,' so-called, which I think must be mostly for deception purposes—like your 'fleet'—but they must have some real strength, and, as I calculate it, the united real parts of these fleets would make us much stronger than we are now."

Hunter said, "You want to gather your strength, so you need time for these units to come in?"

"Yes."

Hunter looked thoughtful.

"There are a few stunts we've worked out that we'd like to try on these birds. Sir, if we could have permission to operate completely on our own—"

"Granted," said Horsip promptly.

Hunter saluted, and went out with a look of creative enjoyment.

Moffis put down a phone, and turned to Horsip.

"*Another* Mikeril attack! The commander of the guard says ten thousand have hit the outskirts of the capital in the last hour. They avoid the troops and hit the populace. Fifteen thousand more *went by overhead,* to attack the outlying districts."

"Overhead?"

Moffis said, "It's impossible, but they do it."

Chills ran up and down Horsip's spine. A verse from school days went through his head:

> By day, by night,
>   In eerie flight,
>   Their shadows pass across the sky.
> They stoop, they dive.
>   Their numbers thrive.
>   Through air and space in hosts they fly,
> Drawn by unseen cords that tie
>   Sinners to the Mikeril hive.

Moffis said, "If it gets any worse, we're going to have an invasion on our hands. You can't call it anything else, when they start coming in like this."

"Where do they come from? Moffis, you know that poem . . . ah . . . 'Through air and space in hosts . . .' "

Moffis shivered. "I know it."

"That part about 'space'—that, at least, should be impossible."

Moffis nodded. "It *should* be. But how do they fly through air?"

Horsip considered it. How *did* they fly through air? It was impossible. The Mikerils were big, hairy, clawed creatures, as large as a man, hiedous to look at, and according to legend they could tie a man up in invisible strands. He had seen at least part of it confirmed. But . . . the creatures had no wings.

Horsip shook his head. They had troubles enough without this complication.

In the following weeks, the Mikeril attacks didn't slacken. They got worse. They swept over the planet like a hurricane. As the reports flooded in, Horsip found it impossible to separate fact from panic, chose a newly arrived brilliant staff officer, and let *him* read the Mikeril reports. Horsip went out with Moffis to visit the troops.

"Here they come, sir," roared a sergeant in charge of a squad with a big splat-stitcher.

Straight ahead, low over the trees, came a thin grayish blur. Swiftly it enlarged into countless black dots.

The sergeant shouted, "Ready! Here they come!"

Somewhere there was a blast of a whistle.

The sergeant shouted, "Loaders back! Aim high and sweep! *Fiiire!*"

The gunner shook in his seat, the numerous belts of ammunition fed up to their separate guns, the frame blurred, streams of glowing tracers arced out. All around Horsip was a hammer and rattle that deafened him. Then the nearest gun ceased fire, and the loaders ran up with fresh belts of ammunition.

In the distance, the dark cloud sheared off.

The sergeant bellowed, "*Ceeease fire!*"

Horsip and Moffis went up with the colonel in charge of the unit to look over the slaughter. The Mikerils were strewn in grisly heaps. . . . And not one had wings.

Horsip returned from his inspection tour to find that, while the population was being decimated by the Mikerils, the balance of force between Centra and the dictators had again shifted.

The dictators, locked in their savage battle to exterminate Columbia, were being diligently sabotaged by Able Hunter, whose brief battle reports spoke of fine strong wires that opened up the Snard ships like pea pods, and of undetectable leech-mines that sought out the enemy ships and blew them up. But Hunter could only inflict painful bites on the gigantic mass of the enemy fleets.

What altered the situation overnight was the unexpected arrival of Battle Fleet II of the United Arms of Centra. Battle Fleet II, it quickly developed, was as powerful as Battle Fleet V. Even allowing for the mushrooming production of the dictators, Centra was now very nearly as strong as either of them.

Horsip at once lifted his command ship from its landing place, and led his fleet against the enemy fleet at the height of its siege of Columbia.

The big screens in Horsip's command ship showed the situation plainly. The outer planets of the Columbian system were under the control of Snard and Ganfre. The system had an asteroid belt, in which the battle for control was apparently going against the outnumbered Columbians. The dictators had also succeeded in seizing a huge satellite closely circling the Columbian sun. The inner planets remained under Columbian control, but a huge invasion fleet was preparing to attack the home planet itself.

Horsip was promptly challenged by one Supreme High Commander Strins Rudal, a subordinate of Ganfre's, who ordered that the "dummy fleet" be withdrawn at once.

Horsip, wishing to defeat the dictators separately, listened politely as Rudal delivered his warning from the communications screen.

"I am aware," said Rudal, "of your deception fleet, General Horsip. I suggest you put it back in your asteroid belt before we blow it up."

Horsip looked stern, but kept his voice level. He selected the name of a powerful Snard dictator none too popular even among his fellows.

"I am not interested in attacking *you*, General. My quarrel is with Q. Schnerg, who is, I think, in this group of ships somewhere."

"High Leader Schnerg is a member of the Coalition. What of it?"

"I have told you, General. I have a quarrel with Schnerg."

"High Leader Schnerg."

"I don't care what you call him. I want him."

Rudal looked blank.

"Surely, General Horsip, you can see we are occupied here. High Leader Schnerg is not available."

"Schnerg will either come out, or I will go in and get him."

"You do not have the ships to challenge the Coalition."

"I don't challenge the Coalition. I want Schnerg."

"Would you mind telling me why?"

"I would mind. I will tell Schnerg."

"General Horsip, I will pass the word to the High Leader. It is not fit that one of his rank be approached by—"

Horsip said coldly, "Do *you* now question the power of the Integral Union to defend its honor?"

Rudal looked uneasy. "I didn't mean that. I meant I would take your message personally. But—"

Horsip looked Rudal in the eye. "My message for Schnerg is not something you can *hand* to him. It can only be *fired* at him. Where is he?"

Rudal lowered his voice.

"General Horsip, I mean no offense, of course, but the real portion of your fleet cannot defeat High Leader Schnerg. Besides, the Coalition is one solid force. We are as one. We will defend each other as if we ourselves were attacked."

Horsip smiled and said nothing.

Rudal looked uneasy.

Horsip said politely, "I have no quarrel with you, or with the Coalition. But I am going to get Schnerg. Now, don't tell me you are going to stop me. I can see the situation you are in as well as you can. If you let go of Columbia to stop me, the Columbians will take back everything you have won. Don't tell me my ships are dummies. Just show me where Schnerg is, and I will show you what my ships are made of. Now, either you get me Schnerg, and get him fast, or I will go in and get him myself."

Rudal looked browbeaten and exasperated. His feelings showed on his face. Why, he was obviously asking himself, had this mess had to come about at *this* moment? Horsip, calculating that anyone with Schnerg's traits would be bound to make enemies, was not surprised to hear Rudal say, "General Horsip, I . . . ah . . . must admit I am not surprised that the High Leader has given you offense in some way. . . . But, could you not possibly wait until some more propitious moment?"

"I want Schnerg," said Horsip, "and I want him now."

"To separate his ships from the rest will create chaos!"

"That is too bad," said Horsip, straining to look regretful, "but if Schnerg does not come out, I will go in after him."

"Just a moment, General. I will take this matter to our leaders."

There was a short delay, which Horsip used to beam messages at the Columbians, pointing out that he was neutral in that fight, and interested only in getting Schnerg. Since Schnerg was one of Columbia's main enemies, the Columbians were only too happy to recognize this kind of neutrality. Then Dictator Ganfre came on, to offer to mediate the trouble between Horsip and Schnerg. Schnerg, said Ganfre, claimed that he had never had anything to do with Horsip *or* the Integral Union, and was not interested in either of them.

"Ah," snarled Horsip, "he is not interested in either of us, eh?"

Ganfre made an earnest plea for Horsip to wait until the battle was over, then he could do anything he liked with Schnerg. Schnerg apparently intercepted that message, and didn't like it, as Horsip promptly received a note from Moffis that the Coalition Fleet was breaking up, large units pulling out in the midst of the battle. Ganfre obviously learned the same thing at the same time. His eyes narrowed and a look of calculation passed across his face. Horsip thought he could follow his train of thought. Schnerg was temporarily allied to Ganfre, but that alliance would break up as soon as Columbia was beaten. If, therefore, Horsip beat Schnerg now, Ganfre would not have to beat him later. If Schnerg beat Horsip, that would simplify the calculations too.

"May the best man win," said Ganfre.

"Thank you," said Horsip. "I hope to."

Then he led his fleet against Schnerg.

Horsip had a sizable numerical superiority over Schnerg alone, but did not dare to use it. If he got into a vulnerable position, the other dictators might decide to rid themselves of this nuisance by letting go of Columbia to attack Horsip. Schnerg maneuvered as if to take advantage of this possibility, and Horsip had to use a large part of his fleet to guard against a possible attack by the rest of the dictators. Halfway through the battle, a huge host of Mikerils, their bodies rigid and unmoving, passed through empty space around his ships as if traveling on unseen wires. Shaken by this sight, Horsip was none too sure of victory or anything else, but his tactics worked, and the Centran Fleet destroyed the dictator's fleet.

Horsip now found himself in the rear of the other dictators, with a fleet approximately half their size, while their attack on Columbia was out of gear because of Schnerg's withdrawal.

The dictators at once offered Horsip a share of the spoil if he would join the attack on Columbia.

Horsip declined.

The dictators proposed a mutual accommodation.

Horsip, certain they would stay together against him now that their own danger was clear, considered that he had done all he could for the moment, and was inclined to agree, as they outnumbered him two to one. He asked for time to consider, and as the screen went blank, Moffis, looking pale, stepped forward.

"A message," said Moffis, "from the High Council."

Horsip unfolded the yellow slip of paper. He looked at it, and chills ran up and down his spine. It read:

By Command
The High Council

We, the guardians of the essential strength of our race, in accord with the ancient law, do hereby proclaim throughout the Realm of Centra the edict of the *clokal detonak*.

We hereby vest in our loyal servant Klide Horsip that power gathered to us from all the race, to reduce the aberrant of the Realm to obedience, or by death cleanse them of their abomination.

Let the sinful lay down their arms, abase themselves before the Great One, admit the error of their ways, seek the aid of the Holy Brotherhood in again finding the True Way, and the sword of chastisement will be withheld.

If they fail so to do, we require General Klide Horsip, Commander of the United Arms of Centra, to destroy the traitors utterly and without mercy.

This command is absolute and binding, it cannot be questioned or negotiated, its effect is immediate, and its term shall last until the submission or death of the last traitor.

> By command
> The High Council
> J. Roggil
> Chairman

The hair at the back of Horsip's neck bristled. He glanced at the battle screen, which showed in stylized symbols the strength of the enemy, and his own strength. He glanced at Moffis.

Moffis looked helpless.

Horsip glanced back at the message. There in front of him were the words "it cannot be questioned." Horsip straightened his tunic. "Get Ganfre for me."

High Commander Strins Rudal appeared on the screen, trying to look cordial.

"Well, well, General Horsip, we are very busy, of course, but always glad to talk to an old friend. I am sorry we will have to make this quick, but—"

Horsip said evenly, "Are you *still* convinced my fleet is made of dummies?"

Rudal looked uneasy. "We all make mistakes—"

"I have just received a message from the High Council which requires—"

Rudal burst out, "We all know, General, that you *are* the Integral Union. We have to admire the way you have pulled the pieces together, but spare us this playacting!"

Horsip observed Rudal's nervousness, and hid his own.

"I am merely the tool of the Integral Union," said Horsip, "and if I break, I will be tossed aside, and another chosen to do the work. I am the servant of the High Council."

Rudal struggled to cover a look of long-suffering.

"Of course, General. Certainly. I will pass the message on at once."

Horsip spoke slowly and distinctly.

"By command of the High Council, the *clokal detonak* is proclaimed throughout the Integral Union. By this command, an absolute obligation is imposed upon you, and upon every living person of Centran blood, to lay down your arms, abase yourselves before the Great One, and seek the aid of the Holy Brotherhood in again finding the True Way. If you fail to do this, you will be destroyed without mercy. You cannot negotiate. This command is absolute."

Rudal swayed on his feet.

Horsip looked at him steadily.

Rudal opened his mouth, closed it again. "I will inform our leaders of this, General Horsip. Now, excuse me."

The screen went blank.

Moffis said uneasily, "It doesn't say anything in there about persons of Centran blood. Maybe it just means . . . well . . . in our *own* territory . . ."

Horsip smiled.

"I know what it means, Moffis. The Council isn't commanding the people in *our* part of the universe to lay down *their* arms. The Council is commanding the 'aberrant of the Realm.' I know who the 'aberrant of the Realm' are."

Moffis nodded unhappily, and looked at the battle screen, where a new large force of the dictators' ships was separating from the battle with Columbia.

Moffis said, "It didn't say we should attack them at once."

"Truth," said Horsip, "but we can't wait until Columbia is captured."

The screen came on again, to show Dictator Ganfre, backed by a vague, out-of-focus semicircle of figures. Some trick in the transmission made Ganfre look larger than life, and his words came out with subtle undertones of power.

"I am surprised, General Horsip, that one victory over a fraction of our forces should create such . . . presumption."

Horsip said, "I will read the command of the High Council." Horsip read slowly and distinctly, lowered the paper. "I can't question it, I can't negotiate it. I can't soften it. You have two choices—obey or die."

Ganfre looked blank.

There was an uproar behind Ganfre, and for the next fifteen minutes Horsip monotonously beat down offers of partnership, threats, attempts to buy him off—until at the last the incredulous dictators saw he meant exactly what he said. Then there was a change in the atmosphere.

The communications screen at once went blank.

On the battle screen, the entire battle fleet of the dictators began to break free of Columbia. At this distance, it appeared a slow movement. But Horsip knew what it meant.

✽ XXIII ✽

The Phantom Fleets

Horsip didn't wait for the enemy to take the initiative, but attacked at once, to pin a portion of the dictators' fleet back against the Columbians. As Horsip drove this enemy force into the eager grip of the Columbians, the rest of the dictators' fleet curved around behind him, so that he was between two enemy forces.

Horsip, eying the battle screen, turned to his communications officer.

"Ask permission of the Columbians to enter their territory."

"Yes, sir."

The enemy in front of him was being slowed by the missiles, beams, and drifting minefields of the Columbians, while the enemy behind was gaining steadily.

A staff officer at another screen called, "Sir, we have a fleet showing up here."

"What recognition signal?"

"None yet, sir."

There was the rap of a printer.

The staff officer said, "Here it is ... Fleet 99, United Arms of Centra ... Bogax Golumax commanding."

Horsip looked blank. "Bogax Golumax?"

Moffis said, "*That's* no Centran."

Horsip's communications officer spoke up.

"Sir, the Columbians grant permission to enter their territory."

"Good." He looked at the long-range screen, where an enormous fleet was beginning to loom into view, then glanced back at the battle screen.

Between Horsip's Centrans and the Columbians, the trapped section of the dictators' fleet was melting away like a light snow in a hot sun. But the main force of the enemy was gaining relentlessly.

Horsip spoke to his communications officer.

"Signal to Ganfre: 'You are trapped. Surrender or be destroyed to the last ship.'"

Moffis grimly studied the screen. "That won't scare him."

"It will if he looks around," said Horsip.

The battle screen now showed symbols on both sides flaring up and winking out as the enemy fleet thrust into range.

Meanwhile, "Fleet 99" loomed ever more gigantic, a monster phalanx whose numbers suggested a traveling galaxy.

Horsip said, "Signal to Fleet 99, both in code and in clear: 'We have the enemy in position. Close and destroy them.'"

Horsip's ships were beginning to get the worst of it. Not only were they heavily outnumbered, but with rare exceptions they could bring beams, missiles, and other weapons to bear better to their front than to their rear. As long as Horsip fled, which he had to do, his disadvantage in fighting power was worse than his disadvantage in ships.

But now the enormous Fleet 99 began to appear in the background of the battle screen.

The enemy symbols on the screen abruptly underwent a peculiar writhing motion.

Horsip spoke sharply, "*General order:* 'Reverse course. Turn by squadrons.'"

The screen showed Horsip's fleet undergoing the same peculiar motion. Now he was pursuing the enemy. Though still outnumbered, this disadvantage was offset as his heavier armament came to bear on the dictators' ships.

The gigantic Fleet 99 closed at high speed, with a smoothly flowing ease of maneuver that put the other fleets to shame.

Horsip said uneasily, "What are the characteristics of Fleet 99's ships?"

"Still not clear, sir."

"H'm . . ."

On the battle screen, Fleet 99 was moving with an ease which suggested something supernatural. The desperately fleeing ships of the dictators were getting the worst of it as their overloaded fire-control centers tried to deal with both Horsip and Fleet 99 at the same time.

On the screen, the enemy's ships winked out, but now the ships of Fleet 99 began to disappear faster.

The communications officer shouted, "Message from Fleet

99, sir! Bogax Golumax to Commander United Arms of Centra: 'The enemy is armed. Now what do I do?' "

Horsip kept his voice level:

"Transmit general order: 'Reverse Course. Turn by squadrons. Maximum acceleration.' . . . Signal Fleet 99, Commander of United Arms to Bogax Golumax: 'Go back and get your guns.' "

There was an astonished murmur in the room. Experienced officers were looking around as if they had lost faith in their senses.

The screen showed Horsip streaking for the protection of the Columbian system, while the dictators tore into Fleet 99, which folded up with only the most pathetic resistance. While part of Fleet 99 was still coming forward, another part was leaving faster than it had come. Still other ships were vanishing while out of range of the enemy.

Moffis said suddenly, "That must be Able Hunter's deception fleet!"

Horsip growled, "Who else would send a message like that?"

The officer at the long-range screen shouted, "Another fleet, sir. Approaching on the same course as Fleet 99!"

"How many ships?"

"Too distant to be sure, sir. It looks big."

"What characteristics?"

"Lead squadrons seem to fit Centran standards."

Horsip glanced at the battle screen. The enemy had given up pursuit of Fleet 99, and was coming after Horsip at high speed. But Horsip now had too great a lead to be caught. Once in the Columbian system, the dictators had the little problem of dealing with Horsip *and* the Columbians.

There was the rap of the printer.

"Sir, message from Gar Noffik, Commander Battle Fleet VII, to United Forces Commander: 'Shall I join you, or attack them from the rear?' "

"Signal: 'Join me.' "

Moffis snarled, "Is *that* fleet real?"

"I hope so. But I'm not planning to take chances."

The battle screen showed Horsip drawing within range of the Columbian defenses. The dictators' fleet was well behind him. Fleet VII loomed up solidly on the long-range screen, though by comparison with Fleet 99 it looked modest.

"Sir," shouted an officer, "ships of Fleet VII have Centran characteristics!"

Fleet 99 had now vanished entirely.

An officer at the long-range screen began reading off numbers and types of ships.

On the screen, the enemy ships shifted position, and Horsip, watching closely, could see the possibilities. Ganfre might lead his whole fleet against Fleet VII before it reached the protection of Columbia. To save Fleet VII, Horsip might have to leave the Columbian system. Ganfre could then turn and attack Horsip.

Watching alertly, Horsip could see that, without Hunter's deception fleet, the position was clear enough. Ganfre still held the advantage, and obviously intended to use it. Already the dictators' fleet was swinging around to get between Horsip and the reinforcing fleet—if it was a reinforcing fleet, and not another of Hunter's phantoms.

Horsip, studying Ganfre's movements, and the continuing approach of Fleet VII, cleared his throat, and turned to his communications officer. "*Signal Fleet VII:* 'Enemy force outnumbers our present combined fleet strength. Stand off until you see a chance to join us.' "

Fleet VII answered, "While they attack us, you can attack them from behind."

Horsip smiled. "Send: 'I like your spirit, but they could split their fleet in two, and outnumber both of us.' "

"My men are impatient to kill traitors."

"There are too many of them. We need some advantage before we hit them."

"Fleets IX and XV are coming behind me."

Horsip looked blank, and turned to his staff officer at the long-range screen.

"Well sir, there is *something*. Just what it is, we don't know yet, but—"

The harsh rap of the printer interrupted him.

"Sir, message from Sark Roffis, Commander Battle Fleet XVI, to United Forces Supreme Commander: 'Where is the enemy?' "

The printer gave another rapid-fire burst.

"Sir, message from Brok Argil, Commander Battle Fleet VI, to United Forces Commander: 'Which ones are the traitors?' "

Horsip looked around blankly.

The officers at the long-range screen turned wonderingly to look at other sections of screen.

"Sir, there are more coming in from another direction!"

Chills ran up and down Horsip's spine.

"Are they ours?"

"Ship characteristics match, sir."

The printer went off again.

"Sir, message from Nark Rokkis, Commander Battle Fleet IX, to United Forces Commander: 'Show us the enemy!' "

Horsip stared at the long-range screens, then turned to look at the battle screen.

Ganfre, with the equivalent of four battle fleets, was sliding his ships past the Columbian solar system, where Horsip waited with Centran Battle Fleets V and VI, and he was already between Horsip and Battle Fleet VII. Ganfre could not attack Horsip without coming into range of the Columbian defenses, while Horsip could not attack Ganfre without leaving the Columbian defenses, and fighting at odds of one against two. Battle Fleet VII, meanwhile, at odds of one against four, belligerently faced Ganfre as Ganfre eased forward to get this fleet into his grip. As the dictators' fleet reached out for Battle Fleet VII, Battle Fleets XVI and VI approached at high speed, with Battle Fleet IX looming up ever more solidly on the long-range screen.

Now Ganfre had his ships almost in position, and at any moment might begin his attack on Battle Fleet VII, which, if anything, was edging forward to hasten the moment.

The printer clacked.

"Sir, message from Gar Noffik, Commander Battle Fleet VII to United Forces Commander: 'Do I have permission to attack?' "

Horsip, calculating the odds, said, " 'Refused. Avoid contact with the enemy until I give the word.' "

Ganfre now chose to begin the attack on Fleet VII.

Each individual ship in Fleet VII simultaneously pivoted 180 degrees and accelerated sharply.

Ganfre closed the gap, to run into a ferocious barrage. Then Fleet VII drew out of his reach.

Battle Fleet XVI now began to show up on the battle screen, along with a gigantic Battle Fleet 88, "Snar Gorible" commanding.

Horsip had seen enough. Fleet VII was unquestionably real. And if the Concealed Zone of the Integral Union could put forth three such fleets as II, V, and VII, it followed that there was every reason to think the approaching Battle Fleet XVI was also real—and that fleet, for the first time, made the odds even.

Horsip at once gave his commands to the Centran battle fleets.

The ships of Fleet VII simultaneously turned ninety degrees, to bring their main fore and aft armament into action, the entire fleet moving in a wide lattice toward the right edge of Ganfre's fleet, which was approaching them head-on.

Out from the Columbian system came Horsip, with Centran Battle Fleets V and II opening out into a thin lattice, and heading for that same right wing of the dictators' fleet.

At high speed, Battle Fleet XVI raced for the juncture where the other three Centran fleets should join, approaching the "upper" edge of that right portion of the enemy fleet.

Ganfre, his right wing suffering under the simultaneous fire of the main fore and aft armament of Battle Fleet VII, while his own ships could bring only their forward beams, missiles, and other weapons into most effective use, and with his left wing completely out of action, had ordered a ninety-degree turn to the right by his ships, to equalize the rates of fire on the right wing, and hopefully to enable him to curve his left wing around behind Fleet VII.

But now Battle Fleets V and II were approaching his right wing, so that it would be sandwiched between two Centran forces, and struck simultaneously from both sides.

Ganfre at once saw his mistake, and signaled a 180-degree turn to withdraw from the Centran trap.

Ganfre's fleet, however, was a coalition, not trained to the same level. Where some of the ships obeyed with precision, others turned late, and some had rejected the first order to turn ninety degrees by ships as being too difficult in this situation, and instead had turned by squadrons. When the second order, to turn 180 degrees, followed on the heels of the first order to turn ninety degrees, the ships turning by squadrons were caught with the first maneuver uncompleted. Again the response varied. Some units elected at once to turn back the leading ships of the squadrons, while others elected to finish the first maneuver before beginning the second. In the resulting chaos, Horsip did not even turn his ships to conform to the new enemy direction, but instead exacted the full toll of his advantage on the enemy's right wing.

Ganfre now swiftly curved back the left wing of his fleet, turning this wing 180 degrees, the huge fleet formations curving around to take Battle Fleets V and II in the flank, and hopefully to sandwich Horsip's left wing as Horsip had sandwiched Ganfre's right wing.

Horsip turned the ships of Battle Fleet V and II ninety degrees "down," each individual ship now headed at right angles to the ships of Ganfre's fleet, as Centran Battle Fleet

XVI, slightly altering its course on Horsip's command, approached the "upper" edge of Ganfre's formation.

Battle Fleet XVI, already spaced for maximum effect, threatened to bring to bear on the thin upper edge of Ganfre's fleet the concentrated fire of all the forward weapons of its ships. The ships on the upper edge of Ganfre's fleet could not hope to equal that concentration of fire. The danger existed that Battle Fleet XVI might chew its way through the whole of Ganfre's fleet from top to bottom, taking the whole fleet in the flank.

Ganfre, seeking to avoid the chaos that had come about before, signaled a ninety-degree turn by squadrons, to swing his whole fleet "down," paralleling the direction of Horsip's Battle Fleets V and II away from Fleet XVI.

Horsip, meanwhile, turned Battle Fleet VII 180 degrees, by ships, aiming it from the right of the formation back toward the left.

The accumulated momentum of the various maneuvers now exacted its price.

Battle Fleet XVI was already moving at high speed before Ganfre gave the order to turn. As Ganfre's ships turned, Battle Fleet XVI passed down through the gigantic lattices of ships, working murderous execution on the enemy, but finally ceasing fire because of the intermingling of the other ships, enemy and Centran, once the upper wing of Ganfre's fleet was passed.

Battle Fleet VII, moving to the right of the other fleets, continued in that direction even after the order to turn had been obeyed. While Battle Fleet XVI was still passing through the formation, Battle Fleet VII was fighting its own inertia, and slipping farther to the right—out of the way. Then, gaining speed, it slid back across the decimated formation of the dictators' fleet while their ships were gathering momentum downward.

Horsip, totally concentrated on the job, now reversed the direction of Battle Fleet XVI.

Ganfre, clubbed and battered, the condition of his fleet varying from iron discipline to chaos, now had the added treat of seeing Centran Battle Fleets IX and XV loom up on the screen.

Horsip brought Battle Fleet IX in from the original left flank of his fleet. Battle Fleet XV he had stand by, on the far side of the battle from the Columbian system.

Ganfre at once: (a) offered sizable concessions to Horsip; (b) threatened the use of new secret wapons if Horsip did not accept the concessions; (c) signaled Earth, calling for help: (d) gave orders for the disposition of new reserve forces of the NRPA; (e) proposed a permanent alliance with Snard, until Centra should accept his terms.

Horsip repeated the original demand of the High Council, and brought in Battle Fleet IX to sweep the enemy formation and be out of the way before Battle Fleet XVI should pass back through the remnants, while Battle Fleets V and II, parallel to the enemy formations, were laboring at the task of destruction, and Battle Fleet VII was getting into position for another pass.

With this in store for it, the enemy coalition abruptly broke into fragments, each fragment suffering multiplied destruction as it clawed for safety, the surviving enemy groups splitting into small formations, and even into individual ships.

Horsip at once signaled Battle Fleet XV, which divided into pursuit groups to run down those enemy ships unfortunate enough to be within its reach.

The other fleets Horsip kept out of the pursuit. Fleets IX and XVI he turned against the home planets of Snard. Fleets VII and VI he sent against the home planets of the NRPA. Fleets V and II, together with Hunter's formidable-looking Fleet 88, he kept together as he watched to see if there should be any truth in Ganfre's threats of new fleets and secret weapons.

Off the home planet of Snard, the Centran fleets met and smashed a reserve fleet half their size just setting out to join the battle.

Near Ganfre's home planet, the leading ships of the Centran fleet began to vanish in bright explosions, out of range of any known weapons.

Horsip suddenly found himself in a war of attrition. The enemy, with the advantage of his weapon, tried to pick off Horsip's ships from a distance. Horsip sought to seize the enemy planets still unprotected by the weapon, and meanwhile used Able Hunter's phantom fleets to get some real ships close enough to pick off Ganfre's sniper-ships. Meanwhile, watching quietly on the far fringes of the action were ships Horsip suspected to be from Earth.

Not liking the looks of things, Horsip got in touch with the High Council.

"Don't worry," said Roggil. "The Concealed Zone is working at its highest pitch, and has been for years, while the

Earthmen in the Integral Union have had every opportunity they might want to waste their effort on extravagances."

"This new weapon," said Horsip, "makes it impossible to finish the job."

"We expected something like that. Keep working on them and don't worry. More reinforcements are on the way."

As Ganfre multiplied his weapon, Centran Battle Fleets XVIII, XI, III, and X came in. The *clokal detonak* still applied, the power of Centra was rolling in like a tide, the Mikerils in gigantic numbers ravaged the main planets of the enemy—but Ganfre's factories labored night and day, turning out new ships armed with the new weapon.

Horsip could see the end of the Integral Union. He had Able Hunter multiply his deception apparatus, and prepared to lead the massed Centran Fleet, masked by Hunter's phantoms, against Ganfre's new fleet. At once, the changing balance of power showed up as Ganfre slid out of reach, his improved detectors ignored Hunter's phantoms, and with easy mastery he destroyed Centran ships in rapid dazzling flashes of blue-white glare. In the midst of the slaughter, with all hope lost and nothing left but grim persistence, several squadrons of ultrafast Centran ships ripped through the edge of the enemy fleet, their passage marked by the dull glow of enemy ships fading off the screen.... Centran laboratories and workshops had produced their own new weapon.

The Centran ships armed with this weapon proved also to be carrying cargoes made up of the new weapon, and Horsip lost no time distributing it. Then, as Ganfre's fleet avoided battle, Horsip led the attack on his main planets, capturing them one after the other to deprive Ganfre of nearly all his base. Horsip was about to finish the job when, once again, his ships began to be destroyed beyond the effective range of his own weapons.

Horsip resorted to tricks and subterfuge, using Hunter's improved phantom fleets to screen his movements. But Ganfre was exacting a heavy toll. Horsip again got in touch with the High Council.

"We are," said Roggil, "sending you an improved version of our own weapon, but it will take time to reach you. Don't worry. They have lost too much of their base to recover.'

Nevertheless, Horsip's ships were vanishing.

Trying to trap Ganfre, Horsip sent a fresh fanatical fleet head-on against the dictator's main fleet, with the order to simulate panic. Ganfre's ships, mercilessly destroying the fleeing Centrans, followed them into a region filled with an improved version of Able Hunter's multiplied phantoms. Hidden by these phantoms were Horsip's massed fleets, which surrounded the enemy fleet, and closed in at high speed. The enemy went to work with his long-range weapons, and the outcome wavered in the balance as the printer clacked, and Horsip's communications officer called, "Sir, message from J. Smith, Major General, Columbian Space Force: 'Request permission to join fighting units of the Centran Fleet.' "

" 'Granted,' " snapped Horsip. "Ask their course, relay it, and warn our ships not to fire on the Columbians."

As the little force of Columbian ships showed up on the screen, abruptly the enemy weapon stopped working.

On the screen the enemy fleet turned almost as one ship and attacked the thinnest portion of the Centran Fleet.

But now the Centrans' ordinary weapons, as well as their long-range weapons, came into action.

Horsip broadcast his surrender ultimatum, to receive no reply.

Faster and faster, as the Centran Fleet brought its full strength to bear, the enemy collapsed.

Suddenly it was all over.

Horsip and Moffis stood looking at the screen.

Moffis said, disbelief in his voice, "We've beat them."

Horsip nodded. But all he said was, "Maybe."

❋ XXIV ❋

The Sun of Right

The collapse of the remaining territory of the dictators followed like an avalanche. With only remnants of a fleet to guard them, with the *clokal detonak* backed up by still mounting Centran power, with hordes of Mikerils already overburdening the defenses, the remaining enemy planets earnestly returned to the True Way.

Then, the conquest complete, and the Holy Brotherhood laboring to get the survivors on the right track, the Mikerils were the next problem. But as Horsip turned his enormous military machine against them, they were already dwindling. Before his attack, they vanished.

Horsip found himself looking around among the ruins for an enemy. But there was no enemy. All that was left was the wreckage, the dead, wounded, and maimed, and a populace of survivors devoutly attending worship. The Mikerils were gone.

Horsip grappled with the problem.

"Moffis, do you understand what has happened here? *Where are the Mikerils?*"

Moffis was frowning over a lengthy report headed "The Real Enemy—Projected Mikeril Numbers—An assessment."

"According to this, we've only started to fight them."

Horsip glanced at the report, which was full of words he had never seen or heard before, and which relied heavily on mathematics, summarized in a formidable array of charts. He tossed the report on the desk.

"Do you remember that nursery rhyme—let's see—'When the sun of right' . . . ah . . ."

"I know the one you mean," said Moffis. "My mother used to put me to sleep with the poem that rhyme is in. Let's see . . ."

Moffis nodded suddenly, and cleared his throat.

> "As the sun of right sends forth his rays,
>   Dark shadows flee.
> So the evil band, Great One,
> Flees thought of Thee."

Horsip said, "That's it! . . . Moffis, it is almost unbelievable, but I think that is what is happening—*has* happened. As soon as the people went back to the True Ways, the Mikerils started to let up!"

Moffis looked doubtful, started to speak, then stopped, frowning.

"There may be something to this. It seems to match up. But how *could* it be?"

"Hunter knows. He predicted that we would win, after studying some reports on Mikerils."

"Well," said Moffis, "when we see him, we can—"

They looked around at the steady approach of footsteps.

A messenger, accompanied by armed guards, saluted.

Horsip returned the salute, and took the message, to read:

By Command
The High Council

We, the guardians of the essential strength of our race, in accord with the ancient law, do hereby decree:

(1) Throughout the Realm of Centra, the inviolable edict of the *clokal detonak* is lifted.

(2) The power vested in our loyal servant Klide Horsip, to reduce the aberrant of the Realm to obedience, is hereby withdrawn, as the task is done.

(3) The actions of General Klide Horsip as Commander of the United Arms of Centra are approved by unanimous vote of the High Council, and have attained that purpose which was intended. This appointment is therefore hereby withdrawn.

(4) Command of the armed forces of the Integral Union is hereby returned to the Supreme Staff, except for certain units which shall be held under the direct control of the High Council.

(5) By unanimous vote of the High Council, General Klide Horsip is created a Full Member of the High Council.

(6) By unanimous vote of the High Council, two individual citizens of the planet Columbia, to be selected by the legitimate leaders of that planet, are created Full Members of the High Council.

By command,
The High Council
J. Roggil
Chairman

There was a hush in the room, and the approach of solemn footsteps. Horsip looked up. A strongly built member of the Holy Brotherhood, in black robes with purple collar, strode up the aisle, bowed his head before Horsip, raised his hands, and said solemnly, "Your Excellency, I bring to you a message from the Council of Brothers. The trust vested in you by the Council of Brothers, and the authority, has reached its fulfillment, and the Brothers, with gratitude, withdraw now this awesome power, lest its presence in a sole human vessel might work some harm to the wielder of so mighty an authority. But know this, that the gratitude of the Council of Brothers is no light thing in this world, and if you desire council, or aid spiritual or worldly, you have but to ask, and the Brothers will be at your side. That is the message I have been commanded to give, and I now beg the permission of Your Excellency to report that my task is done, and the message delivered."

Horsip drew in a careful breath.

"Please give the Council of Brothers my thanks, and tell them that their message was delivered."

The Brother bowed, backed two paces, then turned and strode down the aisle and out the door.

After the Brother went out, the door opened up, and another messenger came in.

Horsip braced himself, returned the messenger's salute, and a few moments later found himself reading a message commanding him to attend a special meeting of the High Council.

"Well, Moffis, it looks as if we're not the only people who think the trouble is over with." He handed him the two messages.

Moffis looked relieved.

"But I still don't know *how* they know."

"Able Hunter knows. . . . If I can get a chance to ask him."

Since the High Council, for some reason sufficient to itself, was now situated far from where Horsip would have expected the trip involved special transportation. Horsip soon found himself on an ultrafast ship with simple arrangements, a minimum of luxurious appointments, a well-equipped gymnasium, and a library with a highly unusual selection of books. Horsip, who did little reading—aside from reams of hated reports—found that any volume he picked up in this library held his interest, regardless of the subject. It dawned on him that these books must have been culled from the entire production of all Centra.

"H'm," said Horsip, eying a book titled *The Essence of Combat—Tactics, Strategy, Policy, and Basic Principles.*

He settled down in a comfortable armchair, and was deep in the book when he vaguely heard the door shut, read on, became dimly aware of someone moving around, looked up, and saw Able Hunter frowning as he examined the titles on the shelf from which Horsip had gotten the book. Hunter looked up, and saw Horsip.

"Ah, General Horsip, how are you? You haven't seen a ..." He paused, noting the book in Horsip's hands.

Horsip smiled genially.

"I will be through with this in a few days. Perhaps I could finish it sooner if I could get a distraction out of my mind."

Hunter laughed.

"If there's anything I can do to help ..."

"What are Mikerils?"

Hunter glanced around. Save for the two of them, the room was empty.

"Mikerils are Centrans infected with a microorganism passed on to them by the bite of another Mikeril."

Horsip looked blank.

Hunter said, "A study of the comparative anatomy of the two proves the relationship. It should have been obvious. How do these attacks start? ... Few and far between. Then they become gradually more numerous and finally overwhelming. Why? . . . Because *the more of these creatures there are, the more Centrans they can bite.* And the more Centrans they bite, the more Mikerils there are. But to be susceptible to the disease, a Centran's body chemistry apparently has to be upset in a certain way—what we used to call 'sin,' and what your priests call 'not following the True Way,' upsets a Centran's body chemistry in such a way that he becomes susceptible to the attacks of the microorganism. *That* is what causes the Mikeril attacks."

"But—what started them in the first place?"

"I don't know. Possibly it began as an infection on an early colony planet. Certainly there must be some other host, to act as a reservoir of infection."

Horsip thought it over.

"Their size isn't much different from ours, but ..." He thought of the creatures moving trancelike through empty space, and sweeping overhead by the thousands—without wings. "It just isn't possible."

Hunter nodded. "I know. We've seen it, but in a few decades people will doubt our reports. All I can say is, mystics on Earth claim that men can 'levitate'—that is, in effect, fly—and can do a great many other things, by following disciplines that control certain nerve currents, as I understand it."

Hunter looked exasperated. "That's their *claim*. But they generally refuse to demonstrate. Now and then there are reports of demonstrations, but are they true, or aren't they?" He reached up to a different shelf. "Here's a book I found yesterday titled *The Powers of the Disciplined*. When I open this book I find that it is written in a kind of script I can't read. But the publishing house is the Self-Development Society. If this were Earth, I would be sure this was a mystic book of some kind. . . . Now, if there are such powers, then perhaps Centrans *can* exercise them, but only after so much self-discipline that for most people it just isn't worth the effort. Perhaps the disease strengthens these powers temporarily, just as an insane man shows unusual physical strength."

"Do your people have anything that corresponds to Mikerils?"

Hunter looked uneasy. "Not that I *know* of."

"Then you, at least, can enjoy the fruits of your labor."

"You mean, after we have a good system set up, then we can settle back and take things easy?"

Horsip nodded.

Hunter moodily shook his head. "What happens then is that we get soft—and get overthrown. Centra has had *one* empire. We've had hundreds. They all got soft."

Horsip suddenly saw how it all fitted together. The Mikerils, hideous as they were, were what kept the Integral Union from falling apart. Every time the Centrans started off on the wrong path, the Mikerils turned up.

"Are you," said Horsip, "the first to learn this?"

"Don't think it for a minute. If I'm not mistaken, the Holy Brotherhood knows all about it. And I imagine the High Council does too."

By the time their ship had reached the headquarters ship of the High Council, Horsip and Hunter had each read *The Essence of Combat* several times. Horsip detected what seemed to be a faint air of wondering respect in Hunter's manner toward him, tried to unravel the cause, and concluded that possibly Hunter was surprised that he, Horsip, could read such a transparently clear and well-written book—and could understand it. This thought put Horsip in a bad frame of mind. While in this bad frame of mind, they arrived at the High Council's headquarters ship, were escorted aboard, and, without delay, decorated with a variety of ribbons and shining emblems in gold, silver, and platinum. The citations were impressive, and Horsip should have been beaming with pride. Instead, he was conscious of the blank expression on the face of Able Hunter as the decorations were hung around his neck.

Horsip's mood got worse. Then the ceremony was over, and Horsip was invited to the big H-shaped table. Hunter, bowing with outward respect, went out.

Horsip let his breath out in a hiss, and sat down. He had reached the height of power, had held the most exalted position open to anyone in the Integral Union, his name was a household word, and just one of the decorations he had received should have made him eternally grateful. As a matter of fact, he was in an ugly frame of mind.

Horsip looked around narrow-eyed, his dissatisfaction dying down somewhat as he looked at the faces around the table. They all showed intelligence and strong character—and then Horsip saw the two representatives of Columbia.

They appeared to be out of much the same mold as the Centran members, but the sight of them made Horsip wonder. The authority of Centra had been solidly upheld—but could it have been done without the help of the Earthmen themselves—those of them who opposed the dictators? Meanwhile, Earth was still there. Who could say when the next batch of enterprising individuals might come out from Earth? And now there were two of them—these two Columbians—on the High Council itself.

Just where was this going to end?

It still seemed to be headed toward the same solution—the Earthmen were going to take over the Integral Union.

Across the H-shaped table from Horsip, Roggil growled, "The ceremonies are now over, and the recorders, photographers, guests, and honored citizens may withdraw."

There was a rustle and murmur, then finally several doors shut, Roggil glanced around, and said shortly, "That's over with. All right, gentlemen, we have business to attend to, and it looks like a mess of the first order. Now—"

One of the two members from Columbia said in a low voice, "Just a minute before you get started on the new business."

Roggil glanced around none too pleasantly.

"What?"

Horsip looked on blankly. Was this the legendary High Council in action? Where was that air of smooth functioning he had noticed before?

The member from Columbia said, "We've just been through quite a convulsion. We want to know what it was all about."

There was a chilly silence.

Horsip sat up.

Roggil said in a flat tone, "The convulsion was brought on by Earthmen, my friend. Do you have any more questions?"

The representative from Columbia smiled—it was an unpleasant expression, as if he contemplated slicing off Roggil's head.

"Why, yes," said the Columbian, "I *do* have more questions. Why did you let it get out of hand to start with? You could have held all that nonsense down. You had power enough. Instead, you withdrew your strength, and let the maniacs run wild. Then, when the whole mess had blown up into huge proportions, *then* you came back in and flattened all those people who should never have been allowed to seize so much power in the first place. What was the point of all that?"

Roggil favored the Columbian with an equally unpleasant smile.

"When you open up a box of incomprehensible oddities such as we found on Earth, *how do you know how they work until you try them out?*"

The Columbian blinked. After a considerable silence, he glanced at his companion.

The companion nodded slowly.

Roggil, with no special look of good humor, waited.

The Columbian looked back at Roggil, and spoke carefully.

"Do you mean to say you deliberately exposed millions of your citizens to a horrible death—in order to *test the value of various Earth attitudes and procedures?*"

"Yes," said Roggil, "that's exactly what I mean. We deliberately *found out now* what these Earth attitudes and procedures were, rather than wait three centuries and have them

rammed down our throats step by step, on your Earth installment plan."

The Columbian smiled suddenly.

"So, for mere *principles,* you risked lives?"

"We'll risk lives for the sake of principles anytime. As soon
as you lose principles, your lives are first worthless and next
lost."

"But could you have won without us?"

"You were part of the calculation. We had to assume that
somewhere in the incredible diversity, there was *something*
on Pandora's Planet that made sense."

"So you let everything out to show what it could do, so
you could pick the best of the lot? Well . . . all right. But why
in such a hurry?"

"Very simple," said Roggil. "If we had held the Earthmen
back, they would have had time to multiply. Their undesirable systems would have developed more slowly, and been
backed up by Earthmen from top to bottom. Therefore the
Earthmen were permitted to expand rapidly. While they held
most of the positions at the top, the body of their organizations were made up of Centrans—*who are subject to Mikeril
attack.*"

The two Columbians nodded, and looked agreeably at
Roggil, and the spokesman of the two said, "Your reasons
make sense. We just didn't want to ally ourselves with a collection of . . . ah . . ."

"Dullards," supplied Roggil, smiling.

The Columbian nodded. "That's the word. . . . Well, what's
the business? This mess you spoke of?"

Roggil drew out a thick report, eyed it a moment, and
now there *was* that sense of working in harmony.

The members waited intently.

"Here," said Roggil, "we have a report on a new race discovered at a location . . ." He touched a button, and a star
map appeared on the ceiling of the room. A ghostly pointer
moved around in it, to pick out a star Horsip was not familiar with.

"This," said Roggil, "is at the edge of our latest advance
into new territory. Here we have run into a humanoid race
which poses for us a peculiar problem." He glanced at the
two Columbians. "We will be interested to learn your sugges-
tions."

The Columbians looked interested.

"What's the problem?"

Horsip leaned forward intently.

"The problem," said Roggil, "is that we have discovered a race"—he looked at the Columbians quizzically—"which is more intelligent than we—or *you*."

The Columbians sat up.

Roggil went on, "They are, in effect, a race of geniuses—by your standards as well as ours. On the average, we would say, their general intelligence is as far above yours as Earth's general intelligence is—on the average—above that of Centra."

The two Columbians looked profoundly blank.

Roggil sat back and smiled.

"Now, gentlemen—what do *you* suggest?"

Mill Run

298-2170